CHRISTMAS JIGSAW MURDERS

'A real page-turner'

'A great twist on the classic murder mystery'

'Highly original and really well constructed'

'Keeps you glued to the pages'

'A gorgeous Christmas treat'

'A fun, quirky and very different Christmas story'

'A really well executed work of complete misdirection'

'I read it in one sitting'

'A real masterpiece in intrigue'

'Would make for entertaining reading
at any time of the year'

'An extraordinary whodunnit'

Alexandra (A K) Benedict is a bestselling, award-winning writer of short stories, novels and scripts. Educated at Cambridge, Sussex and Clown School, she has been an indie-rock singer, an actor, a Royal Literary Fund Fellow and a composer for film and TV, as well as teaching and running the prestigious MA in Crime Thrillers at City University. She is now a full-time writer and creative coach, and lives on the south coast of England with writer Guy Adams, their daughter Verity, and dog, Dame Margaret Rutherford.

Follow her on X and Instagram:
X @ak_benedict
⊙ @a.k.benedict

Also by Alexandra Benedict
Murder on the Christmas Express
The Christmas Murder Game

As A K Benedict
The Beauty of Murder
Jonathan Dark or The Evidence of Ghosts
The Stone House

ALEXANDRA BENEDICT

THE CHRISTMAS JIGSAW MURDERS

SIMON &
SCHUSTER

London · New York · Sydney · Toronto · New Delhi

First published in Great Britain by Simon & Schuster UK Ltd, 2023

This paperback edition first published 2024

1 3 5 7 9 10 8 6 4 2

Simon & Schuster UK Ltd
1st Floor
222 Gray's Inn Road
London WC1X 8HB

Simon & Schuster: Celebrating 100 Years of Publishing in 2024

Simon & Schuster Australia, Sydney
Simon & Schuster India, New Delhi

www.simonandschuster.co.uk
www.simonandschuster.com.au
www.simonandschuster.co.in

A CIP catalogue record for this book is available from the British Library

Paperback ISBN: 978-1-3985-2540-5
eBook ISBN: 978-1-3985-2538-2
Audio ISBN: 978-1-3985-2539-9

Typeset by Palimpsest Book Production Ltd, Falkirk, Stirlingshire

Printed and Bound in the UK using 100% Renewable
Electricity at CPI Group (UK) Ltd

For Guy, my matching jigsaw piece

Game 1

Anagrams of novels and Christmas stories by one of my very favourite writers – Charles Dickens – are scattered throughout the novel. I've given the chapter in which each one is found as a hint, and will give the solutions at the end of the book.

A Christmas Carol – Ch.33

A Tale of Two Cities – Ch.3

Dombey and Son – Ch.13

Great Expectations – Ch.23

Hard Times – Ch.37

Nicholas Nickleby – Ch.26

Oliver Twist – Ch.11

The Battle of Life – Ch.42

The Chimes – Ch.54

The Cricket on the Hearth – Ch.58

The Haunted Man – Ch.54

The Signalman – Ch.43

Game 2

In honour of the brilliant Christine McVie, who died in 2022, I've scattered the titles of fifteen Fleetwood Mac songs throughout the novel. The songs and their locations are revealed at the end of the book.

Prize Game 3

At the top of each chapter is a jigsaw piece containing a letter or character. Rearrange the pieces to make a well-known Christmas song and its singer. The first to tweet me @ak_benedict on Twitter or mention me in an Instagram/Threads post @a.k.benedict with the answer wins a special prize!

And for extra larks, Pips, just for fun, I've thrown in lots of references to one of my literary heroes, Charles Dickens. Let me know if you spot some . . .

She tears your heart to pieces – and as it gets older and stronger, it will tear deeper

Charles Dickens, *Great Expectations*

I have been bent and broken, but – I hope – into a better shape

Charles Dickens, *Great Expectations*

'*Bah,' said Scrooge. 'Humbug.'*

Charles Dickens, *A Christmas Carol*

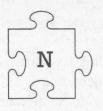

One

December 19th

No one was dead, not to begin with. That was about to change. Sitting at the desk, looking out to sea, the killer felt death's approach as keenly as needles into skin. Hands trembling, they pulled on white gloves that stopped short of the wrists. Santa would come in Reaper's weaves that year. Holly would be berried with murder.

They closed the newspaper, crossword complete. Every piece of the plan was in place; now to make the first move. But they hesitated. Right now, they were many things, but not a criminal. The killer stayed still, watching seagulls sweep across the sky, buffeted by unseen winds, eking out the minutes before their life changed forever.

The killer looked at the clock. There was much to do before dusk. Unlocking a deep drawer, they carefully took out the box and checked the contents. Bile rose in their throat at what they saw.

Rolling black-and-white-squared wrapping paper across the desk, they cut a length. The scissors sighed. Box placed on top, Sellotape already cut into long strips, they taped up the present, adding layer after layer, as if stopping a hostage from getting away.

Arms stretched wide to measure a wingspan of red ribbon, the killer remembered a Christingle service, years ago. Regrets burned in them, as they always did. But those regrets were why they were doing this. Snuffing out the memories, they tied the ribbon around the box, looping it into a bow. The card, the one that would kick everything off, was slipped underneath the ribbon.

Holding the chequered present as reverently as myrrh for a precious child, the killer lowered it into the draw-string sack open on the rug. When they stood, it was with resolve. People would lose their lives before midnight on Christmas Eve. The knowledge sliced at the killer, but it had to be done. They picked up the present.

God bless us, and every one of our victims.

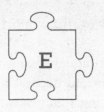

Two

December was the worst of months, according to Edie O'Sullivan. It brought cold memories, and darkness that soaked into her like winter mist. At this time of year, she was never more than a foot away from shadows.

Not even four in the afternoon and day was submitting to night. *Night – a dark, rearranged thing that dismisses the sun.* She couldn't see the details of the jigsaw piece she was putting in place, even with her magnifying glass. With an eye on rising bills, she'd put off turning on the lights and heating for as long as possible, but some things were more important than saving money, and jigsaws were one of them.

She stood, knees cracking like a festive fire, and went over to the light switch. The mess of her living room, with its piles of books and unwashed cups, was now visible to the whole street. The French windows turned the room into a stage, the frames a proscenium arch, and Edie into a character in a farce, hurrying over to draw the curtains before she was seen. She stopped, though, by the window, her hand on the undrawn drapes.

On the other side of the road, Lucy Pringle, a perfectly nice young woman who lived opposite to Edie in every way, was up a huge ladder, fixing yet more lights to her house. They had started decorating at the beginning of November, a worrying trend of which Edie wholeheartedly disapproved. This year, she'd seen baubles and selection packs sold next to barbecue briquettes in August. Edie would rather the festive season turn up on Christmas Eve and bugger off on Boxing Day. She considered that magnanimity itself. If it were up to her, Christmas would be binned, and not thrown back in the recycling bins from whence it came, but rather into the black bins. The ones that wouldn't get emptied for weeks over Christmas.

Lucy was gesticulating to her husband, Graeme, who was standing at the foot of the ladder. He nodded, ran into their garage and, seconds later, a huge Santa lit up above their front door. The shifting lights were supposed to make it look like he was waving, but from where Edie was standing, he looked like he was wanking. A masturbating Santa. That was all she needed.

Lucy came down the ladder and stood back on their lawn to inspect the sight. She clapped and turned, scanning the street to see if anyone else had been watching. Spotting Edie, illuminated in her front room, she waved and made a move as if about to walk across the street.

Edie's face burned. Her heart made arrhythmic kicks. She grabbed a piece of bubble gum from the table and started to chew. Blowing bubbles not only kept her calm, but created a literal barrier between her and others.

She had no idea why Lucy would want to talk to her. Maybe she pitied Edie, talked to her friends about being nice to the poor old woman who lived over the road. If

Lucy came over now, she'd want to make small talk, and Edie would have to stop her in a way that would only come across as surly.

Edie yanked the curtains shut. Best not to encourage pity visits, however bored she was and however much she occasionally longed for company. Besides, she didn't want Santa flashing through her front windows.

She kept still, waiting for the crunch of gravel towards her door, but nothing came. Lucy had got the message. She probably wouldn't come back again. Edie felt relief and sadness, mirror emotions she knew well. Peggoty, a silver Siberian, and one of three cats who deigned to be loved by Edie, shuttled between her slippered feet. Edie bent down and picked Peggoty up, nuzzling into her fur. Peggoty had an unerring, purring ability to know when Edie was unsettled. It prompted her to move, and she headed towards the cool kitchen to put the kettle on. Cats, puzzles and tea: Edie's triumvirate of solace.

As she walked past the dining room that she'd kept locked up for over twenty years, frozen memories began to thaw. Most of the year she could ignore that room, but now she couldn't help remembering the last time she'd been inside. It had been just before Christmas. Sky had been packing up her silversmith kit, laying her handmade jewellery in velvet-lined boxes, like the coffin to which she had just consigned their love.

Sky had turned to Edie, eyes full of pain. She held out a necklace – a silver crescent moon. 'This was going to be your present. I thought you could still have it, to remember us by.'

Edie grabbed the necklace and threw it against the wall. 'I don't want you or your shoddy baubles.' The chain slunk to the ground. She turned to Sky, wanting her to scream, to yell, to hurt.

Sky's voice, though, was low and soft. 'We could end this well. It's up to you. This is where we say our last words.'

If Edie knew anything, it was words. As a crossword setter, she could make them do anything she wanted, apart from wrap up what she was really feeling. 'The word "Baubles" has a perfect anagram. "Bubales". Definition: North African antelope of the genus Alcelaphus.'

Sky's tears looked like liquid silver. 'Goodbye, Edie.' She waited for Edie to say the same, but the word never came.

As Sky left, closing the front door as she had their relationship, not with a slam but achingly gently, Edie longed to run after her. But neither her legs nor her pride would let her. All she could do was step out of the room and padlock it, along with her heart.

Now Edie hurried past, shoving the memories to the back of her mental deep freeze and praying they'd stay there.

Outside, through the kitchen window, lights were coming on in other people's houses. Thin silver clouds swagged across the moon, reminding her of the necklace. But she must try not think of the Sky she once knew.

After making a pot of tea (one teaspoon loose Ceylon, one Assam, and one for the pot of Lady Grey, left for six minutes exactly, then strained in time to a prayer to Mary), she sat back down in the living room with her jigsaw tray on her lap, a cat on either side of her, and continued placing the edges of each piece together. Every match she made helped calm her heart. This was what she could rely on, not anyone else, or even her own mind. The methodical, steady intersection of pieces to gain a complete picture, however long it took.

The doorbell rang. Lucy must have decided to come over after all. She was persistent, Edie gave her that. She wasn't going to give her the satisfaction of answering the door, though.

The footsteps, however, quickly spat away against the gravel, onto the pavement, and along the bin alley that nestled next to her garden. Probably a courier. Every Christmas, her boss at *The National* sent her a Fortnum's hamper, always with the same note: 'For the Nation's Best Crossword Compiler'. Very welcome it was, and if left on the doorstep it might disappear as fast as the purple chocolates in a Quality Street tin, even in this neighbourhood.

Edie dragged herself up again, taking care not to displace any pieces. Peggoty and Fezziwig followed her into the freezing hallway. The outline of a medium-sized box, resting on her doorstep, was visible through the glass.

Opening the door, she picked up the box, wrapped in printed black and white squares and blood-red ribbon. It was as light as the snow beginning to fall, and its contents shifted. The envelope tucked beneath the bow was addressed to her: *Ms Edith O'Sullivan*. Curiosity overcame the cold and, placing the box on the porch parcel shelf, Edie opened the envelope. Pulling out a charity Christmas card with holly on the front, she read the printed message inside:

Ms O'Sullivan,
   You are known for your cross words, but can you set your sights on a murderer? Four, maybe more, people will be dead by midnight on Christmas Eve, unless you can put all the pieces together and stop me. Make sure you do it properly, you never were a good cheater.
   Yours,
   Rest In Pieces

Edie's mind wouldn't move, but her hands shook, and her heart turned over as she ripped the paper off the present and took out a white, square box. She eased off the lid and stared down at six jigsaw pieces. Habit took over and she began placing them together, finding their matching edges. Her chest tightened as she slowly realised what she was seeing.

One piece had what seemed to be part of a handwritten sign. The other five pieces showed black and white tiles, covered in blood, and the partial chalk outline of a body. A crime scene in a box, and she was to try and solve it.

Merry bloody Christmas.

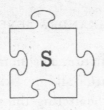

Three

'If the sender thinks I'm going to play their stupid game, they're very much mistaken,' Edie said, when she'd drunk enough of Riga's 'Livener' cocktail to stop shaking.

Riga Novack was Edie's ninety-year-old next-door neighbour and one of the few people other than Sean, Edie's great-nephew and adopted son, that she could stand being with for any length of time. Within minutes of Riga moving in fifteen years ago, she'd come round to Edie's house, wearing vintage Chanel and carrying a tin of homemade lavender *kolaczki* biscuits. 'This is to make you like me,' Riga had said. 'But in the unlikely event that you do not appreciate biscuits, then I have booze.'

They'd been friends ever since.

Now they were in Riga's garden room. Vines and leaves covered the glass ceiling and walls, and sitting inside it gave Edie the strange sensation of being slowly digested by a carnivorous plant. More garden than room, it smelled of all the herbs Riga grew for her concoctions. She was a herbalist to some, kitchen witch to others. Best friend to Edie.

'You must be curious, though?' Riga said, handing back the box with the pieces in and taking off the gloves Edie had made her wear to prevent contaminating the evidence. 'You are part cat, after all.'

'That's the most flattering thing you've ever said to me. No offence intended, Nicholas.' Edie looked over to Riga's favourite armchair, where Nicholas the dog was huddled on his blanket. Nicholas looked at her and sniffed. He was a very judgey pug. 'And of course I'm curious. It's a puzzle.' Edie settled back into Riga's second-best wicker chair. 'A big, shouty part of me wants to find out everything, including who sent it to me . . . I've got more questions than I've had Christmas cards this year. But this isn't like anything I've dealt with before.' She took a bite of Riga's shortbread. It was fragrant, rich and delicious. Much like Riga. 'Someone is threatening murder.'

'You always told me you could solve anything.' Riga moved with no sign of the pain that Edie knew she was in, other than the slowness with which she lowered herself into her third-best armchair.

'I meant word puzzles, not murder.'

'Are there no similarities between them?'

Edie thought for a moment. 'I suppose both have clues. And with a crime I'd start with clues that are easy to solve. Then I'd pencil in suspected answers until I could cross-reference guesses to see if they were correct.'

'Sounds like you'd make a good detective.'

'But why send the box to *me*?'

Riga read through the card again, bringing it close to her face. 'It mentions your crosswords, so it could be any one of thousands of nerds who've done your local or national puzzles. Especially since that feature on you in *The Times* where they dubbed you the Pensioner Puzzler.'

Edie scowled. People had called her that for months after the article came out. She had always been known as a know-it-all, a brainbox, a swot. Now they had another name to call her.

'Whoever it is wants your puzzle-solving nous.'

'If they'd sent me a crossword then I'd agree. But jigsaws? Hardly anyone knows that's how I unwind.'

Riga's forehead cross-hatched in thought. 'So, it's personal, then. A grudge?' She pointed to the word 'cheater' in the message. 'I wouldn't have put you down as a cheater.'

Edie looked away. Not even Sky knew about the time Edie had been unfaithful to her. At least Edie hoped she didn't. 'Like anyone my age, I've cheated death a few times, but that's not a game any of us win. Otherwise, I don't see the point in cheating. I prefer winning fair and square.'

'Could it be a prank? Let's face it, you're not averse to pissing people off.'

'True. I said that to Sean when I left him a message.' Sean had recently been promoted to Detective Inspector in the Weymouth Constabulary. He'd know what to do. Edie kept looking at her phone to see if he had replied.

'Have you asked Lucy Pringle if she saw who delivered the package?'

'I came straight across to see you.'

Riga's eyes glinted. 'Because I'm more likely to be curtain-twitching?'

'Because you're more observant.'

'I was once. Glaucoma has turned my eyes into the silicles of *Lunnaria annua*.' Riga leaned forward and stroked one of the silvery seed pods of her Honesty plant. In summer it had been full of purple flowers, but now the opaque ovals looked like the ghosts of coins, hung from dead branches. Edie made a mental note of the Latin name for her next crossword. Riga was a compost heap of riches for a crossword compiler.

'I was out the back here, obviously, but if I *had* seen anyone,' Riga carried on, 'they'd have been a blur. But you knew that. You just didn't want to talk to Lucy.'

'I'd get stuck on her doorstep, hearing about her latest half-marathon or the papier-mâché monstrosities her countless kids have made.'

'You should be careful, you know. Or you could end up like me. Nobody coming to see you other than gossipy neighbours and grumpy women like you.'

'Any gossip to share?

Riga's eyes flashed. 'Guess where Graeme asked Lucy to be his wife? A Costa toilet!'

'Not sure I wanted to know that.'

'Then you shouldn't have asked. As my prodigal family will tell you, I often say things people don't want to hear.' Riga's cackle was edged with spikes. She took another large mouthful of her Campari and soda, heavy on the Campari. At times like this, Riga reminded Edie of a dowager vampire, existing on blood-red drinks and witticisms.

And it was true that Riga had few visitors from her family. The last argument with her daughter had washed away the final vestige of soil that nourished their relationship and now, despite Riga's ill health, there was nothing left.

Edie was jolted out of her reverie as Riga clapped her hands together. 'Enough about me,' she continued, eyes glinting. 'I'm practically a ghost. Take this warning from a root-bound crone whose skin is almost see-through. Get on with your life. Meet someone, have adventures, be happy.'

'I'm eighty, Riga.'

'Exactly. There's still time.'

'I'm fine,' Edie lied.

'You know what I call you when I write letters to my pen friend? The Weeping Widow.'

Edie flushed. 'I'm not a widow. I never got married.'

'You may not have double-barrelled yourself or thrown yourself down wedlock's waterfall, but you never moved on from the relationship's death. You're the Miss Havisham of the Jurassic Coast, only you jilted yourself.'

Edie's heart hurt. 'That's very you, Riga. Blunt but poetic.'

Riga shrugged. 'Those nearest to death have little to lose.'

Edie's phone vibrated in her pocket. It was Sean. He was out of breath when she answered, and the sounds of the busy police station competed with his voice. 'Sorry, Aunt Edie. Got back to you as soon as I could. What's all this about jigsaws? I couldn't hear your message properly. Is it a present you're after?'

Edie explained about the box and the goading message in the card.

'I'll be over after my shift,' Sean said. 'Around half seven.'

'Meet me in The Bell.' Edie didn't want to go home, but she wasn't going to tell Sean that.

Shouts broke out over the phone, and sounds of a scuffle. 'Got to go. It's kicking off here.'

As she hung up, Edie felt a swell of relief at Sean being able to help with the puzzle, but also a shiver of unease. She had long ago pledged to keep him safe. Involving him could do the opposite.

'How's the adoption going?' From the swimmy look in Riga's eyes, her sundowner had gone down well.

Sean and Liam, his husband, were in the long, heart-tearing process of adopting a child. They'd gone through the classes and assessment, and were now approved adopters. 'They've been tentatively matched with a little girl called Juniper and are meeting with her social worker tomorrow.'

'Juniper,' Riga said. 'I like that.'

'Of course, you do. You love gin.'

Riga laughed. 'True. But juniper berry is also protective and healing, good for keeping bad at bay. It's a shield of a name for a child.'

'I'm trying not to think about it until we know for sure; it's too painful to hope.'

'And if all goes well?'

'She could be with them within a month or two. Ten weeks after that, they can apply to officially be her parents.'

'And you'll be a great-great-aunt. And, kind of, a grand-mother.'

Edie looked down at the jigsaw pieces. 'Great great-great-aunts, or good grandmothers for that matter, don't get death puzzles boxed up as Christmas presents. What kind of example is that?'

'It makes you unique, certainly. But that's not what's important. You've looked after Sean all his life. You didn't want to be a mum, but you've been a great one.'

'Hardly.'

'However many mistakes you made, you were there for him. And he's now a wonderful young man.'

'He is. Although he'll probably tell me to drop the case.' Sean always gave Edie a jigsaw puzzle for Christmas, but she bet he'd want to take this one away from her.

'Since when have you paid attention to what anyone else says?'

'But it can't end well, can it?' Edie continued. 'It's not like I can drop everything and go full Poirot. I don't have the facial hair for a start. Although the older I get, the more it's going full hedgerow.'

Riga stroked her chin as if it were covered with a lustrous beard. 'Wait until you're ninety.'

'I love how, no matter how old I get, I'll always be younger than you. So don't go dying on me, okay?'

'Death is a train that can be delayed but not derailed.' Riga took a sip of her topped-up Campari and nodded, pleased with both drink and aphorism.

Edie thought of the 'Murder Train', the Scottish sleeper on which three people had died last Christmas. It still puzzled her, that crime. Didn't quite fit together. Part of her itched to work it out. Maybe she *could* be an armchair detective. Better still, a recliner detective.

'What time are you meeting Sean?'

'Half seven.' Something about that snagged in her mind, reminding her of one of the jigsaw pieces.

Edie took a magnifying glass out of her handbag, put on gardening gloves, and picked up the piece in question, examining it closely. It showed the outline of a hand lying on black and white tiles, with a real watch lying where the wrist would be. Edie froze. The face of the watch was smashed, the clock showing half past eleven.

'What is it?' Riga asked, leaning forward.

'The watch,' Edie said, hardly able to get the words out. 'It's Sean's.'

'Are you sure? Watches can look the same.'

'Certain.' She had given it as a birthday present to her brother, Anthony, Sean's grandfather. Then, when he'd died, she'd given it to Duncan, Sean's father.

Edie reeled as the past crashed into her . . .

Storming out of the house on the night of Christmas Eve, 1988, slamming the door on Sky's entreaties. Fuelled by anger and the Bucks Fizz that Sky had insisted on mixing, as if Christmas was to be celebrated, Edie had walked for miles. Sleet stung her skin as she continued the argument in her head. Looking up at last, she realised that she had no idea where she was. Shivering, she continued walking until she found a phone box and rang Anthony with the coins in her coat pocket. She sat on the kerb for an hour, waiting for Anthony to pick her up. Only he never came.

When she could no longer feel her feet from the cold, she phoned Sky, who came for her and held her despite everything Edie had said, and held her tighter when they found out that Anthony had died in a car crash on iced-over roads while coming to get her. Edie had collected his things from the hospital and pressed his still-ticking watch to her broken heart.

Then she was slammed into Swanage police station on another Christmas Day, holding the same watch: 1990, the day after the car crash that killed Duncan and Melissa, Sean's parents, as well as his older brother, William. They'd been to see a panto, while Edie babysat nine-month-old Sean. He slept in his pushchair as she stood in the station that smelled of bleach, sweat and the mince pies that were being shared around the officers. The man behind the desk handed over William's blood-covered teddy bear in its plastic shroud and the broken watch as if they were yellow-sticker items at a checkout, not the last connections she had with Duncan and four-year-old William.

She took sleepy Sean from the pushchair and held him close, whispering things she didn't believe, like, 'It's going to be okay.' If Christmas hadn't already been poisoned for Edie by her mother dying while giving birth to Anthony on December 25th, 1946, then that day would have done it. What's there to believe in when things like that happen in the world?

When she'd officially adopted Sean, Edie had decided to keep the now repaired watch to one side, giving it to him on his confirmation day. He'd worn it every day since.

And now that same watch was on a painted jigsaw

piece, the face fractured again. Edie felt as if one of the ivy vines was wrapped around her heart, strangling it.

'You still there, Edie?' Riga was tapping her glass like she was about to give a speech.

'Sorry. I got lost in the past.' Edie wished she could close her eyes and, when she opened them again, it would be New Year. Every December, she became a cut-and-shunt vehicle, made up of broken memories.

'Maybe it's time to see why it's being dredged up.'

Edie shook her head. 'The past is dead. It should stay submerged.'

'Tell that to ghosts,' Riga replied. 'Anyway, why would Sean's watch be on there?'

'I have no idea.' Turning the jigsaw piece around in her hand, Edie suddenly began to feel for the first time in years the thrilling fizz at finding a puzzle she might not be able to solve. Although she had never played a game with such stakes before.

When she looked up, Riga was staring at her. 'Your eyes are shining, and it's not just my Livener. You're going to investigate, aren't you?'

Edie felt an unaccustomed smile on her face. 'I'm the Pensioner Puzzler. Of course I'm going to investigate.'

Four

Adrenaline streamed through the killer, screaming at them to sprint. They ignored the urge; running would make them more conspicuous. Above, tree branches reached for them like the bony hands of hair-ruffling aunts. Beneath their feet, roots unsteadied their steps. The dark woods of Godlingston Heath were full of traps, and that was before they'd set one of their own.

Rustling came from nearby bushes and the killer's heart beat faster. They looked around but couldn't even see the path in front. They mustn't switch on their head torch, or even their phone, in case it gave them away, but their breath came like smoke signals in the cold dark. No one had followed, they were almost sure of that, but a single dog walker or jogger catching sight of them and the whole plan could be ruined. They must act as if they were meant to be there, taking a night-time winter stroll, as if that was a perfectly normal thing to do.

Maybe then they would get away with being found carrying a log that was not meant for the heat of a Yuletide fire, but the head of the first victim.

They started trembling at the thought, and concentrated on how this was just their body preparing them for action. It was providing them with cortisol and more adrenaline. They must use it wisely. An excess would cause them to mess up the plan.

Owls sounded above. In the distance, the killer heard a car door slam.

The victim was right on time. There was no backing out. Not now. Tonight would bring an end to one life, and change that of the killer forever. Darkness was coming for them all.

Carl Latimer was racing himself to the oak tree at the end of the path. Two days ago, he'd achieved his all-time record and he was absolutely going to smash Past Carl's achievements into the soggy ground. *I am the best*, he said, over and over in his mind, convincing himself with every step on the woodland floor. He could already see the faces of his running group when he told them of his success. They were still smarting from him winning the Chase the Pudding race on the beach yesterday – he'd been the fastest Santa across the Weymouth sands. He loved seeing their envy, their jealousy, their pride.

It was dark, but he knew the terrain. He was always in command. His feet were quick and true and knew what to do on every root that twisted out of the ground.

Carl always ran here at this time of night. He felt at one with the owls, with the badger that stood frozen on the path before bowing its head and shuffling away in supplication. The birds that roosted in leafless trees, unable to be alone. Unlike Carl. He excelled on his own. Always had. Always would. Fuck any woman who turned him down; he'd show them. He was fast. He was strong. He had a will of iron.

Music floated over the treetops, getting the night birds to stop talking for a moment. He recognised the song, though he didn't know where from.

But the music meant that someone else was there in the woods with him. Right where he was heading. Someone was on his track, trying to take up his space. He picked up speed. He'd beat them and himself at the same time. He'd let himself have two pints later, after his protein balls.

The words of the song drifted through his thoughts. Something about pictures. A light flashed, too. Teenagers, probably, snogging and groping on a tree stump, drinking cider that wouldn't give them a headache or ruin any chance of athleticism the following day. Young people didn't know they were born. They had bodies that could run for miles without stopping or hurting, and they didn't deserve them.

The wind blasted through him, sending a cold challenge, and he fought against it. Let it rage. The music seemed to die down, as if it too was buffeted back by his prowess.

He accelerated again on the home stretch. Legs burning, lungs stretching, heart beating so loudly it sent birds screaming and flying out of the trees into the swallowing dark. The oak was a huge shape at the end of the path.

He felt its solid, ancient, English presence. Get there and he was home.

And then suddenly his sure foot was uncertain, hitting something. He was falling. The ground punched him in the face and chest. He was on the woodland floor, pine-cones pressed against his cheek. Mud on his hands. Pain in his arm and ribs. Winded, but not out of action. He felt for his water bottle and, yelling at the searing pain, found instead a long branch that was stretched over the path. It must have fallen in the previous night's storm.

The music grew louder, and an image popped into his head of backcombed hair and eyeliner.

Twigs snapped. Footsteps. Someone was coming.

He tried to push himself up, but his wrist wouldn't hold him.

The person was right behind him. They were here to help him, of course they were. Carl tried to turn to see who it was.

Then he felt something hit the back of his head. The pain rose to a scream, then was eaten by the dark.

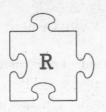

R

Five

Like so many pubs of its kind, The Bell was dying. The smell of woodsmoke, wet dog and mulled wine couldn't cover that of black mould. Across the road, The Anchor had, at some point in the 2010s, gone from spit and sawdust to Chenin Blanc and charcuterie boards. As it also provided free popcorn, Edie was all for it, but The Bell still had a place in her coal-fired heart, despite its gaudy Christmas decorations. She had pogoed to punk bands and skanked to ska in here. Plus, The Bell was quiet, and that was what she needed tonight.

Edie ordered at the bar, making sure she didn't touch the counter. She had no wish for her Westwood peacoat to adhere to drying beer.

Nerves firing, she tried to calm herself with words. 'The Bell' was an anagram of 'Bet Hell', which was exactly like one corner of the bar – fruit machines flashing and jangling. Like Christmas, 'Amusements With Prizes' promised more than they could ever deliver.

Sophie, landlady of The Bell, placed a double brandy on the bar and next to it slapped a newspaper opened to the puzzle page. She pointed to the cryptic crossword. 'This one of yours, Edie?'

Edie shook her head. 'I don't work for that rag.'

'Shame. I was hoping you'd help me.'

'I didn't know you did crosswords, Sophie.'

'I've always wanted to. I just don't know where to start.'

'Like anything, once you know the rules it's simple. The first or last word, or phrase, often defines the whole thing, and then there's an S.I., a Subsidiary Indicator.'

'A what now?'

'A fancy way of saying a clue within a clue, to help you work it out. It might be a synonym, or a metonym, or a suggestion that there might be an anagram – "scramble" often points to this – or the word itself might be hidden inside the clue.'

'Do crosswords always play fair?'

'If there's a question mark, or "maybe", then the setter's toying with the rules. And sometimes there's a rebus, an answer where part of the clue has several letters that must be fitted inside one square. But that's rare, and should be pointed out.'

Sophie looked less the wiser. She tapped the crossword. 'Show me.'

Edie scanned the clues. 'Four across is a crown jewel of a clue. "An august fillet will destroy all".'

Sean came in as Sophie was looking at the five-letter stretch of spaces. Her face was as blank as the squares.

'Oh, come on,' Edie said. 'It's fucking easy.'

Sophie squared her shoulders and glared. 'No need for that, mate.'

Sean bent to kiss the top of Edie's head. 'Are you tormenting people with crosswords again?'

'You'll know the answer.' Edie had taught Sean how to do crosswords before he'd learned how to skateboard. 'Another word for "an august" person?'

'Noble man or woman? A peer?' Sean suggested.

'Similar. And what do you think of if you see "fillet"?'

'That the answer might be inside the skin of the clue.'

'So, what's the word Sophie needs?'

Edie felt a flush of pride as Sean wrote 'royal' into four across.

Sophie groaned. 'How is that easy?'

Edie underlined where the word 'royal' was hiding like King Charles I in a priest hole within 'destroy' and 'all'. 'I also said it was "fucking easy", emphasis on "*king*".'

Sophie shook her head as if despairing. 'You also said it was a crown jewel of a clue. You didn't tell me that you were helping.'

'She'll do that.' Sean gave his great-aunt a quick hug. 'Try and help without you even knowing.'

'What can I get you?' Sophie asked Sean.

'Draft cider, please. And I love your decorations.' Sean pointed to the ceiling strung with multi-coloured garlands; the ones that came flat and could be stretched out like garish concertinas. These ones were mottled and broken, like they'd been bought in Woolworths in the eighties and should have stayed there. Sean, though, meant what he said, as he always did. He loved Christmas as much as Edie hated it.

'I'm getting the tree tonight,' Sophie said. Even *her* eyes, who had seen it all and more, lit up with the thought of hacking down a living thing and placing it in the corner of the room. 'I've made baubles out of beer bottles.'

Sophie and Sean continued to talk about the darling nature of Christmas and other irrelevances. 'Can we get on?' Edie said after a while, interrupting a heated discussion concerning how to bake gammon in Pepsi Max Cherry. 'Sean and I have important things to discuss.'

As they walked into the empty snug, Sean put his arm around his aunt. 'I'm glad you called me. Bet you're glad now that I joined the force.'

Edie had tried to convince Sean to do pretty much any other job – well, anything that wasn't potentially fatal. The idea of him being placed in dangerous situations still made her feel sick. 'Let's not dwell on that, shall we?'

'This would all be a lot easier to deal with if you'd got a doorbell camera like I told you ages ago. We'd be able to see who left the box.'

'Do you think I don't know that?' Edie strode over to the corner table and plumped herself next to the window. A vinyl Santa was peeling off the glass. '*Santa Claus*', she thought, trying to distract herself from her own failures, *can be anagrammed into 'casual ants'*.

'What about your neighbours? Do any of them have cameras?' Sean asked, ducking beneath the hanging swags of tinsel that criss-crossed the ceiling. Edie had the urge to tug on one sparkly strand and bring down the whole crass fire hazard.

'A few, but they point to their doorsteps in case someone steals an Amazon package. I'd have words if I thought they were directed anywhere near my house. Privacy is a right that's under threat, you know.'

'When someone leaves a crime scene on your doorstep, a lack of privacy would be helpful.'

Edie crossed her arms and scowled. 'And that is useful now how exactly?'

'I worry about you, that's all.'

'No need. Eighty is the new thirty. I saw it on *The One Show*.'

'What does that make me?' Sean's pint spilled as he sat down. He mopped it up with the sleeve of his jumper, reminding Edie of when he was a little boy.

'A bizarrely tall zygote.'

Sean grinned. His laugh turned into a cough. The wheeze that came from his chest made her own breath hard to catch. As he grabbed his blue inhaler from his top pocket and took a puff, she remembered those terrifying nights in hospital during his infancy with him on a nebuliser. He had always been what used to be known as 'a sickly child', like Anthony, his grandad, her brother. Nowadays, he was looking thinner than ever, if a little more muscular from working out. That was Liam's fault, Sean's husband. He was always encouraging Sean to better himself, as if Sean could be bettered. Liam had got Sean a personal trainer and her great-nephew might now be beefier, but he was as pale as milk after it had been skimmed.

When Liam had first met Edie, he was training to be a florist and had brought her a bouquet that was bigger and more beautiful than any she'd ever been given by a lover. It was a monochrome arrangement of pale lilies, ranunculi and peonies, fanned out like a white peacock tail. She'd received such a deep pang of pain at the prospect of never experiencing love again that she'd said, words dusted with poison like pollen, 'Don't think you can buy your way into my heart like you have with Sean. I'm not so naive.' Sean had left with Liam immediately. It had taken weeks before he forgave her. Not that she'd apologised. Liam was now one of the best florists in the South, but he'd never made her a bouquet since, and rarely visited. Not even Edie could blame him for that.

It reminded her of something Sky had said the day she left. 'You do all you can to push people over the edge and out of your life.'

Edie packed away the intruding thoughts as she would stray puzzle pieces.

'Can I see it?' Sean said. 'The jigsaw?'

Edie fished her gardening gloves out of her coat pocket, but Sean shook his head. Opening his rucksack, he handed her a sealed packet of crime scene gloves and took one for himself.

Gloves on, she took the white box out of her tote bag and laid it on the table. She eased off the lid and it gave a sigh.

Sean leaned forward and picked up the pieces of jigsaw. He turned them over, arranging them in the box with his long, skinny, gloved fingers.

'There were only five?' he asked.

Edie's heart started to beat too quickly. If she showed him the piece with his watch on, the one ticking near his pulse point right now, and it became an official police investigation, then Sean would be taken off the case for being involved. Without Sean's help, she'd have less access to information to help her solve the puzzle.

Edie looked to her knees so he couldn't see her eyes. 'Yup. Four that fit together, presumably combining with others to make the outline of a body, taking up a fair bit of space and possibly from the centre of the puzzle. And the other piece is the top left-hand corner.'

Sean looked at each in turn. 'Do you recognise the black and white tiles under the outline?'

'Not that I know of.'

'It looks like a collage, several images combined. I'll see if we can get the pieces and box tested for fingerprints, and also if there's budget for a digital forensic specialist.'

Edie was relieved that they might be tested, and even more relieved that she had taken photos of the pieces. 'Yeah, there's a shadow between the markings of the supposed missing body and the black and white tiles that reminds me of early Photoshop.'

Sean's eyebrows were raised so high they touched his fringe.

'Don't look so surprised. You millennials didn't create the digital world. This technology has been around for a long time – not as long as me, sure, but I'm no stranger to it. Underestimate octogenarians at your peril.'

'I wouldn't dare.'

'Good.'

Sean picked up the corner jigsaw piece that didn't fit with the rest and turned it round in his gloved hand, feeling the edges. He kept taking glances at it and frowning.

'What is it?' Edie asked.

'This piece is bugging me. Reminds me of something, but I can't think what.'

Edie looked at it again. 'Parallel bars, maybe wood, with a sign on them, not that I can tell what's written on it.' She took out her magnifying glass and tried to read the writing, but it wasn't a high enough magnification.

'Let me.' Sean took out his phone, opened his camera and took a picture of the piece. Then he zoomed in.

She took the phone from him and read the words that were handwritten on a large piece of paper, sellotaped to wooden bars.

The only person to bring you down is you
  The only person to bring you success is you
  You are your own downfall
  Be your own crashmat

She read the sign out loud, her tone stuffed with sarcasm, then said, 'What absolute crap. Gobbledygook for the Goop Generation.'

'Crashmat!' Sean said, hitting the table so hard the jigsaw pieces jumped in their box. 'That's where I saw it. In a school hall I went to a few weeks ago, doing my "Don't do drugs, kids" assembly.'

'Which school?'

'St Mary's, I think. On Martyr's Hill.'

'I know where it is.' Edie took a very large gulp of brandy.

Sean nodded. 'Didn't you teach there, before you did supply work and crosswords?'

'I did.' More memories came back to her in a tide that contained secrets she'd thought she'd drowned. Just after, though, came a wave of curiosity. For once she didn't know it all. And that was thrilling.

Sean leaned forward. 'I don't want to scare you, but is there a possibility that you've been approached for a personal reason, not just because you solve puzzles?'

'There's a big difference between setting puzzles and solving them,' Edie replied, hoping he wouldn't notice that she hadn't answered the question.

'You didn't answer my question.'

Edie pictured the other jigsaw piece, sitting in a pot on her mantelpiece, next to her brother's ashes. Sean's watch, and now St Mary's, linked her directly with whatever was happening. 'I don't see what it could have to do with me,' she said, then shifted the subject. 'Is it enough for you to make it an official investigation?'

Sean shook his head. 'Not yet.'

'Then what should I do?' She tried to arrange her face in a way that suggested she was helpless.

Sean laughed again and held his chest in case he coughed. 'Don't try and look helpless, Edie. It *really* doesn't suit you. Tell you what. I've taken the day off tomorrow, as our adoption meeting is in the afternoon. How about we pay a visit to St Mary's first thing?'

Edie hesitated. St Mary's had been the site of so many poor choices.

'It'll help take my mind off the meeting. It's all up to

the social worker now, to see if she likes us. You'll be doing me a favour if you come with me to the school.'

'Excellent,' she lied. She looked down at the outline on the pieces. There were so many dead bodies in her past, not all of them buried.

'What are you thinking?' Sean was staring at her with concern.

'I always thought one day I'd have a grand house with an entrance hall with parquet floor or black and white tiles.' Lying seemed the best approach in the circumstances.

'You still could!'

Edie laughed. 'There's no cash in crosswords.'

'I know someone with an Only Fans account who does puzzles naked on live webcam.'

'I'm glad you're supporting the arts, Sean.'

'She's my mate, Edie. And that's clearly not my thing. Now if it were a man, solving the *Times* crossword wearing only a cardigan and horn-rimmed glasses, *then* I'd subscribe.'

'Well, I won't be stripping off for online wankers. It's cold enough in my house as it is.'

Sean drained the last of his pint and stood. 'Same again?'

'Don't you have to get home to Liam?' She hoped her lip didn't curl when she mentioned Sean's husband's name.

'He's out tonight, running as always, then he's seeing some friends, again, for a Christmas drink. He's already said I shouldn't wait up.'

'Will you?'

''Course I will. I like to make him tea, give him

Ibuprofen and a pint of water. It's also the only time he'll eat carbs, so I take advantage by eating loads of Biscoff-topped toast with him. I wouldn't be able to sleep anyway.'

'The adoption meeting?'

'I know you told me not to get invested, but I can't help it. So. Drink?'

'Bottle of Sol for me this time. And don't bother with the lime wedge stuffed in the top. I'm sour enough already.'

As Sean went to the bar, Edie tried not to think of memories of St Mary's. Instead, she jumbled it into an anagram. 'My stars.' She didn't believe in astrology, but she hoped both his stars, and hers, were in alignment.

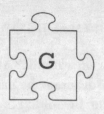

Six

Blood pooled on the ground around Carl Latimer's head and leg. The killer shivered, and not from the cold. Something moved behind them and they twisted round. An owl rose overhead, calling who-knew-who for help. There were witnesses to what had been done.

Latimer's hand twitched like the killer had seen happen to the dying on television. They had never seen someone die in front of them before. There was no sense that anything spiritual was taking place. No spectral light, no barely perceptible shift in the surroundings, no wisp of spirit heading for the treetops.

The killer shook. They had never hit someone before, not even a punch in jest, and bringing down the log on Latimer's head had needed more force than they'd anticipated. They'd had to go in for a second hit, terrible executioner that they were. But at least Latimer was unconscious, face down, leg bent to the side like a frog, by the time the killer brought the log down on the Games teacher's knee. Those charged with wielding death should do so responsibly.

Blood pulsed out, soaking into the soil and leaves of the woodland floor. Closing their eyes, the killer whispered an atheist's prayer, then stopped. A god who would take a murderer's offering was not one from whom they wished benediction.

Opening their eyes, the killer realised they were still grasping the log. They had to drop it, leave it for the police to find, but their fingers wouldn't uncurl. They gripped onto the wood as stubbornly as Latimer held on to life. It was as if the killer was stuck there until Carl Latimer died. Perhaps that was how it should be. Latimer might deserve to die but, as a human, his life should be respected, even if it was taken. The killer stood taller under the dark forest sky. 'I'm sorry.'

Carl's fingers trembled still. Perhaps they should hit him again, put him down like one would a fatally wounded animal.

Bile coursed through the killer. It burned, and they were glad. Both because they deserved that pain, and more, and because it meant they felt something again. For too many years, the killer had been dead inside. Now there was a chance they could feel alive. They swallowed the sick as it surged into their mouth. No DNA would be found from this killer.

The song was still playing, and they knew that they would now hate that song until they themselves died.

Carl had stopped moving. His eyes were closed. The killer was glad they didn't have to bend close to touch him; it was clear from the cessation of breath in the air. Carl was dead. They had become the killer.

Taking the jigsaw piece out of their coat pocket, they looked at it one more time. It was the next step in their expiation and the next clue for the Pensioner Puzzler. Only when Edie O'Sullivan spoke of what she'd done would the blackboard be wiped clean and they would, at last, be free.

Seven

December 20th

St Mary's School looked out over the sea. Made of dark red brick with mullioned windows, it had changed so little since the bleak day Edie had left that, for one moment, she felt as if she was being shown round her past.

Even the smell was the same when they walked through the main front doors: floor polish, sweat, tray-baked cake and the citrus smarting of egos and hearts.

'DI Brand-O'Sullivan.' The St Mary's receptionist stared at Sean with eyes so narrowed their whites were hardly visible. The glass screen in front of her was smudged with handprints and had a small envelope of an opening. Her scowl seemed fixed, the dark shadows under her eyes making it look as though she hadn't slept. She had the general appearance of a bank teller who would refuse to give out money.

'Pleasure to see you again, Mrs Challis. And I asked you last time to call me Sean.' Sean gave her one of his most winning smiles.

Mrs Challis, however, was not won over. 'I didn't know

37

you had an appointment, Inspector. Let's see if you're on the list.' She flipped through the huge academic diary in front of her, not even looking at it. Instead, she stared Sean right in the eyes without blinking. 'See? No appointment.'

Sean shuffled and seemed to shrink. His cheeks went blini pale and his neck, salmon pink.

Edie was torn between feeling defensive of Sean and admiring of Mrs Challis. She was in the presence of what used to be called a 'tartar', a woman so formidable her passive aggression punched into straight-up aggression. Everyone needed a Challis on their side.

'I've come on a potential police matter, Mrs Challis,' Sean replied. 'I was hoping we could have a quick look around the school hall.'

Mrs Challis shook her head. Her hair was so firmly lacquered that it looked as if not even a force ten wind would trouble it. 'Absolutely not. We can't just let people wander around the school.'

'Even police officers?' Edie asked.

Mrs Challis picked up a neatly folded copy of *The National* and opened it. She pretended to read, clearly hoping they would both go away. On the other side of the page, Edie's mini crossword-of-the-day was already neatly filled in, along with all the other puzzles. The bookshelf behind the receptionist featured box files and Elly Griffiths' latest novel, which had Post-its sticking out the sides like Sean's tongue from his mouth when he was thinking.

Sean stood a little taller. 'We have received a possible threat connected with the school gym.'

Mrs Challis tilted her head. 'A threat?'

'Or a warning, we're not sure.'

'I'll have to know more than that before I can give you access.'

'I can't give you information that may be essential to an investigation.'

Sean and Mrs Challis stared at each other, locked in a stalemate.

'But I can,' Edie said. 'It involves quite the puzzle, including mysterious jigsaw pieces, one of which features wooden bars, like the climbing equipment in your school hall, and a sign stuck to them.'

Mrs Challis blinked and turned to her. 'And you are?'

'Edie O'Sullivan.' Edie pointed to the newspaper. 'I write—'

'You're the Pensioner Puzzler!' Mrs Challis said, a genuine smile now climbing up her face.

'I don't go by that name.'

'I do your puzzles every day. I time myself. Sometimes, Dr Berkeley and I race each other, just for fun.'

Edie suspected that Mrs Challis' idea of fun involved immense concentration, fierce competition and very little actual merriment. She could see how school administration, with its parents and pupils to be wrangled, was a lot like one of those puzzles where you move pieces around a square to form a picture.

'I can't rival him on philosophy, education or science. As a chemist, Dr Berkeley knows the periodic table back to front, so those symbols you use don't faze him. He's obsessed with history, too. But I hold my own.'

'I bet you do,' Edie said.

'I'm a literature fiend, not bad on music and very up on current events. We can't wait for your next one.'

'And I am grateful for your interest. You keep me in a job.' Edie hoped that she appeared more gracious than she felt. 'Now, do you think I could take a quick look in the school hall? We don't even know what we're looking for, but we must start somewhere. It's like working out a crossword or a jigsaw.'

Mrs Challis nodded slowly. 'It is a process.'

'A ritual even,' Edie replied. 'Tea on, biscuit dunked, brain engaged. Doing a crossword or a sudoku is like a rosary, going through each mystery in turn.'

Mrs Challis kept nodding and blinking, as if she couldn't believe she was being seen and understood.

Edie, however, felt a little sick at the intimacy of Mrs Challis' gaze. 'So, do you think we could pop in to take a look? We'll only be a few minutes, won't we, Sean?'

Sean was looking at Edie in absolute amazement.

'I'll show you in.' Mrs Challis was already on her feet and coming out of the reception, cradling *The National* to her chest as if it were a kitten. Abruptly, she held it out in front of her. She looked like a shy teenager rather than a no-more-flak-taking fifty-ish-year-old. 'Would you sign this, please?' She pointed to Edie's name, sitting above the crossword.

Edie signed, caught between feeling pride in her work and embarrassment for Mrs Challis. She added an extra flourish under her name like she'd seen authors do, then handed the paper back.

Mrs Challis stood still, looking down at the signature. She looked as if she were about to cry. 'Thank you, Ms O'Sullivan.'

'Call me Edie.' Edie hoped her smile was ingratiating, instead of looking as if she was grinding her teeth.

'And I'm Sandra.' Sandra Challis' eyes opened so wide that Edie could see the green flecking her blue irises. She wasn't moving, as if she'd forgotten that she was supposed to be leading them into the hall. Edie knew the phrase 'never meet your heroes' but decided that there should be a phrase from the heroes' perspective: 'never meet your acolytes.'

'After you, then, Sandra?' Sean tried to prompt her.

Edie winced, anticipating Sandra's response.

'It's Mrs Challis to you, Inspector,' Sandra snapped.

The school hall was larger than Edie remembered. Their footsteps echoed on scuffed yet still shiny floorboards that had seen over a century of children sit on their laps as they pretended to listen to teachers. Edie could almost hear the shouts and laughs and sobs of kids past, struggling with a pommel horse or trying to climb the rope that hung from the ceiling. The clock on the wall ticked towards ten o'clock, as if to remind all that time slipped like rope through burning hands.

She was swung back to an early December evening in 1999. Sky had come to the school after Edie had been supposed to meet her at home after work. Edie was up a ladder, here in the hall, instead, putting up Christmas decorations. When she came down, they were standing under the clock, like lovers meeting at a railway station.

41

Sky dropped to one knee and held out her palm. On it was a little blue box, opened to show a diamond ring. 'Edith Katherine O'Sullivan,' she said. Her hair was in two long plaits. 'We have been together many years, but I really want to be your wife. The law won't let us be together, but we can jump over brooms, and have a party, and set up our lives together. We'll have children and as many cats as you want. Will you marry me?'

Panic surged. 'Children?'

'I know we talked about it when we got together, and you said you didn't want children. But, since then, you've adopted Seán, and you've been such a wonderful parent. We could be mums to our own child.'

'I'm fifty-six, Sky!' Edie's raised voice echoed round the hall. 'I am so tired at the end of the day I can hardly see. Sean will be an adult in a few years and then I can retire from full-time teaching and do my own thing, not have a toddler.'

Sky's eyes were shiny. 'What about me? What about what I want?'

'*You* said the age gap wouldn't make a difference. *You* agreed you didn't want kids.' Edie's finger jabbed towards Sky. A red ball of fury blazed inside her. 'You didn't even want to co-parent Sean. You said you wouldn't be any good.'

'I know. But in the last few years I've really wanted a child of my own.'

'Why didn't you say?'

'I *am* saying.'

As Edie imagined holding Sky as she gave birth, and

the two of them cradling and raising their child, her heart swelled like blown glass. Then she pictured Sky pregnant, and then Sky dying, as Edie's mother had, on Christmas Eve. It wasn't 1946 anymore, but still, as an older mum the risk of complications would be greater. Edie's heart would shatter if she lost Sky.

'I know me being pregnant would freak you out, because of your mum. But we'll be okay. Please, Edie. Think about it at least?' Sky looked so young and earnest standing there. The sixteen years between them had never felt so significant.

'No,' was all Edie could say.

'I really need to do this.' Sky's voice was quiet and bruised. 'I would love to do it with you, or at least have your support.'

'You will never have my support for this. It's my way or no way.'

'Please?' Sky was now on both knees, hands out in supplication to Edie, waiting to receive a sacrament.

Her naked desperation filled Edie with fear and anger. 'You were right all along. You'd make a terrible mother.' Milliseconds after she said it, Edie knew she was calling time on their love. But she couldn't bring herself to unsay the words.

Sky's face clouded. Tears fell.

They parted under that clock, lovers leaving rather than meeting. Sky's trainers shushed away across the floor.

'Are you with us, Edie?' Sandra Challis, and Sean next to her, were looking at her with concern.

Edie tried to drag herself back to the present by focusing

on the clock as it was right now, each tick chipping away at the time before Sean's adoption meeting.

But the meniscus of the past wouldn't let her go. One end of the hall was taken up with the unseen stage. Edie remembered being behind the curtains that hid it from view, waiting for her last full school assembly. It had been weeks after Sky had left her and the day after the event that had changed everything. Standing there, her heart a bad actor, she had felt like a corpse waiting to be viewed at a funeral parlour.

'Edie?' Sean said gently, pulling her away from the curtains.

She had to swim away from these memories. She was here to solve a puzzle.

'Are these the wooden bars you mean?' Mrs Challis asked as they walked over to the climbing wall that reached up to the high ceiling.

'When I saw the sign, it was around here.' Sean pointed to the centre of the bars at his head height, and then at a small area where lighter wood was exposed. 'Looks like something was taped on and ripped off.'

'I tell the teachers time and time again to use the right materials for the job,' Mrs Challis said. 'They're worse than the children. At least I can get kids put on detention. It's the teachers who should be sat down after they finish work for the day and made to miss out on their bottles of red wine. Maybe then they wouldn't mess up the fabric of the school and society.'

'Well, quite.' Edie thought it best to steer the conversation away. Those kinds of chats, like great societies across time, never ended well. 'Do you remember a sign going up here? It would have been . . . what? . . . two weeks ago at least,' she said, raising questioning eyebrows at Sean.

Sean nodded. 'That's when I saw it.' He showed Mrs Challis the picture on his phone.

'I remember that poster. Made me think that my climbing days, socially, professionally or literally, are over.'

'Do you know who made it and put it up?' Sean asked.

'Mr Latimer often makes so-called "motivational" posters for his classes. Not that they work. Kids can be very lazy.' Mrs Challis tutted.

'Not just kids, Sandra.' Edie leaned closer to Mrs Challis in a stab at being chummy. 'As you've said, adults can be just as lackadaisical.'

'Lackadaisical! That was in yesterday's crossword! I was pleased with myself for getting that one.'

Edie had to stop herself shouting that it was an incredibly easy clue and of course Mrs Challis got it, and that Edie had only said 'lackadaisical' to try and build a bond between them to exploit. She could feel the words building up, filling her mouth.

Just then the double doors opened, and a tall man with grey-black hair strode into the hall. His back was dead straight and his suit well-fitting. Only a sprinkling of shaving rash over his granite jaw showed anything less than authority and precision.

Edie would put money on this being the headmaster. 'There you are, Mrs Challis!' The man was smiling, but there was a jagged edge to his voice. His right hand played with his tie pin.

'Sorry, Dr Berkeley,' Mrs Challis said, smiling back up at him, suddenly flushed. She took a folded handkerchief out of her pocket and dabbed at the sweat that had appeared at the sides of her neck. 'I was showing my guests the school hall.'

Dr Berkeley wasn't looking at Mrs Challis. He was too busy staring at Sean. 'You're the police officer who came a few weeks ago for the drugs talk,' he said. 'Have you been sent to enquire about Mr Latimer?'

'Mr Latimer?' Sean turned to Mrs Challis. 'As in—'

'The Games teacher I was telling you about.'

Edie felt a crypt-cool prickle of disquiet. 'Why would we be asking about him?'

Dr Berkeley looked to Edie at last, eyebrows raised, probably only just realising she was there. Edie was used to being invisible – even orange-haired older women managed to disappear.

'Can I talk to you in private please, Mrs Challis?'

'Of course, headmaster.' Mrs Challis' face was fully alert as she searched the headmaster's for information. She turned to Edie and bowed her head. 'I'll be back as soon as I can.' She held the signed newspaper to her lips as if praying upon it, before following the headmaster across the hall and through the doors.

'You've got a fangirl, Aunt Edie.' Sean's eyes twinkled.

'At least give her the dignity of being a woman, Sean.'

'A fan*woman*, then.'

'Without her being a crossword kook, we'd never have got in. Not that there's anything to look at. Why on earth would we be sent here?'

'Whoever sent you the jigsaw pieces wanted us to be aware of something.' Sean started taking pictures of the climbing bars to compare with the jigsaw.

The headmaster opened the double doors again and ushered the receptionist back through. 'I'll leave that in your capable hands, then, Mrs Challis.' Edie suspected this was not the first time he'd said that. Mrs Challis seemed to be a woman who cleared up the messes of others, tutting all the while.

Sandra Challis weaved a little as she came towards them, as if her usual equilibrium had tipped. The newspaper had gone, and instead she was holding a torn-off note and staring at it with a frown, as if it were a puzzle she had to solve. She was biting her lip. When she reached them and looked up, her eyes were glazed.

'What is it, Sandra?'

'You said jigsaw pieces?' Her hands were shaking.

'Has something happened?'

'Mr Latimer was found in the woods this morning, with a head wound and a broken leg. He's at the hospital.'

'What's that got to do with—'

'They think he was attacked. He was holding a jigsaw piece in his hand.'

Eight

Carl Latimer's hospital ward smelled of food cloaked in plastic cloches. Each bed was occupied. One man was crying behind blue curtains; another was on the phone, lying about where he was to a loved one. Edie hated hospitals almost as much as police stations. Both suggested death. At least festive decorations hadn't hit the ward. Christmas was hardly sanitary.

Latimer was sitting up in bed. As they approached, Sean glanced at his watch. Edie looked, too. He had an hour to get to the adoption meeting.

'You should leave, come back later,' Edie whispered.

Sean shook his head, although she could tell he was torn.

'Which station are you from?' Latimer asked when they'd both sat down. His leg was in plaster, his elbow in a sling, his chest strapped. His pupils were dark moons, swollen with opiates, and his skin was grey. He looked little like the energetic, half-marathon-winning man that Edie had googled on the way over. His speech came out slowly and slurred, and he gripped the side of the bed as if trying to hold on to his words.

'Weymouth,' Sean said.

Latimer sucked his teeth. 'I was hoping you were from Swanage. My mate works there.'

'You'll have to put up with me, I'm afraid,' Sean replied. 'I'm DI Brand-O'Sullivan.'

'And I'm his associate,' Edie said. Sean gave her a stern look. He'd asked her to keep quiet during the interview and she'd agreed, not something she ever found easy. She distracted herself by making up anagrams. *Latimer = maltier. Ward = draw. Kidney dish = hides dinky.*

Not that Latimer seemed to notice she was there. Edie popped some gum in her mouth and started chewing.

Sean got out his notebook. 'I'd like to ask you some questions about what happened to you last night.'

Sean had talked to his boss, DCI Leyland, on the way in, keeping him up to date with developments. Leyland had made clear that until it was certain that Latimer had been assaulted, rather than it being an accident, there wasn't enough to launch an investigation. As the DCI had stated, though, the jigsaw piece was too much of a coincidence to ignore. He had instructed Sean to officially question Latimer. He had also agreed to have the area where Latimer had fallen in the woods cordoned off as a potential crime scene, although there wasn't yet sufficient evidence to get forensics in, or to have anyone secure the site properly.

Sean had argued that without SOCOs and security on site, the scene would be compromised. Any additional evidence would be destroyed by intruders, weather, animals etc.

'What do you want to know?' Latimer reached with some difficulty for the glass of water on his over-bed table.

Sean gently pushed the table closer to help. 'We'll need some initial information. Full name, address, occupation, date of birth, etc.'

Latimer sighed exaggeratedly, as if he had somewhere more important to be than a hospital bed with everyone around him trying to help. 'Carl Benjamin Latimer. 25 Ashton Road, Weymouth. Born 13th March, 1987. Head of Games, St Mary's School. Anything else I can help you with?' His sarcasm was strong and bitter.

Edie imagined him marching behind the puffing stragglers on a cross-country course, mocking them. She had a long-standing hatred of PE teachers.

Sean scribbled down the details. 'Take us through exactly what happened before the event that landed you here.'

'I was out running, as usual, and doing well.' Latimer spoke with difficulty, taking sips of breath, holding his ribcage. 'Exceeding my markers. All that good stuff. I was nearly at the end when I tripped on something, a large branch across the path. I fell, badly. I was in pain, but I was about to get back up, keep running, you know, every second counts, when I heard someone coming up behind me.'

Sean looked up from his notes. 'Did you see who it was?'

'I tried to, but then I felt a massive pain in my head, and everything went black.'

'Anything else you remember?'

Latimer tilted his head, as if that would help roll his memories out like marbles. 'I heard music, and there was movement in the bushes, but then there always is. Some of the birds in the trees seemed startled, but I thought that was because of me.'

I bet you did, Edie thought, but managed not to say. She felt like a game of Kerplunk with only a few sticks left to pull before she spilled. She used to play it with Sean. And maybe she'd play it with Sean's child soon, too. 'What music was it?'

Latimer frowned. 'Who's that?' He gestured towards Edie, clearly seeing her for the first time.

'I'm his great-aunt.' Edie's tone was as cold as if it were kept in a hospital mortuary.

Sean glanced at her, trying to tell her to be quiet with his eyes. But he didn't use his mouth, so she decided to keep going.

'And how was it played? The music?'

'Is she allowed to ask me questions?' Latimer asked Sean. 'What's she with you for, anyway? Do you always bring old ladies with you?' He laughed, then clutched at his chest.

Any sympathy Edie had evaporated. The gum now softened, she started blowing a bubble. The air filled with the smell of fake cherry. She held eye contact with Latimer as the bubble grew bigger and bigger. His eyes were horror-blown, growing wider as he watched.

'She looks like a troll,' Latimer said to Sean. 'You know that right? One of the ones with sticking-up hair.'

Sean's jaw tightened. 'Answer her questions.'

Latimer broke his gaze away from Edie's and shuddered. It was as if he had never seen an eighty-year-old woman blow a bubble before. He tried to fold his arms into a toddler sulk then cried out at the pain. 'The song had something to do with pictures.'

'"Picture to Burn" by Taylor Swift?' Sean asked.

Edie popped the bubble.

Latimer jumped, grimacing first in pain, then in distaste as she placed the gum in the cardboard kidney dish by his bed.

'No, it was a bloke singing.'

Sean tried again. 'Ed Sheeran's "The Photograph"?'

'It was definitely "Pictures of . . . something". An old song.'

'"Pictures of Lily"?' Edie asked, remembering playing The Who in her bedroom.

Latimer frowned. 'Maybe, don't know. Made me think of goths.'

Edie snorted. 'Not "Pictures of You" by The Cure? Because that's hardly ancient.' She counted back – somehow it was over thirty years old. Sky had played *Disintegration*, the album the song was from, over and over, so many times that Edie had come to see it as their album. 'Lovesong' had been their anthem. She'd deliberately avoided it since Sky left.

Time doesn't just fly, it flytips. Dumps the old by the side of the road as everyone else drives on.

'That's it!' Latimer looked animated for the first time since they'd arrived. 'That's the song.'

Edie realised that she was singing, and that Sean was looking at her strangely.

'And it came from a phone, I think. Tinny, but loud. I thought it was kids up to something.' He paused. 'I remember the music got louder after I fell.'

'As the footsteps came nearer?' she asked.

'I suppose.'

'Would anyone have a reason to harm you, Mr Latimer?' Sean asked.

'Other than my crazy exes?' Latimer laughed, but Sean didn't, and neither did Edie. 'My running group probably wants to nobble me so they can win something for once.' When Sean wrote that down, Latimer added, 'Only joking. No one wants to hurt me. I'm a bloody dream.'

Edie rolled her eyes. 'I bet you are.'

Sean took a quick look at his watch. Edie checked her own. Just over fifty minutes till the meeting. 'So, what happened after you blacked out?'

'Next thing I know, someone's shaking me and shouting.'

'When was this?' Edie leaned forward.

'Early hours of the morning. I could see the person crouching over me with their phone torch. And the huge face of their dog trying to lick my blood.'

'You shouldn't let animals do that,' Edie said. 'They can catch diseases from you.'

Sean sighed.

Edie shrugged. It was true.

'You're really starting to piss me off, you know?' Latimer looked over at the button to press for help. 'I'm in a shit ton of pain, and you're just trolling me.'

'You're the one who said I looked like one. Trolls gonna troll.' Sometimes it paid to be the older parent of a millennial.

'Let's get back to what happened, shall we?' Sean said quickly. 'Did you get their name? The person who found you?'

Latimer shook his head, then winced. 'They rang for an ambulance so it might be recorded, I don't know.'

'And what have the doctors said about your injuries?'

'That one of my head wounds could be from falling, but the other one, on the back of my skull, is more likely to be from being hit. I've got one cracked rib, and some others are bruised. My right elbow's broken but they can't put a cast on apparently, so that's shit. My knee's the worst thing.' Latimer's lip started quivering. 'It looks like someone smashed it into pieces.'

Edie locked eyes with him. 'Pieces?'

'My kneecap is shattered. The doctor doesn't know when or if I'll be able to run again.' He looked down at his leg and his eyes began to shine. A little boy trying not to cry.

'I'm sorry,' she said. 'That must be very hard for someone like you.' She meant it, too.

A tear fell, and he swiped it away with the heel of his hand. Then his brow furrowed, and his eyes angered over. 'What do you care?'

'You make it hard to, it's true.'

'Did you make this notice?' Sean asked, showing Latimer the enlarged photo of the sign.

Latimer nodded. 'Classic motivation. Get them learning self-reliance early.'

'And there's nothing in it that people would take against?' Edie asked.

'Only the weak.'

Sean checked his watch again and stood to leave. 'If we find out anything more we'll be back in touch, Mr Latimer.'

'The jigsaw piece,' Edie whispered.

Sean closed his eyes and nodded. 'We were told that you had something in your hand when you were found.'

'Yeah, it was weird. A jigsaw piece.'

'Do jigsaws have any significance to you at all?' Sean asked.

'You take a picture, break it up, then put it back together again. What's the point?'

'Where is it now, the piece that was in your hand?' Edie tried to hide her excitement.

'In my locker.' Latimer's eyes slid to the cabinet next to him. 'Help yourself. I don't want it.'

Sean opened the locker and looked inside. He slid on a pair of plastic gloves and pulled out a grey paper tray. On it lay a bottom left-hand corner jigsaw piece with what looked like a brick wall on it and something white.

Edie took her phone out of her handbag, spilling tissues and a packet of bubble gum. She popped another piece in her mouth and started chewing. It helped her think.

After taking a picture of the jigsaw piece, she enlarged it, as Sean had the day before. Who said old dogs couldn't learn new tricks? Although Edie was more of a cat.

'What can you see?' Sean asked.

'The edge of what looks like a street sign, on a brick wall.'

'What's on it?'

'Only the first letter, then it breaks off. "P".' She enlarged it further. 'And there's something that looks like blood on the walls.'

'I'll call it in, get someone looking for a street sign on a wall beginning with "P", but . . .'

'It'll be like finding a clove in a bag of nails.'

'At least it's a start.' Sean stood and walked away, already on his phone.

Latimer's eyes were beginning to close, his mouth slackening into sleep. Without Sean there, it was like she had disappeared again.

'Mr Latimer?'

His eyes opened a little more. 'What?' His tone was grudging.

'Look after yourself, would you? When you leave, I mean. I have a feeling that whoever hurt you meant to kill you. And kudos for not dying and all, but they may attempt to finish the job.'

Latimer scoffed. 'They can try.'

Anger flared in Edie. 'I'm trying to keep you alive.'

'Go back to your old people's home.'

'Old ladies know more than you, have seen more than you, and, as you have shown, are largely invisible.'

Sean walked back over and stood by Edie's chair.

'If you had taken an old lady with you last night,' Edie continued as she stood, 'she'd have been able to tell you what happened. Or stopped it happening in the first place.'

Latimer's laugh was sardonic. 'Sure.'

'Old ladies don't just wear tweed, you know.'

Latimer turned away from her. Some people just won't take advice.

'You *are* wearing tweed, Aunt Edie,' Sean whispered as they walked to the door.

'Yes. But this is Vivienne Westwood, darling.'

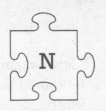

Nine

'That bear is glaring at me.' Edie was looking through the rear-view mirror at the huge yellow teddy Sean had bought from the hospital shop. Wherever he went now, he kept finding things for Juniper. Edie had told him it was bad luck to be presumptuous. Sean had said that he thought it was more like trying to manifest the adoption by acting as if it was already happening, then told *her* off for being superstitious.

The bear was now sitting in the middle of the back seat, amber eyes glinting with reflected streetlamps.

'It's keeping an eye on you,' Sean said, keeping his own gaze on the road. 'Protecting you in case the jigsaw puzzler is dangerous.'

'If I'm going to have a security detail watching out for jigsaw-wielding menaces, it won't be a three-foot ursine. Anyway, I'm your elder; I look after *you*.'

'You know I love you and appreciate everything you've done for me, Edie, but I'm a married police officer in my thirties. You can stand down now.'

'Never. I have few purposes in life, one of which is to make sure you're safe.'

Edie stared, unblinking, in front of her as the windscreen

replayed her memories. Standing in front of Sean's incubator in the Neonatal Unit in the days after his birth, his lungs learning how to breathe. Standing by the graveside of Duncan, Melissa and William, holding Sean as he grasped his toy elephant by the fluffy tusk. There was a photo of her throwing soil onto the coffins, two large, one heartbreakingly small, next to each other in the ground. With her silver jumpsuit, pink hair and straight back, she looked like a knight with a punkish plume, daring death to come any closer.

'Even so,' Sean said. 'You must leave all this to me from now on. Right? If you receive anything else, you hand it over and don't get involved.'

'As if I would.'

'Edie . . .'

'This is your job, not mine. I'm not qualified, and you are. You needn't worry.'

A call came through the speakers, from Liam.

'I'm on my way, love,' Sean said, before Liam could say anything. 'I should be able to get there on time, or just after it starts.'

'You said you'd be here with me before.' Liam's voice was urchin-spiked. 'That was why you took the morning off, so we could prepare together.'

'I know, but a case came up.'

'Of course it did. Not that jigsaw thing Edie lured you over with yesterday?'

Sean winced.

'I'm sitting right here, Liam.' Edie kept her voice level.

A beat of silence.

'I'll tell you more later,' Sean said quickly. 'I'm just dropping Edie home, then I'll be over to you straight away. Maybe, on our way back, no matter what happens, I could get us something nice for dinner. Your choice.'

'Let's see, shall we?' Liam's voice was tight.

'See you soon. Love you!'

Liam ended the call without responding.

Sean stared out of the windscreen like a glass-eyed bear. Edie knew he couldn't stand letting anyone down. The slightest sign of conflict made his insides turn and twist like a fortune fish. He'd need to get over that once he had a child.

Edie folded her arms and crossed her legs, bumping her arthritic knee on the glove box. 'You can't prioritise me or work over your family, Sean. Believe me.'

'You *are* family, Edie. You are my aunt, my guardian.' He paused. 'My mum.'

Edie had to stop herself gasping. Her heartbeat increased. He hardly ever called her that.

'And, as family, you're coming to us for Christmas, right?'

So, he'd just called her 'mum' because he was trying to get her to do what he wanted. 'Absolutely not.'

'What are you going to do all on your own?'

'I have cats. I'm never alone.'

'You've got to do something special, though.'

'I'll treat Christmas as I do every day: getting up at six, having my walk, doing a jigsaw, writing a crossword, watching a gig on YouTube, going to see Riga and getting pleasantly pissed . . . If I'm lucky, I won't even remember it's Christmas at all.'

'We'd love you to be there.'

Edie laughed. 'You're joking. Liam wants me with you for Christmas dinner?'

Sean didn't say anything.

'Exactly. Anyway,' Edie continued, 'this is your last Christmas before you have a kid. You and Liam should be having as much sex and romance as you can, while you can.'

'*Aunt Edie!*'

'Don't tell me it's not true. Soon it'll be no-sleep-nights, not date nights. Last thing you need is me there in an appalling Christmas jumper.'

'You in a Christmas jumper would make my year.' He smiled as if imagining it. 'You'll babysit for us, though, won't you, when we have a kid?' His urgency made her melt a little.

'Who else is going to teach the child how to set cross-words, alongside other essential life skills?'

Sean smiled. 'If you change your mind about Christmas, we'll have enough food in.'

They pulled into her street as silence filled the car, along with sadness. They both knew she never changed her mind.

Edie watched Sean drive away, satnav already set for the café-bar in Swanage where they were meeting the social worker. She said a quick prayer to Monica, patron saint of parents and lost children. May Sean be the parent he wished to be.

'Edie!' A breathy shout came from the access path at the end of the street. Lucy Pringle was running towards her in an unseasonal singlet and shorts. Her skin was red and blotchy, her ponytail a sweaty pendulum.

Lucy stopped in front of Edie and bent over, hands on her knees. As she stood, she pressed 'stop' on her smartwatch. 'Not bad. Twenty seconds quicker than yesterday.'

'Very good,' Edie said, with no sincerity at all. 'You must be very pleased.' She turned to go, but Lucy placed a perspiring hand on her tweed shoulder.

'I was hoping to catch you. I took in a package for you earlier.'

A chill slid down Edie's neck like sleet.

'If you wait a sec, I could get it. Or you could come in?'

'I'll stay here,' Edie replied.

Lucy jogged across the road to her house. She picked up a brown padded envelope from the shelf in her porch and padded back, handing it over. 'Here you go.'

Edie looked at the printed label addressed to 'The Pensioner Puzzler'. Inside, she could feel through the envelope, were more jigsaw pieces.

'Police are asking for witnesses to an incident in Godlingston Woods last night. A local teacher has been left injured but in stable condition. If you saw something suspicious around midnight last night, please ring Weymouth Police on—'

The killer tried to focus on the words coming from the radio, but it was as if church bells were tolling a tinnitus.

Nothing was solid. They held on to the edge of the desk, but even that felt like water.

They'd killed Carl. They were sure of it. They hadn't checked for his pulse, but there'd been no breath coming out of his mouth. That was surely conclusive.

But, unless this was a trick or trap on the part of the police, Carl had lived. The killer wondered if their cut-off prayer had been intercepted by a trickster god, or Lord of Misrule, who had turned their plans upside down. But they had to fall back on what was most likely: they had messed up. Again.

They would have to make up for their mistakes, but how? It would have to be when Latimer went running again but, with a broken leg, how soon would that be? The killer had ruined their own plans before they'd even started.

But they had to keep going. The thought of taking the life of the next victim made them want to cry, but they had so much to make up for, so many Christmases that they'd got wrong. *This* was how they'd prove themselves worthy. Piece by piece, murder by murder, they'd make it the perfect Christmas.

Ten

Sean parked up and sprinted along Swanage seafront. Sleet stung his head from the outside, his thoughts from the inside. What would the social worker think of his lateness? Would it count against them that he'd chosen a café-bar? What if he'd ruined everything before the meeting had even begun?

Sean slowed as he approached The Cellar Bar, nestled under the Mowlem cinema, facing Swanage Bay. He and Liam had come here for espresso martinis on their first date, eight years ago, and they'd been together ever since.

Liam was sitting at a table in the corner; a woman, the social worker presumably, sat opposite him. She had pink hair in a tousled bun and was wearing a big brown jumper. The mighty Mariah Carey's 'All I Want For Christmas Is You' was playing through the speakers. Sean decided to take it as a sign that things would go their way.

Liam looked up and relief ran across his face, quickly pursued by annoyance.

Sean hunkered down to give him a hug, and a kiss on the cheek. Liam patted his shoulder. 'So sorry I'm late,' Sean said, sliding into the spare chair. Through the large glass windows, the rough sea stilled, as if listening. 'The traffic from Weymouth was terrible.'

The woman blinked at him, eyes huge behind thick, round spectacles. She looked like an unbelieving owl.

'Also,' he admitted, 'I left late.'

'Liam told me you were racing from a case.' She stuck out a hand that jangled with bangles. 'I'm Sunny, Juniper's social worker.'

They shook hands. 'How is Juniper?' Sean pictured the four-year-old with red-gold hair, who, in every photo, stood unsmiling against the nearest wall or door, hands behind her back. The first time Sean had seen her photo and bio in the heart-tugging brochure full of unfamilied kids (he'd told Edie off for dubbing it 'an Argos cata- logue of adoptees'), he'd felt a kinship that his therapist was helping him understand. And then when he had met her, at a picnic in Lodmoor Country Park, she'd come over to their picnic blanket with her Lego set. They'd constructed a tower in near silence for an hour.

'She's looking forward to Christmas. She's already put out her stocking.'

Sean's hand went to his heart as he thought of all the activities they'd be able to do with Juniper next Christmas, if all went well – the Weymouth Elf Trail, panto at the Pavilion, the Polar Express at Swanage steam railway . . . Edie had never so much as taken him to see Santa.

Liam took and squeezed Sean's hand. 'So, what would you like to know about us?'

'Actually, there are a couple of things I wanted to raise with you both before we go any further. Firstly, Juniper's biological mum has got in touch with us – she's five months pregnant and finding things a struggle. We don't know yet if she'll want to care for this child, or what social services will think best, but, as you know, if we can keep siblings together, we will. So, I was wondering if—'

Sean and Liam looked at each other. 'Yes,' they said, at the same time.

Sean felt as if his heart was swelling to twice its usual size. 'In case that wasn't clear, we'd love to also adopt Juniper's brother or sister, should it come to it.'

Sunny smiled. 'I was hoping you'd say that.'

'Is Juniper's mum being well looked after?' Sean asked.

Sunny nodded. 'She's getting all the help we can give her. So that only leaves one more thing I wanted to talk to you about, before we just chit-chat. I need to ask you something, Sean.'

Fear shivered through him. Outside, waves surged, spume rising over the sea wall. 'Ask away.'

'I've read in your files that you've recently been promoted to Detective Inspector.'

'That's right.' His fear increased. What if his job stopped them from becoming parents? How would Liam react?

'Sean passed his exams with the highest percentage in the region,' Liam chipped in. The pride was clear in his voice.

'Will that mean,' Sunny asked, 'that you'll have more, or fewer, dangerous situations to deal with? It's just that Juniper has obviously been through a lot. I need to make sure that her home life is stable and safe.'

Sean pushed his anxiety down, doing his best to keep his voice steady. 'We want that for her too. And while I was party to some dodgy situations when I was a PC, since becoming a detective, there have been far fewer. And the higher I go in the force, the more deskbound I'll be. The only dangers will be paper cuts and fighting over the hole punch.'

The social worker's magnified gaze seemed uncertain. 'Be honest with me. It will make everything work so much better.'

'There will always be some risks, I can't avoid that. But I'm sure it won't be a problem.'

'You look stressed,' Riga said when Edie sat down at the big table in her friend's kitchen. Riga was wearing one of the many Christmas jumpers she collected. This one was red and slim fitting, elegance itself apart from the words 'I LOVE SANTA'S SACK' on the front. 'Look at me. Show me your irises.'

Edie rolled her eyes.

'That wasn't what I meant, but no matter. I've seen all I need.' Riga walked slowly into the adjacent garden room. The sound of her secateurs snipping cut through a robin's song. She came back in with sprigs of chamomile, thyme and sage, adding them to a saucepan on the hob and whispering to Hekate. She then opened the apothecary drawers over her sink, taking out pinches of various dried herbs. Edie was used to Riga making potions – as long as the herbs were steeped in brandy and sugar, she didn't mind in the least.

'So, what's happened?' Riga asked.

Edie filled her in on the day's events, ending by telling her that she'd received new jigsaw pieces.

'*That's* why you've brought your jigsaw tray. I was worried you were going to force me to do one with you.'

'Never again. I've learned my lesson.'

Edie's one attempt to get Riga hooked on jigsaws had led to Riga throwing pieces all over the floor in frustration. Even Nicholas the pug had sniffed them and looked disgusted.

'You're so great at being a sounding board for my crosswords, I thought I could talk to you about the jigsaw clues.'

Riga raised meticulously pencilled eyebrows. '"Sounding board" makes me sound a little . . . flat.'

'My enabler, then.'

'Much better.'

Edie placed her tray on the table and laid out paper versions of the first jigsaw pieces she'd received, along with the piece she'd kept back from Sean.

'Did you make those?'

Edie couldn't tell from Riga's tone if she was mocking her artwork. She sat up straight, defensive. 'I know they're not perfect. I was in a hurry.'

'I was just marvelling. They're exactly as I remember.'

'Easy when you've got pictures.' Edie swiped to the photos on her phone. 'And I could use today's ones for scale.' She added the pieces from the padded envelope Lucy Pringle had given her. 'These three expand the crime scene section that probably makes up the centre of the jigsaw. Same black and white tiles, but this time with scattered holly leaves.'

'Nothing says Christmas like festive foliage and an outlined corpse.' Riga's tone was as dry as her thyme martinis.

'The other five, however, are more useful.' Edie laid down one that showed the next letter in the street sign: 'O'.

'"PO",' Riga mused. She leant over and took several A-Zs from a messy drawer.

'I haven't seen one of those in ages,' said Edie.

'I remain more comfortable with the analogue world.' Riga flicked through each to the end. 'If we assume we're dealing with victims from the Weymouth, Swanage and Studland area, we have Pocket Lane, Street or Avenue; Point Road and Lane; Pointer Lane; Polar Road and variants; Poole Road and variants; Pound Street and—'

'Wait,' Edie said, getting out a notebook and writing down all the possible streets. This kind of thoroughness was where she felt comfortable. Even so, there was no evidence that they should be restricted to this area.

Following the rules of crosswords, one should move on to the next clue. The next pieces were two that joined to show the acronym 'VIP'.

'"VIP",' Riga said. 'A Very Important Person, so maybe a dignitary, a councillor? Or someone famous?'

'Possibly.' Edie knew, though, that the first answer, unless on a mini or easy puzzle, was a misdirection. 'Although the letters are interlocked, so maybe it's an insignia?'

'Could be a VIP area in a club? The times I had in those in the sixties.' Riga's eyes were misted by time as well as glaucoma. 'Do they have such things in Weymouth?'

'How would I know?' Edie chewed gum to take away the medicinal taste of Riga's tincture. 'How about we look at the next clue?' She laid the last two puzzle pieces down. Across them lay a figure of eight made of twisted rope. 'Infinity symbol, invented by mathematician John Wallis in 1655.' Edie had used variants of it in crossword clues for years. 'Also called a lemniscate in algebraic geometry. Or lazy eight in livestock branding. Or a way of writing the Greek letter omega. Or could be for the brand Meta, as in Facebook and Instagram. I've also used it as a clue for the answer "Möbius strip".'

'It can also mean many things in different cultures,' Riga said, gently as usual, reminding Edie that there was a world beyond facts and puzzles. 'Including peace, tranquillity, endless love and the survival of the soul beyond the body. Maybe it's to do with someone's death not being the end.'

Edie was chilled at the thought. 'All of which widens possibilities, rather than narrowing them down.' Edie felt a rare sense of being out-puzzled by a better compiler. 'Maybe the rope helps?' She was getting desperate.

'How?'

'I've no idea.' Edie discreetly spat her gum into the hankie hidden up her sleeve. She read again the typed note that had been in the envelope with the pieces.

```
Ms O'Sullivan.
    These pieces are just for you. I know
you know how to keep secrets. Maybe you
can use them to prevent a death, rather
```

```
than be responsible for one. If you
take these, or any others, to the
police, both you and DI Sean will be in
my sights.
   Yours,
   Rest In Pieces
```

Riga glanced over to read without touching the paper. 'This isn't good.'

'You are a mistress of hyperbole, Riga.'

'What does that mean, "you know how to keep secrets"?'

Edie shook her head. 'I don't know.' And she didn't want to think about it. Secrets should be left at the bottom of the sea.

'Well, try not to blame yourself if you don't get it straight away. It's not like you can solve a jigsaw without all the pieces.'

'But that's what they want me to do, if I'm going to stop someone dying.'

'What does Sean say about this new batch?'

Edie didn't reply.

'You haven't told him yet, have you?'

'He made it clear that I shouldn't get involved. I don't want to be cut any further out of the investigation.' The puzzle had her gripped.

'Promise me you'll tell him in the morning.'

'Maybe.' Edie never made promises she couldn't keep.

Eleven

A new wreath was hanging on the door when Sean got home, not long after Liam. Eucalyptus, lavender and blue thistles created spokes that radiated outwards from reindeer moss that was covered with deep red roses, flowering white jasmine and pomegranate halves. Ivy trailed down to the doorstep like the tail of a comet.

Sean bent to smell the jasmine, feeling a whisper of the spirit of Christmas.

The door opened and Liam stood before him, holding out his arms.

Sean put down the big yellow bear and the takeaway bags he'd picked up on the way back. 'It's beautiful,' he said as they cuddled. 'Your best wreath yet.'

'I wanted something that felt like a good luck wreath.'

'It worked. Sunny *loved* us! One step closer to having our own little family.'

'Maybe not as little a family as we thought.'

'Let's hope so.' Sean had wondered on the way back whether to grab a bottle of champagne to celebrate, but had decided not to tempt fate. They'd been through so much to get to this point. But from what Sunny had said, it was all going ahead. Sean couldn't wait to tell Edie.

71

He carried the South Indian takeaway through to the kitchen, pausing to kiss Liam under the huge bough of mistletoe over the doorway. Liam was holding the bear, making them all a snuggly throuple.

As they laid out the food, Liam unwrapped a dosa and placed it on Sean's plate before helping himself to a large piece of fish wrapped in a banana leaf. 'So, why was Edie in the car? Is this the jigsaw thing?'

'Yeah.' Sean spooned aloo masala onto his dosa. He took a bite and realised just how hungry he was. 'A man was found unconscious and injured in Godlingston Woods, with a jigsaw piece in his hand.'

Liam's eyebrows raised. 'Do you mean Carl Latimer?'

'You know him?'

'He's in one of my running clubs. I heard on the group WhatsApp that he'd had an accident in the woods.'

'It may not be an accident. He was the one I went to interview in hospital.'

Liam's eyebrows shot up further. 'Is he going to be okay?'

Sean nodded. 'Yeah, although he won't be back running with you for a while.'

'He never could keep up anyway.' Liam was using his jokey voice, but he'd gone pale, his hand shaking. He couldn't deal with violence. 'And this has got something to do with Edie's jigsaw?'

'The blood on the piece Carl was holding suggests another crime might take place.'

Liam looked grey and queasy. 'Real blood?'

Sean knew he shouldn't say any more, but he couldn't stand to see Liam so shaken. 'Looks like Photoshop, but the pieces will be sent to forensics. The puzzle setter seems to be goading Edie into solving the clues before more people are hurt.'

'Why her? I mean, I know better than most that Edie can turn even the most supportive person into an enemy.'

'Yesterday I thought it could be one of her fans, but not now.'

Liam still looked rattled. 'So, is Edie in danger?'

'Whoever sent her the pieces seems to be needling her rather than threatening her. Feels like an ego trip.' Even so, the very idea of the one person who had been there all his life being at risk made Sean even more determined to keep her out of it.

'But what connection has she got to Carl?'

Sean dipped his dosa into the delicious sambar. 'I don't know.' It was bothering him, though. Especially as he sensed Edie was keeping something from him.

Liam picked at his fish. 'Perhaps you should be looking into Edie's past.'

'How do you mean?'

'Come on, love. If it had been anyone else, you'd have been investigating their history right away. What if she's the one who's done something wrong? Remember how she interrogated me when we got together? How she tried to get you to back away?'

Sean felt the usual conflict whenever Liam talked about Edie, or Edie about Liam. He was always the one in the middle. 'She was being protective. It takes her a long time to trust anyone. That's hardly the same thing as provoking someone into murder.'

Liam didn't look convinced. 'As long as you protecting her now doesn't put you in danger.'

'I know. I don't want to jeopardise the adoption by something happening to me.'

Liam grabbed Sean's hand. 'No, that's not what I mean. I love you. I can't lose you.'

Later, on the sofa in front of the fire, Sean shucked Ferrero Rochers and ate them. He'd bought the big box for Christmas, but it was close enough, surely. He could always get more. He turned to his husband. 'I'm really sorry that I didn't spend the morning with you and that I was late. I should have prioritised us.'

Liam opened his arm as if it were a wing and Sean snuggled in. Liam laid his head on Sean's. The bear sat in the big armchair in the bay window, seeming to smile. 'I know it's going to be like that sometimes. It's your job. It's not like you skipped being with me to go to the gym.'

'Isla would be amazed if I voluntarily worked out.' Isla was Sean's personal trainer, when he actually turned up. He should get back to her; she'd sent a message reminding him it was Bootcamp on the Beach tomorrow. Not that Liam would have let him forget. While they both attended, Sean was by far the least enthusiastic. He'd reply later, not mentioning the takeaway or the shiny pile of Ferrero Rocher wrappers. 'Are you going running tomorrow, too?'

'Depends on what everyone else is doing. Given Carl was running by himself, it makes me not want to go alone, you know?'

'Of course.'

They sat in silence, watching the fire twist and turn. It danced across the bear's shiny eyes.

'What shall we call it?'

'What?'

'The bear.'

'Aberystwyth.' Liam's accent stepped up a gear when pronouncing his home country's place names.

'Why?'

'Because I called my first bear Carmarthen, so that name's already taken.'

Sean gave Liam a chocolate-hazelnut kiss. 'Makes sense. Aberystwyth it is.'

'Juniper will love it.' Liam paused. 'Any luck getting Edie to come for Christmas?' His tone carried complications.

'As much luck as if I'd tried to get Aberystwyth to come to life and have a Christmas picnic.'

Liam twisted and placed his feet on Sean's lap. 'Do you think she'll ever get over what happened?'

'I hope so.' As he rubbed Liam's feet, however, Sean thought of all the terrible things that had happened to Edie at Christmastime, and couldn't see how anyone could ever recover from that, least of all Edie.

'I forgot to ask, with all that's happened, what time did you get in last night? I waited up till one but couldn't keep my eyes open any longer.'

'It wasn't long after. The party was still going when I left.' Liam looked at the clock. 'Which reminds me, I need to pop out later. One of my hotel customers is having Christmas drinks for *their* suppliers. They invited me when I dropped off this week's bouquets.'

'We could go together!' Sean said. 'It's been ages since we went out. The last time was probably the night on the beach when we decided there and then to redo our vows. It relit our spontaneous side, for a while.'

Liam shook his head. 'Sorry, baby. This is work, I won't be having any fun. I'll be back as soon as I can, but don't worry about staying up.'

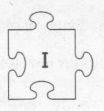

I

Twelve

Dr Veronica Princeton hadn't stopped laughing all evening. They'd had cocktails at Nook, more drinks with dinner in the harbour, then shots at every bar that would take them. The whole town seemed full of Christmas spirit, from the theatregoers hey-ho-ing their way out of *Snow White* at the Pavilion earlier, to the carol-bellowing lads in Santa hats weaving across streets. Best of all, she was with her mates. She couldn't remember a time when she had felt so accepted, understood and at home. She definitely didn't feel like that at her actual home.

'Come back to mine,' Helena said as she got into the taxi, spilling chips everywhere. 'I've got a bottle of tequila at the house.'

'Slammers!' India shouted. 'Like the old days.'

Veronica held the door open, wavering. It was gone two in the morning. She could just hop in. All she had wanted to do this evening was pretend she was twenty years younger again, when things were a lot less complex emotionally.

But would it be as fun?

'Next time.' She slammed the taxi door and waved as her friends headed off to lick salt off their fists, exchange salty stories and shed salty tears before passing out, lights still on.

While she paid a visit to the dark.

The killer couldn't even remember getting back to their room. All they knew was that the first murder was complete. 'I'm so sorry, I'm so sorry, I'm so sorry.' They paced back and forth, floorboards keening. 'I'm so very sorry.' They no longer knew who they were saying it to, only that if they stopped, they would immediately call the police and confess.

They peeled off the gloves and placed them on the table, not knowing what they'd do with them, only that they couldn't wear them anymore, as if the gloves were the ones that had hit Veronica over the head, then strangled the last seconds out of her, not the killer.

Her face wouldn't leave their head. And she was definitely dead, they'd made sure of that this time. They would never forget her eyes as she died. Her pupils fixed on theirs, inches away, not moving. All that life she'd had, replaced with forever death.

The killer lurched forwards, hands to their mouth, as the coffee they'd drunk to stay awake to the dead hours and the whisky they'd drunk to dull the pain resurged. Leaking through their fingers, the vomit ate into the floor. The boards were silenced.

Somewhere deep in the darkest of cupboards within, the killer had wondered before this happened if they would revel in causing the death of another human, but there hadn't been even a kindling of joy as the spark of life had left her. Now in the anguish of that knowledge, the killer thought again of the path they had chosen. Of their reasons. Of their vows. It reignited a spark of resolve deep inside them, despite it all. Whatever the cost, they must continue. There was no other choice. 'I'm so sorry,' they whispered. 'For everything.'

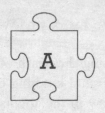

Thirteen

December 21st

Sean couldn't hear the sea over the beating of his heart. From the squat that already had his quads screaming, he forced his legs into a plank, then back again before standing. Hoping that Isla was watching one of the other fools attending her Bootcamp on the Beach, he took a breather. No matter how deep his breaths, though, he couldn't get enough oxygen – his lungs felt like they were made of concrete. Burpees were not his friend.

From her imperious position on the lifeguard chair, Isla held up her loudhailer. 'Get back to it, Sean! I can see you!'

Lucy Pringle, Edie's neighbour and Isla's right-hand woman and deputy, bounded up to him. 'You can do it!' It was too early for their voices to be so full of exclamation marks. 'Look at Liam to see perfect form.'

Liam, as she suggested, was burpee-ing with ease and grace while humming 'God Rest Ye Merry Gentlemen' at the same time. Once again, Sean wondered what Liam saw in him.

'Battle rope time for half of you, running between cones

for the rest!' Isla announced. Lucy dragged over a stretch of interwoven black and red ropes that lay on the cold sand like wrestling snakes.

Moving over to the ropes, Sean took one in each hand, and started moving them in waves.

Next to him, a woman wearing a Fleetwood Mac T-shirt was flicking the ropes as easily as if they were string.

'Impressive!' Sean said to her.

'It's hell!' she replied. 'I'm Nina, by the way.'

'Sean.'

'I know.' Her smile was lopsided and loaded.

'Faster, Sean!' Isla's enhanced voice swept over the sea. She was clearly following her own hallowed and bellowed advice – even when swamped by her black hoodie it was clear that she was even slimmer than when she'd taken him on as a client. Sean wasn't sure he could say the same, but he had at least gained a bit more muscle tone. He could now wear short-sleeved T-shirts with less shame.

Liam was running between traffic cones at speed, distracting Sean from the burning in his shoulders.

'On your backs for core workout,' Isla called.

Lucy was standing by the mats she'd laid out on the grass. 'And it's going to be the most intense yet!'

Sean winced in anticipation. Last week, his tummy had hurt so much after the core exercises that it'd been hard to reach for biscuits for days. Just as he was lying down, though, his phone went. 'Sorry,' he shouted to Isla, peeling himself back up. 'Work. I've got to answer it.'

Isla laughed. Through the loudhailer it sounded weirdly like a seagull. 'I'll believe you this time.'

Sean reached his bag in time to answer the call from the DCI. 'Yes, boss.'

'We need you in, Sean,' DCI Leyland said. 'Your jigsaw gig is definitely no hoax. A woman has been murdered.'

Riga was giving a pep talk to a poinsettia when Edie let herself into her friend's house. 'You really should be showing off by now,' she was saying to the plant. 'I'm not angry. I'm disappointed.'

'You really believe it can hear you, don't you?' Edie said, taking her usual seat at the garden room table. She wore purple plaid and a green shirt to give her more confidence than she felt.

'Embarrassing it makes the cheeks of its leaves turn red. Ask anyone. Here, have a croissant.' Riga gestured towards the plate of breakfast pastries on the table. 'I'm trying out a new bakery.'

Edie chose a huge croissant that looked like an armadillo with flaky armour. It was crisp on the outside, cloud-soft in the middle and utterly delicious. She offered the plate to Riga.

Riga, hazy behind vape smoke that smelled of candy cigarettes, shook her head. 'The sourdough nearly broke my tooth earlier. Doubt those will be better.'

Edie doubted Riga had eaten anything at all but played along. 'Yet you offered them to me?'

Riga grinned. With her green turban on and the sweet smoke that curled around her, she reminded Edie of the

Caterpillar from *Alice's Adventures in Wonderland*. 'You're my guinea pig. Any advance on the clues from yesterday?'

'I was up for hours trying to find every street beginning with "PO" in Dorset that had a VIP connection.'

'And an infinity symbol.'

'Yeah, you'd think that would be an easy win of a clue, wouldn't you?'

Riga's laugh turned into a cough. She took a puff on her nebuliser, reminding Edie of Sean.

Images of him in hospital at two days old crashed in, as they always did. Of his stuttering lungs fighting to rise and fall. Jaundiced, feverish, so small. She hadn't managed to look after Anthony, but she would make sure she protected his grandson. Her son.

'I asked the neighbours if they'd seen anyone around the time the box arrived.' Riga took a sip of her bitter coffee. 'And it so happens that Lucy *did* see a figure in an anorak, hood up, putting the present on your doorstep. She *thinks* it was a man but couldn't swear to it.'

Edie blinked. She knew she should have gone over to talk to Lucy. She had no problem interrogating strangers; neighbours were the scary ones. 'Thanks for asking.'

'If you'd joined the cul-de-sac WhatsApp group, you'd have known that by now.'

'I'm not a joiner, Riga.'

Riga sighed. 'But it would help if you were. Everyone with cameras has gone through their footage for you. Mr Pickwick said whoever it was didn't come in a car – his CCTV shows the road.'

'They're just being nosy arseholes.'

'Edie, they're trying to help. If you could just—'

'It's the obsession with true crime podcasts. Everyone's trying to be backseat detectives.' Edie knew her wave of defensiveness was hiding something, but she didn't want to look inside at what it was.

Riga raised her pencilled eyebrows. 'And what does that make you?'

Edie looked away. In the garden outside, a robin flew onto a bird feeder. The silver frost on the ground made the scene look like one of the Christmas cards she ripped up every year.

'You're going to get a door camera, though, right?' Riga pointed her vape stick like a magic wand.

Edie felt a jolt of reluctance. Why should a criminal make her change her life? 'When I get the time,' she lied.

'Liar!' Riga barked.

'I simply don't like being told what to do.'

'No shit! Have you ever been told to look into Pathological Demand Avoidance?'

'No, and if I had I wouldn't have done it. Nobody amends their behaviour. Not really.'

'Oh, Edie. What am I going to do with you?' A strange charge twisted between them.

Edie's phone buzzed in her bag.

It was Sean. He was phoning from the car; she could hear the indicator. 'The jigsaw piece with the edge of a sign. It's Pocket Lane, a narrow road between the High Street and the seafront.'

Edie felt her stomach drop. Pocket Lane had been one of the roads she'd looked at. She should have known. But how? She also knew the place. She and Sky had shared a chippy snog there on their second date. 'How did you manage to work that out? Did you get any more pieces of jigsaw?'

'The body of a woman was found in Pocket Lane.'

'Oh no.' Edie felt sick. 'How did she die?'

'Not sure yet, and I wouldn't tell you anyway.' Sean paused. 'But there were jigsaw pieces in her hair.'

Fourteen

The wind chased Sean along Esplanade, pushing him towards Pocket Lane. Passing the Georgian houses, hotels, cafés and guest houses that faced the salty stare of the sea, he felt fear as well as excitement – it was his first murder investigation. This type of thing didn't happen often in Weymouth. He could already see the blue lights flashing and an officer standing guard at the entrance to the skinny alley that cut through onto Crescent Street. As he turned into Pocket Lane, he saw Edie sitting in the window of the Corner Café. She had cleared a viewing spot in the condensation and waved to him, blithe as you like.

Sean felt a rare flash of anger towards his aunt. He loved her with a fierceness that usually surpassed irritation, but this was different. His boss had made it clear that Edie should steer clear of any further part of the investigation, as she was the recipient of the clues. Before he could go in to tell her to go away, though, he was spotted by Helena Rice, his favourite SOCO.

'Sean! I was hoping you'd be the investigating officer.' Helena was climbing out of her plastic suit and shoes and placing them in an evidence bag. From their nights out in pubs and clubs he knew that she hated the restrictions of both the suit and the job. She said she heard the sound of the rustling suit in her sleep.

He nodded. 'What's been found so far?'

Helena took her hair out of its bun and it Gorgoned in the wind. 'A woman was hit over the back of the head and then strangled sometime in the early hours. From blood spatters and marks on the ground, she was killed near the Crescent Street end, then dragged further down so she wouldn't be seen.'

'Any idea of motive?'

'Unlikely to be a chance robbery as she still had her handbag and purse, with quite a lot of cash inside. But that's your side of things.'

'And then there are the jigsaw pieces,' Sean said.

Helena nodded.

At the other end of the lane, the body was being lifted onto a stretcher to be taken to the forensic pathologist.

Sean was silent for a moment, making a pledge to the victim that he'd find out who had killed her. 'Any identification?'

'A driving licence in her purse in the name of Veronica Princeton. The picture on it looks like her. She lived on Redcliffe View.'

'Fancy.'

'Extremely. I also found a card for the fertility clinic she owns.'

Sean thought of the IVF clinics he and Liam had visited with Jinn, their friend and one-time potential surrogate. The amount of money it would have taken was staggering, in no way affordable for them. With no guarantee it would work. That could lead to some unhappy people, though it would hardly be cause for murder. You never knew, though, what could make someone break. Considering the money and emotions involved, there was always scope for crime.

'Any sign of a weapon?' he asked.

'Not in the alleyway. Mark has sent SOCOs out to search the bins around the seafront and surrounding streets. Although if the attacker was throwing something away, it'll probably be—'

'In the sea.' Sean loved the sea, but it was a fickle friend, so often working against the police. Sometimes it kept secrets; sometimes it spat them onto the shore. One of the first jobs he'd had on joining the force was attending the washing up of a bloated corpse. The smell and the stress had stayed with him for weeks. When he'd confided in Edie one night how hard it had been to tell the victim's family, she'd said the sea was at fault. It should have swallowed the secret. Kept it to itself. Sometimes Sean really didn't understand her.

'The jigsaw pieces, have they been sent off to forensics?'

'Yes, but I took pictures of them, both in her hair and on their own. I'll send them to your phone. I had to stop myself trying to put them together. I love a jigsaw.'

'You and my aunt both.'

'I know. She had our class make them.'

'I'd forgotten you were taught by her.'

'I hadn't. Hard to forget a teacher like Edie. And "taught" is a bit of a stretch. When we had her as a supply teacher, we knew we wouldn't have to do anything.'

'Apart from jigsaws. She always made her students do them. I guess you've probably already heard, but yesterday she was sent a wrapped jigsaw box with the first pieces inside, along with a card that said she had to solve the puzzle.'

'No pressure, then.' Helena tied a scarf around her neck and pulled on a woolly hat that stopped the wind playing with her hair.

'The difficulty will be keeping her far enough away from the actual investigation.'

'Good luck with that. Doesn't really sound like Edie.' Helena laughed. 'Right, my shift's over; I'm clocking off. Going home to a hot bath and a cold bed.'

'Don't forget to send the photos. See you on Christmas Eve for drinks?' Sean asked as she walked towards the sea. They had a tradition, if three years constituted a tradition, of going out after work, getting drunk, then going to midnight mass. The lapsed Catholic in them both.

She nodded.

'I'm trying to get Liam to come. He's got all these work do's, so I haven't been out with him in forever. And if we get the kids soon—'

'What?'

He knew that would hook her. 'We may be adopting a little girl called Juniper, and possibly also her sibling. Fingers, everything, crossed.'

'That's amazing! Well then, he's got to come with us. I'll be seeing him later; the running club are meeting up for a quick run and a long pint in honour of Carl. I'll badger him then.'

'I'd forgotten you'd know Carl Latimer, too. Is anyone *not* in the running club?'

'*You* should be.'

'You sound like Liam. I keep telling him that running's bad for you.'

'Look what happened to Carl . . .'

'Do you know why someone would hurt him?'

'Are you interviewing me, DI Brand-O'Sullivan?' Helena sounded like she was teasing, but her eyes flashed.

'I'm just a bit behind everyone else. I don't know him at all.'

'Well, he's a bit of a lad, or at least was; being a lad in your thirties is really sad. I went to school with him, and he was a twat, got into trouble a lot. Nothing that bad though. As far as I know. And I don't think people get attacked for being a bit of a wanker. In pubs, maybe, but not in the middle of a wood.'

'Thanks, mate. If you think of anything else . . .'

'I'll let you know. Now, I'm off.' Helena was almost knocked back by the wind when she reached the end of the alley. He could hear her swearing at the elements as she turned the corner.

Sean phoned his DCI.

'What is it, Sean?'

'I want to investigate the attack on Carl Latimer as attempted murder linked to this latest death. I need authorisation and funds to search and thoroughly secure the crime scene in Godlingston Woods.' He hoped that the delay hadn't already compromised any evidence, but kept that to himself.

'Permission granted. I'll get a team over there and expedite all forensics.'

Sean breathed out in relief. 'Thanks, boss.'

'Watch out for press; we've already had calls requesting information on the death. We may need to do a conference.'

Across the road, on the promenade, Sean recognised Della Ingrit, a reporter from the *Dorset Echo*, hurrying towards Pocket Lane in her characteristic red beret. It was rumoured she even kept it on in bed. 'They're already here, boss.'

'Keep them at bay, would you?'

'My pleasure.'

Sean ended the call and strode straight up to the reporter. 'Ah, Della. First to the party as always.'

'Have you got a quote for me, Inspector Brand-O'Sullivan?' Della's head jutted forward. 'Cos, if not, I need to talk to someone who does.'

'I have nothing official to say to you, Della. We don't know for sure what we're dealing with yet.'

'I heard it's a prominent local businesswoman. And that is pretty certain, according to my source. We've also learned that there may be a connection with an attack made on a local teacher. You know how much our readership is concerned by anything that affects members of the local community.'

'Everyone in Weymouth is a member of the local community.'

'Sure, but former councillors and teachers, they're a bit different, aren't they? People pay more attention. They're pretty much local VIPs.'

Sean tried to keep his face unreactive to discovering that Veronica Princeton had been a councillor. 'I don't suppose you'd like to tell me who your source is?' He hoped it wasn't someone on the team.

'You suppose right.'

Sean stood taller and stared at Della with intent. 'If you, or any of your friends, approach the victim's premises or family, I'll arrest you.'

'How dare you, Inspector. As if I'd even think of it.' Della winked at him, then went to talk to one of the rubberneckers of death.

Sean looked up and down Pocket Lane. The buildings loomed high over the alley, making it feel even narrower. It was a good choice for a murder site. No CCTV at either end, although even if there was, the likelihood of it working was fifty-fifty at best. He'd check Esplanade and Crescent Street for cameras next, but he had a great-aunt to reprimand first.

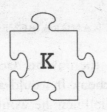

Fifteen

The Corner Café looked out to sea and smelled of Christmas, but Edie forgave it both these sins for its proximity to the crime scene. Trying to ignore the olfactory clash of cinnamon, clove, orange, marzipan and Stilton quiche in the air, she watched as officers bustled around the entrance to Pocket Lane. Gulls swooped over them like paparazzi. Dark clouds overclapped the sky, huddling together as if they too were gathering for the dead.

Edie kept going over the clues she'd received, wondering if she could have done more. If she *should* have done more.

Her chair was turned towards the counter, but she could still feel the sea's presence behind her. Goading her. She diverted herself from the guilt and thoughts and memories that wanted to surface by making anagrams. *Shore = horse. Channel = hen clan. Hidden secret = decreed hints*.

Jennie, the proprietor, came over with Edie's second order of the morning. She laid out the big teapot and the Dorset apple cake Edie had ordered for Sean. It was his favourite. She had made it for him every Friday from when he was small until the day he had left home. She still made it for his birthday. It would appease him when he came in shortly. Edie knew he wouldn't be able to resist telling her off once he'd finished talking with his SOCO mates in their rustly onesies.

'Heard anything about what's going on?' Edie asked.

Jennie leaned forward. 'I was out the back and saw a body being put in a private ambulance. I heard one of the officers say it was a local woman, killed in the early hours. And someone else recognised her. Veronica Princeton.' Jennie had clearly been spying out her back window. Edie approved.

Veronica Princeton. The name seemed familiar. Initials VP. 'I don't suppose you know her middle name?'

'Why, do you know her?' Jennie leaned closer, hungry for information that could be picked up like crumbs.

'I'm not sure.'

'Terrible business.'

'Although not terrible *for* business.' Edie gestured round the café – it was completely full.

Jennie shook her head slowly, as if despairing of the gossiping customers, even as they filled her till and decimated her Victoria sponge. 'Sky's looking lippy,' she said, looking at the clouds as she picked up her tray. 'Could be a storm later.' She nodded decisively, then left.

Edie had long ago got used to how meteorological prognostications functioned as a Dorset farewell. She preferred, of course, being of Kilkenny descent, the Irish goodbye, slipping away without anyone noticing. She peered at the tea in the pot. It was barely yellow. Jennie was stingy with her tea bags. Edie took two of her own out of the little plastic baggie she kept in her pocket for such occasions. Tea must be steeped to a mahogany finish, or at least the post-tan shade of Claudia Winkleman, and you couldn't do that without a ton of tannin. Glancing through the window, she could see the sea being tousled by the wind, just as she used to ruffle Sean's hair.

And there her great-nephew was, coming round the corner towards her as if summoned by her thoughts. The door tinkled as he entered the café. His face was set to scold.

'Sit down,' she said when he got to her table. 'I got you a pot of tea and some breakfast.' Edie pointed at the wodge of apple cake.

'Are you trying to bribe me into forgiving you?' Sean was looking up to the ceiling, not at her. He always did that when he was angry. 'Because it won't work. I'm not hungry.' His stomach gave him away by rumbling.

Edie tried not to grin in triumph and failed.

Sean sighed and sat down. Picking up a fork, he tapped the thick brown sugar crust on top of the cake with satisfaction. 'I thought I said you should keep away.'

'I wanted to get an idea of where it happened. And I haven't questioned anyone involved.' Edie decided that Jennie didn't count as an interviewee. It would be more conspicuous if she *hadn't* asked in a place like this.

Sean took a mouthful of cake, closing his eyes as he savoured it. 'Not as good as yours,' he said, grudgingly.

Of course it wasn't. 'What do you know about Veronica Princeton?' Even as she said the name, Edie remembered Veronica. One of the few pupils she'd taught at St Mary's that she *did* recall. She'd tried to blank them all, bury that time. But Veronica had been a star pupil, full of sparkle, brilliance and challenge. And now she was dead.

'Edie!' Sean looked around to see if anyone was listening. Which they probably were. 'The victim's identity has not been confirmed. I have to talk to the next-of-kin so they can be formally identified.'

'Come on, there must be something you can share with me?' Edie looked at him with the nearest she could approximate to the look a cat gave when trying to convince a sucker it was starving.

Sean lowered his head and speared a large piece of apple with his cake fork.

Edie leaned back in her chair and stretched. 'What was on the jigsaw pieces?' Her voice, she realised too late, had grown loud again. She wanted to know if they had received the same ones she had yesterday. And wondered whether she would receive some new ones today.

'Sssh!' The couple at the table nearest to them were staring.

'Keep your eyes on your buns, you two,' Edie said to them. They looked back to their Bath buns, whispering to each other.

'I'm serious, Edie.' Sean's own whisper was harsh. 'This isn't a puzzle you can do from the comfort of your home. Someone has died, and someone else has been seriously injured. This isn't your hobby.'

'Sure.'

'You've got to listen and do what I say for once. You're eighty. You shouldn't be playing with murder.'

'Will you at least come and see me tonight for a drink?'

'You said yourself that I need to put Liam, and the adoption, first. Especially as it looks like we might get Juniper, and maybe her baby brother or sister.'

'Wait, what?' Edie placed her hand on his, her heart flexing. 'Is that what happened at the meeting?'

'You'd know if you'd asked.' Sean's phone buzzed. He opened a message and Edie leaned over to see. 'Oi!' He slapped his hand over the screen.

Edie, though, had already clocked that the message was a picture of jigsaw pieces arranged on an evidence tray, and was calculating which of them would fit with the pieces she already had. She took a sip of tea. Feeling the tannin discolouring her teeth, she gave a satisfied smile.

Sean ate the last of the cake. 'Later.' He strode towards the door, brushing crumbs off his coat, taking part of her heart with him. Edie felt the beginnings of regret for not obeying him. Then he turned to her, face softening. 'Thanks for the cake. And be careful, would you? We still don't know why you were targeted. I don't want you hurt as well.'

'You be careful, too.' Edie's voice was a whisper again, and nobody, let alone Sean, could hear it.

Edie left a tip on the table – a piece of paper from her notebook with the handwritten message 'more tea bags needed in the pot' – then left the café. She stared down Pocket Lane as she went past. It was a passage as narrow as Dublin's Dame Court, if slightly less stinking of piss. No sign of CCTV cameras on its high walls, nor on this section of the seafront.

Across the road, on the promenade, a tall man was watching from under the lip of a seafront shelter. Seeing her stare, he turned away. People loved to soak up other people's tragedy, as if doing so meant they kept their own at bay. She was the same, always slowing at a traffic accident, or reading the details of a death while shaking her head at the inhumanity.

In this case, though, she knew the victim. Memories of Veronica drifted around her. Of the first time seeing the girl's quick maths brain in action as she solved a quadratic equation without hesitation; of Veronica getting the highest mark in the county for Maths GCSE and running round St Mary's hall, waving her results in triumph; of Veronica coming to Edie in tears when she hadn't got into Oxford first time, and Edie not knowing what to do other than pat her awkwardly on the shoulder and help her piece together another plan.

Even so, part of her was glad Veronica was dead and not Sean, though the rest of her was steeped in fear that the same fate would come for him.

The wind seemed to pause, then changed direction, bringing with it a blast of brass-band-played carols. Rather than festive bombast, it had a mournful sound – a melancholia that, to Edie's mind, very much suited the season. Without even thinking about it, she started walking towards the source. It was coming from the middle of town – New Bond Street, maybe, or the harbour.

Snicking through the next alleyway, she followed the sound through interlocking streets, trying to ignore shoppers and their bags rammed with landfill. People were a lot easier to ignore from the safety of her house.

Turning into Hope Square, she caught the smell of doughnuts and hot dogs and realised, too late, that the brass band was at the Christmas Market. She'd had a flyer through the door a week or so ago, and it had obviously gone straight in the bin, but now she wished she'd looked at the date first.

Stalls lined the sides of the harbour, curving from Cove Row into Cove Street and filling the space in front of gingerbread-house-esque Brewer's Quay. She walked quickly past a stall-holder bullying sugar into pink candyfloss beehives, and another selling craft cider, offering samples in little cups. Someone else was selling preserves made from local produce, including damson jam and, most horribly, chutney made from Poole Quay seaweed. Edie didn't care about the health benefits, there was no way she was spreading bladderwrack on her crumpets. It smelled of the previous summer, when the soft sands of Weymouth beach had been striped by a stinking band of seaweed.

There were, however, stalls that sold more pleasing items – handmade bags and silk scarves, woollies knitted by a woman sitting on a fold-out chair as her needles clacked out another hat. Edie should, she knew, buy presents for Sean and Liam, and she wanted to get something splendid for Riga.

Cutting through an area where people were drinking boozy hot chocolates smothered in cream, she lingered at a stall selling big wheels of cheese and shook some free samples into a napkin. The cats would like those later.

She realised as she continued walking, nibbling blue vinny, that she hadn't been shopping for pleasure in ages. She was almost having fun. People were a bit too close to her, sure. She could also do without the general Christmas bonhomie but, overall, it wasn't bad. High praise, for Edie. Maybe the proximity to death was giving her an appreciation for living. That would be a change.

And then Edie stopped. A woman with long curly hair, skeined with silver, was standing behind a jewellery stall. From this distance Edie couldn't see her features, but from the line of her shoulders, the tilt of her head as she replied to a customer, and the way she waved them goodbye, it looked like Sky. But Sky had moved away over twenty years ago; there was no way she could be here, in Weymouth.

Edie had deliberately not asked anyone about where Sky had gone. Had steered clear of searching on Friends Reunited and then Facebook when they became the way to stalk exes. She hadn't wanted to know where Sky was, or whether she had become a mum or not. Whether she was happy with someone else. But she'd never stopped thinking about it.

Someone bumped into her back, but Edie hardly noticed.

She was moving towards the stall as if pulled by a giant

rope. She had never felt less in control. She didn't even know if she was hoping that it was her ex, or if she was hoping that it wasn't.

When she was within a few feet of the stall, standing to one side, she knew for sure. That smile could only have been Sky's. Her skin was more wrinkled, but the lines around her eyes made them stand out even more. And the jewellery was based on celestial objects, though the pieces were more refined. One of the pairs of earrings was shaped like crescent moons, the surfaces bumped and pocked. Edie's hand went to her earlobe. She was pierced with jealousy at the thought of someone else giving Sky those laughter lines, and Sky giving someone else that jewellery.

Sky took out a tray of necklaces from under the stall and started arranging them on a velvet plinth. Like her, they somehow shone without any sun.

Edie's heart stuttered, as if it had been buffering ever since Sky had left her.

Or she had left Sky, depending on how you saw it.

Sky looked up, then. Saw Edie.

The magnetism was still there. Their eyes held each other. It was as if they'd never lost one another, but Edie knew that wasn't true. She didn't even know if Sky recognised her.

'I wondered if I'd see you here.' Sky's voice was silk wrapped. No apparent edges. It somehow made everything worse. If Sky had sounded bitter, unforgiving, then Edie would have had something to press against. This, though, flattened her.

Words came into Edie's head. They fizzed inside her, screaming. Some were arches – welcoming, curved gateways. Others arching, arrows intended to be shot into the sky. And Edie couldn't say any of them.

Turning, she stumbled away, not able to see what was in front or feel the ground beneath her.

'Edie!' Sky shouted after her.

Edie lurched towards the Red Lion. Holding onto the wall, she looked back. Sky hadn't followed her. Of course she hadn't, why would she? Still, though, Edie's arrhythmic heart seemed to stop dancing.

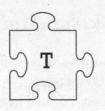

Sixteen

Veronica Princeton's house was one of the big ones on Redcliffe View that looked out to sea. A four-storey Edwardian, with a front garden full of winter-quiet roses. Her private fertility clinic in town obviously made a lot of money.

The house had high hedges on all sides to keep the world away. Yet death had found a way in regardless. Opening the gate, Sean breathed in deeply and walked up the path, DS Jessica Michaels behind him. He wished that he'd been assigned DC Ama Phillips, as Michaels had yet to forgive him for beating her to the one detective inspector role.

His phone buzzed with a message from Edie. Aunt Sky was back. Sean tried to put aside the sweep of feelings that threatened to overwhelm him. Sky had clouded Edie's life since she left, but he couldn't think of that now. He had to concentrate. He'd told people their loved ones had died before, but never as a result of murder.

The front door was a shiny red, and the song 'Paint It Black' played in his head. The door knocker was in the shape of a lion's head. Sean hoped that whoever answered would have its courage.

A stiff-backed man with a bald head opened the door.

He was wearing a brown silk dressing gown and carrying a pink shirt and a bow tie, and seemed disappointed to see Sean. Sean wondered if he'd been hoping for his wife. 'What is it?' Behind him, an enormous Christmas tree stood on black and white tiles.

'I'm Detective Inspector Brand-O'Sullivan,' Sean said. 'And this is DS Michaels. Are you Mr Princeton?'

'There is no Mr Princeton. I'm Dr Samuel Newman.' He said all this while waving his hand as if swatting away inaccuracies. 'Is there a problem? It's just I have to get ready for—'

'May I please come in, Dr Newman?' Sean felt like a grief vampire, requesting an invitation over the threshold.

The other man paled and grabbed onto the door frame. 'Not . . . Ronnie?'

'It'd be better if we talked about this inside.'

Newman backed into the long hallway, his hand dragging against the dado rail. He was hunched, already looking ten years older.

Without being asked, or asking, Michaels disappeared into the kitchen to make a pot of coffee, and Sean sat on the edge of a sofa in Princeton and Newman's living room. It was huge, at least twice the size of Sean and Liam's whole downstairs. A veranda stretched along windows that showed a bright belt of sun on the horizon, separating fish-grey sea from corpse-grey sky. In front of the view was a large desk.

Newman sat in a plush armchair, then stood up, then sat back down again. 'I don't know where to be.' He sounded so vulnerable, Sean wanted to hug him. Protect him. Instead, he had to find out if Newman had killed his wife.

'Please, be wherever you feel most comfortable.'

Newman went over to a large mantelpiece draped in greenery. He picked up a picture in a large gilt frame. From where Sean was sitting, it looked like a wedding photo.

'Can you tell me what's going on?' Newman was sweating. His hands trembled. This could be as much of a sign of anticipatory shock as it could be of guilt, or fear at being found out. One way or another, the body was preparing itself for bad news.

'Do you know where your wife is, Dr Newman?' Sean hated having to ask this, rather than immediately answer him, but if Newman was involved, these first questions were crucial.

The other man's eyes were wild. He came over, grabbed Sean's arm. 'I've no idea. I thought she'd stayed at the clinic last night, or with friends, but you obviously know.' He looked down at his hand, and seeming to realise what he was doing, let Sean go. He sat down on the rug, legs crossed, now looking like a little boy. 'Please. Tell me.'

If someone withheld information about Liam, Sean wouldn't be able to stand it. 'I'm so sorry to have to tell you that a body has been found, and we have reason to believe it could be your wife.'

Newman shook his head but didn't say anything other than, 'No.'

'Her identification was found at the scene. I am so sorry.'

Newman blinked. 'A body.'

This must be so abstract for him. The woman he'd shared a life with, alongside all the unique intimacies and vulnerabilities that brought, was now being described as 'a body', as part of a 'scene'. His wife and her life were suddenly in quotation marks.

Michaels came through with a cafetière and three cups on a tray. She'd managed to find some shortbread fingers and had fanned them out, so they looked incongruously like a crude depiction of sun.

Seeing the cups laid out seemed to shake Newman from his trance, if not from his denial. He stared at the cafetière as if he too was being pressed down. He picked up a cup and, wrapping his hands around it, held it in front of his heart. But good coffee couldn't prevent bad news. 'The body . . . she . . . hasn't been identified yet. Is that correct?'

'We need an official identification,' Sean replied.

'Then I need to go, see it . . . her . . . then I'll be able to say it's not my wife.' He stood and walked to the door, looking more like the man of business who had first answered it.

'And once you're dressed and ready, we'll take you. But I'd like to ask you a few questions first.'

'*Why?*'

'If we haven't found your wife, then we need to know why her identification was in the possession of someone else, and, indeed, where she is.'

Newman seemed mollified by the use of present tense. 'I wish I knew.'

'Does she often stay overnight elsewhere?'

Newman bristled as he sat back down. 'If you're implying there's a problem between us, you're wrong. She often has drinks and a meal out with friends, and then crashes at theirs or in the back room of the clinic if she's too drunk to drive.'

'She wouldn't get a taxi home?'

Newman shrugged. 'Everyone needs to relax sometimes.'

Behind him, Michaels was writing down his every word. 'Are you frequently unaware of your wife's activities?' she asked.

Newman frowned. 'I'm often working late shifts at the hospital. Ours isn't like other relationships.'

'And were you on a late shift last night?' Sean asked, trying to infuse his voice with casualness rather than making it obvious that, as with all those close to a victim, Newman was under suspicion.

'You're ruling me out of your enquiries, aren't you?'

'We just need an overview of events, Dr Newman.'

'I was on call. I was here until about half ten when I was needed for an emergency procedure. I got back just before dawn and had a nap. I hadn't long got up when you arrived.'

'That's very helpful, sir, thank you. And I don't like to ask this, but do you know of anyone who would wish your wife harm?'

'Why would anyone want to hurt her?' Newman looked away, for the first time seeming to hide something.

'If you could answer the question, sir.' Michaels' voice didn't carry the same care as Sean's.

Newman folded his arms. 'My wife used to be a coun-cillor. They get a lot of complaints. And she's had threats at the clinic.'

'What kind of threats?'

'Legal ones, mainly. Dissatisfaction if IVF hasn't worked, or if a treatment hasn't given a customer everything they wanted. But there were others which were more . . . personal.'

'It must be a pretty emotive business to be in.'

'Tell me about it.' Newman was shaking his head. 'For the practitioners, too. Ronnie often comes home crying, for one reason or another.'

Out of the corner of his eye, Sean saw Michaels look up, eyebrows raised at Newman's words. He nodded at her to pursue her instinct.

'Would you say your wife is happy, Dr Newman?'

'Are any of us?' he replied.

'I'm asking about Veronica specifically.'

Newman rubbed his eyes. 'Ronnie often looks for happi-ness in the wrong places. But then I do, too.' He looked out at the unsettled sea. 'I'd like to go now, please.'

'Thank you, Dr Newman,' Sean said. 'If you'll come with us, we'll take you to the viewing room. Is there anyone else you'd like with you?'

Newman closed his eyes. 'No.' Pain crossed his face. There was a story there to be read another time.

As Sean led him out of the room and back into the entrance hall, he stopped on the black and white tiles. They looked recently polished. And just like the ones on the jigsaw. 'Nice tiles.'

'Thanks. Ronnie chose them.'

Michaels' eyebrows rose again, and Sean couldn't help imagining the outline of a body on the shining floor.

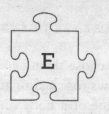

Seventeen

Edie was back at Pocket Lane, the Crescent Street end, to try and take her mind off Sky. It was fascinating to watch technicians in plastic onesies gathering potential evidence in bags. Like the ziplocks she carried everywhere, but with blood samples rather than tea bags.

The crowd had grown, even though the police had blocked off half the street. The cordon didn't stop the curious from pushing forward as far as they could. People always crossed boundaries; they couldn't help it.

A woman in a navy-blue coat with a red belt and matching beret was muttering into her phone and taking the occasional picture. Clearly a reporter. The press were already sniffing around, although this member of their ranks was practically snorting up the residue of information.

'Awful, isn't it?' Edie said, sidling up to her.

The woman didn't look at Edie at first. She nodded absentmindedly and scribbled in shorthand in her notebook.

Edie had learned shorthand, and several other codes and languages, to help her compile her most cryptic crosswords. 'I'd cover your notes up if I were you. Not sure you want everyone with shorthand to know where the victim worked.' She jabbed a finger at the page, which stated 'Family Ties Fertility Clinic'.

Now the woman looked Edie up and down. Once again, a young woman was surprised that an older one would dress in anything other than beige, as if they themselves would be happy to fade out after fifty.

'Like what you see?' Edie said, doing a sarcastic twirl.

The woman laughed. 'Yes, actually. You're unusual-looking, for Weymouth at least. In Brighton, Bristol or Hoxton it'd practically be a uniform.'

Edie bristled. 'And what do you think you look like?' She pointed to the beret and trench coat. ''Allo 'Allo finished years ago.' She was about to say something more insulting, then stopped. This wasn't going to help. She may already have gone too far.

But the woman laughed again, louder this time. 'I'm Della Ingrit, from the *Echo*.'

'Good morning, Della.' Edie checked her watch. 'Afternoon.'

'Were you a reporter, too?'

'What makes you think I'm not one now?'

'It's just . . .' Della's hand rose, as if about to gesture to Edie's creased-up, lived-in face, then floated back down.

'I get it. I'm ancient and should therefore have retired years ago.'

Della blushed and looked at her shoes.

'I do work for the papers, actually. The nationals.' Well, it was true. She wouldn't mention that it was for cross-words.

111

'Sorry. I should know better. Call myself a feminist.'

'Have you been to the clinic?' Edie asked.

'Not yet. Been warned off. But I'm going over after I file the scene. Happy for you to get there first, make up for my casual ageism.'

'I should think so. One day, you too will be flying past eighty and wonder how you got there.'

Della saluted Edie, hand to beret. 'May we all fly past eighty and eye-up ninety.'

Edie almost found herself smiling, but put a stop to that nonsense at once.

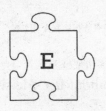

Eighteen

'Holly Tree Lodge?' Dr Newman's tone was spiky as Sean parked up outside the Dorset Coroner's Mortuary. 'Surely that's not an appropriate name for a place of death?'

The journey from Weymouth had felt long and awkward for Sean, so he could only imagine what it must have been like for Dr Newman, sitting in the front of the car and looking out of the window. He hadn't stopped drumming on his knees all the way. Now, he was staring at the gate to the mortuary, rubbing his hand up and down his face.

'And it looks like a chapel.' Newman jabbed a finger at the window. 'Seems wrong for us atheists.'

He had a point. With its whitewashed walls and large window, the building resembled the church in *The Graduate*. Sean and Liam had watched it a few weekends ago on one of their film binges. Sean would never say so to someone bereaved, but he rather liked this cutely named building. If he ever had to identify a loved one's body, as Aunt Edie had had to do, he'd rather it was here.

'It used to be a church,' Michaels said. 'I went when I was younger. It's a very peaceful building, which seems right for a place of rest.'

Sean looked at Michaels in the rear-view mirror. Her

hands were raised to her chest as if praying still. He really didn't know much about her. He should do more to get to know his team.

Both Sean and Michaels got out of the car, but Newman didn't unfasten his seatbelt. Sean opened his door for him, but he just gazed out of the window. 'I haven't willingly been in a chapel for years.' Newman's voice seemed far away, as if trapped in the last time he was in a place of worship. 'And neither has Ronnie. If she's in there . . .'

'I know this is hard, Samuel.' Sean risked using his first name. 'We'll make this as easy for you as possible. But I think you need to know.'

Newman nodded and climbed slowly out.

As they walked up the path, a robin sitting on a nearby wall broke into song, with a joy which could appear insensitive, ill-timed at the very least, to those on the brink of grief. Newman flinched.

Inside, Michaels waited in the entrance, filling out forms, while Sean took Newman into the viewing area. He could feel the doctor's anxiety rise as they got nearer the room at the end of the hall. It came across as anger.

'Is it necessary to put me through this? I'll be making complaints. I'm a very busy man.'

'I completely understand.' Sean kept his voice as soothing as possible.

'And shouldn't this job be carried out by someone much older than you? Someone with more experience of grief and trauma than a child?'

Sean didn't bite. 'I've been in the police force for over

a decade, Dr Newman.' He knew that, like the children he and Liam so desperately wanted to parent, Newman was experiencing big feelings that needed acknowledging. Even if, as was statistically likely, he had killed Veronica Princeton, he should still be granted space to feel. Edie had once said to Sean that he and she were opposites; that Sean believed the best in people, and she believed the worst. It was true, and sometimes it meant people hurt Sean. But he thought he was better off, overall.

They entered the small area off the viewing room, over-full with a sofa, coffee table and two armchairs. Newman gave a half-laugh. 'I suppose this is where you take people who *have* identified their loved ones, to calm them down before they go back out into the real world. So they don't start screaming in the middle of Boscombe.'

'We try and give people what they need.' Sean gestured towards the door, which seemed so innocuous, but was in fact a Schrödinger space. Until that door was opened, loved ones were both alive and dead. 'Come through, Samuel. It's time.'

DCI Leyland answered on the third ring when Sean phoned him after dropping Newman off, silently sobbing, at his house. They'd left him in the care of a Family Liaison Officer. 'Do you have confirmation of identity?' Behind Leyland was the sound of rustling, like a packet of crisps being opened.

'Yes, guv,' Sean said. 'Dr Newman confirmed that the

body is that of his wife, Dr Veronica Princeton. He's with Ella Bishop now.'

'Ella's one of our best. She'll get it out of him if he's guilty.'

'And look after him, either way.'

'Of course.' The DCI's tone, however, didn't suggest this was as much of a priority for him as it was for Sean. Sean heard a clunk, then a metallic click, then balls running through a pool table. Leyland must be at his club. Again. 'What now?'

'I dropped Michaels at the hospital to look into Newman's alibi. She'll then talk to the women his wife was having dinner with. I'm going to investigate the fertility clinic threats. Could be a motive there.'

'And how does that relate to this jigsaw business?'

'No idea yet, boss. I'll be trying to connect the pieces we already have to see if we can prevent further attacks.'

Sean winced at the squeak of chalk on cue.

'Mind you do. We've got the national press digging around now. Teachers and doctors being targeted? That's prime middle-class worry fodder.'

'As long as they're not striking, obviously,' Sean said. 'Then they're the enemy.'

'Quite right,' Leyland said. A cue ball thwacked another ball, which shot into a pocket. 'And it's very important to know one's opponent.'

Sometimes, though, it wasn't clear who the enemy was until right at the end.

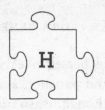

Nineteen

The Family Ties Fertility Clinic was located in a pedestrian cul-de-sac on the outskirts of town. It shared pavement space with an aesthetician, a wholefoods café and a bar that sold cocktails in jam jars. There was not a single charity shop, or bookshop, and therefore the street was of absolutely no interest to Edie.

Not that she was a big believer in charities; it was more that she could always get a cheap jigsaw on their shop shelves. Although you couldn't guarantee that all the pieces would be present. Once she'd had to march back into Cancer Care demanding a refund for a missing baked bean. She needed all the pieces.

The clinic was glass-plated, but covered in grey opaque paint that didn't let you see inside, even when Edie stood close to the window. The 'VIP' interlocked letters from the puzzle were displayed on the door, and the infinity symbol, formed out of rope, was etched into the glass wall.

Guilt etched deeper into Edie. Maybe if she'd shared the jigsaw pieces with Sean, someone could have made the link where she couldn't. For the first time, she wondered if she wasn't a puzzler at all. She'd let Veronica down. Badly.

And then she shook herself. She'd just have to try harder. Puzzles took time and patience, and she had patience in abundance. Time, though, wasn't on her side.

Walking into the clinic, Edie found a large, bright space, filled with flowers and white sofas. A pink clock hanging on the wall provided a physical reminder of the biological equivalent that drove people to the clinic. The place felt more like a hotel reception than a medical facility, only there was no one present. The sole concession to Christmas was a mistletoe-studded garland across the counter. Given that mistletoe would be poisonous to babies, it seemed an odd choice. As were the pale lilies sitting next to the vat of cucumber and lemon water on the reception desk. Just ask Riga. *Lilium candidum L.*, also known as Madonna lily, was used in folk medicine for old-age-related disease.

But then, she supposed, white lilies were associated with the Virgin Mary, and IVF meant it was possible to have a virgin birth. And when Edie had objected to Liam giving her white lilies, saying that in the language of flowers they meant death, he'd argued that they were used in funeral displays because they symbolised rebirth, the release of the soul from the body. Which was true, the Ancient Egyptians considered lilies to show growth, fertility and rebirth, but she wasn't going to concede that. Not to Liam.

Edie flicked through the glossy leaflets showing pictures of plump babies and beatific women. She thought of Sean and Liam when they had first been looking into IVF and what it might involve, and how quickly they'd realised they were nowhere near rich enough. It wasn't in any way fair, but little in life was.

She stopped on a page devoted to the clinic's owner, Dr Veronica Princeton. Veronica had hardly changed at all in, what, fifteen years? Twenty?

Edie felt a pang somewhere near her heart at the image of the beautiful, keen-eyed woman, Photoshopped into softness, with an expression perfectly judged between medical and matriarchal. It said, this is a doctor who can make you a mamma.

Doctor Veronica (no surname, Edie noted – keeping it to first names only for friendliness while they made you penniless) *is one of the UK's leading fertility specialists. Educated at Cambridge and Harvard Medical Schools, she returned to her home town of Weymouth to set up a practice with a passion for helping families conceive. Trained in all the latest methods, Doctor Veronica combines state-of-the-art* (aka expensive) *technology with a personal touch, to ensure that clients get the results they long for. Family Ties Fertility Clinic makes families thrive. Join Doctor Veronica on a journey to what you've always wanted.*

The girl she had taught had grown up, and probably made far more money than Edie could even imagine. And Edie could imagine a *lot* of money. She'd never had it, but often dreamt of spending it.

A flicker of Veronica as a young woman stuck in Edie's

head. They were in a Maths class, looking at quadratic equations. Veronica had understood instinctively that things must be balanced. That all must be reduced to nothing. There had been a darkness to her, a nihilism that Edie had sensed, but she'd had a lightness too. She was balanced.

Maybe the darkness had won out.

A door opened in what Edie had thought was a smooth white wall. A woman in a white coat emerged, hair smoothed into a swoosh of ponytail. Her eyes were red, and her foundation was broached by streaks of black mascara.

'I'm sorry. We're not open today. I should have put a sign up. Unforeseen circumstances.' From the way she was staring blankly around the room, it seemed as if she couldn't see anything at all. She stumbled, holding out her hands but not finding anything to hold onto. Edie glanced at her name badge: 'Lesley, Fertility Practitioner'.

'Come and sit down.' Edie took Lesley's arm and gently led her to one of the soft white sofas. Edie poured her a cup of water from the cooler and placed it on an all-glass table that was so clean it was almost invisible. 'It's a shock, isn't it, loss? Beyond anything anyone can expect or prepare for. Hollows you out.'

Lesley nodded slowly, as if her head were too heavy and might topple off. 'I lost my mum last year.'

'And to you Veronica was . . .'

'My boss. And my friend.'

Lesley stared into the middle distance, and Edie recognised a woman who had longed for more.

'I've had "friends" like that.'

Lesley blinked several times.

Maybe Edie was projecting.

And then Lesley looked at Edie properly for the first time, tears falling. She took in Edie's orange hair, purple suit and red brogues. 'When I'm old, I'd like to wear purple, too. Like in the poem.'

Edie had to swallow her usual tart retorts. 'Wear it now, while you're young.' Lesley was forty if she were a day, an age when one is no longer encumbered by being young. Edie knew, though, that she was the sort to view it as a compliment.

Lesley's smile was so wide it was embarrassing. Then a look of confusion crossed her face. 'How did you know? About Veronica? I only found out from her husband a few minutes ago.'

Edie thought that, as always, the near truth would be most effective. 'I heard a rumour about her passing, and I didn't know where else to go to find out if it was true.'

A look of fear crossed Lesley's face. 'You're not press, are you?'

'Not at all. I taught Veronica at school. She was brilliant. I then took a close interest in her career. I'm pretty much a friend of the family.'

'You've seen it all, then? The problems? The triumphs.'

Edie had the tingling sense that she was on fertile turf. 'You can't triumph without overcoming the issues that come up on the way. And Veronica overcame.'

Lesley's eyes went wide. 'I'm just glad that she had powerful friends.'

'VIPs?'

Lesley laughed despite herself and wiped away a fresh batch of tears. 'Yeah. Friends in high places. They made bad things disappear.' She looked down at the picture of Veronica in the brochure and crossed herself. 'But I shouldn't be talking about that.'

'You must have seen amazing results here, watching couples grow into families and dreams come true.'

Lesley nodded, but there was, again, a bristle of something else, too. 'Family Ties makes families thrive. That's what she always said. Families are everything.'

Edie tried to imagine what her child would have been like if she'd grown a family with Sky. Occasionally she thought of the life she might have lived if she'd continued to love. Not for the first time, she felt a stirring of spring in her wintered heart. And wished for frost to kill it off.

'They don't let you down, like some other kinds of love. Veronica always said that. But she never learned. "Lesley," she'd say to me, "I never learn."' Lesley's laugh was long and manic, surprising even Edie. 'Ironic seeing as she had an affair with a headmaster.'

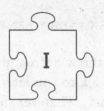

Twenty

The first thing Sean saw as he entered the Family Ties clinic was his aunt sitting on the edge of the sofa. She looked riveted by whatever the woman in the white coat was saying. Irritation swept over him. She could have compromised the investigation already, and then Sean would be taken off the case.

Edie and the woman looked up at the same time. Edie gave a very slight shake of her head and a glare that seemed to say, 'Don't you dare give me away.'

'I'm DI Brand-O'Sullivan. And you are . . .?'

'This is Lesley Maupert, fertility practitioner,' Edie said, as if it was perfectly natural for her to be present. 'And I should be going, Lesley.'

Edie stood, smiling. Seeing his aunt grin was deeply unnerving. It seemed taken from another face and stapled on, wonkily.

'Are you sure? You can't stay?' She was gripping Edie's sleeve.

Don't say Aunt Edie had made a friend?

'Thanks for all your support and information, Lesley, but I'll be off. The police give me hives.'

'I'll see you at the funeral,' Lesley Maupert said.

As she left, Edie threw Sean a glance that could mean anything from 'I'll talk to you later, young man' to 'Why did you interrupt me?' Whatever she meant, he knew she wasn't happy with him. When he was the one who should be livid with her.

When Edie had gone, Sean sat down next to Lesley Maupert on the sofa.

'You're here about Veronica, aren't you? Dr Newman said the police might pop by.'

'Did he also tell you—'

'That she's gone? Yes.' She turned to him. 'I don't really know what to say to the police. I've never talked to one of you before.'

'I'll just be asking you a few questions, to see if we can get some more information about Dr Princeton's death.'

Lesley adjusted her white coat and sat up straighter. 'I'll do anything I can to help.'

'In order to eliminate you from our enquiries – just a matter of formality, you understand – could you tell us where you were last night between midnight and four am?'

'Is that when it happened?' Her lips trembled. 'When she died?'

'We're not sure yet.'

'I was at home, same as every night. I don't really go out. No one to go with.' Her tiny smile had such sadness behind it. 'Veronica promised that one day I'd go out on the town with her.'

'So do you have anyone who can confirm you were home?'

'Only my dog.'

Sean's phone buzzed in his pocket. He took it out and discreetly viewed the message from Michaels. She'd checked out Dr Newman's alibi. There were gaps in his story – he'd said he was in the doctors' resting room, but no one had seen him after three am. She was checking CCTV.

'We've discovered,' Sean said, 'that the clinic received complaints and threats of violence. Could you tell me more about that?'

'It started small – graffiti saying "Hope killers" and "Scamming scum". I had to scrub it off the glass. Then, the next week, the whole window was smashed. Veronica started getting abusive messages, threatening to go to the press.'

'Why wasn't this reported to the police?'

'Veronica says . . .' Lesley stopped and closed her eyes. '*Said* that you have to expect that in fertility clinics. "When you're dealing out dreams, some people get nightmares". She didn't want people who were already suffering to get into more trouble.'

Sean knew couples who had brought their dreams to fertility clinics. All had come away bruised in heart, body and wallet, but a few had also come home with a baby. He didn't know if he'd have been able to bear the process.

'What about you?' He dipped his voice so that it was low, inviting her to confide in him. 'Have you been targeted personally? Because it must be lovely to help people, but horrible to have them turn on you?'

Lesley Maupert's mouth trembled. 'I've had a few

Facebook messages. Veronica said to ignore them, but I still worry.' She paused, then her voice dropped too. 'I don't walk alone at night anymore.'

'I'm sorry to hear that. And I understand.'

Lesley looked in his eyes. 'I can see you do.'

'I'm going to need a list of everyone who has attended the clinic or been in contact.'

Lesley blinked. 'There might be data protection issues.'

'Medical records can be accessed if there's significant reason for the enquiry. And, as Veronica has been murdered, that will cover it.'

'It's that word: murdered.' Her lip crumpled.

'I'm sorry, Ms Maupert. I know this is hard.'

She stared into his eyes again, seeing right through him. 'Yes. You do know that, don't you?'

'Can you show me where the Facebook messages came from?'

She nodded and flicked through her phone, then held up a page.

'Weymouth Running Club?'

'The messages came from an admin for the Facebook group; I don't know their name.'

But the banner for the page had a picture of the Weymouth Runners after a race, and Sean knew which one. It was from the Bournemouth half-marathon. He knew because he'd been there, cheering on Liam, who was standing in the centre of the picture, beaming.

Twenty-One

Edie was sitting on the bench outside when Sean came out of the clinic. She looked up from her phone. He was talking on his, frowning.

She wanted to tell him everything. To work with him again. To be honest.

He hung up and stared at her, unsmiling. Edie was reminded of when his grandad was a little boy. Anthony had been the sunniest of little brothers, until she took a toy away from him, at which point his little forehead would bunch up and his lips quiver. She never could bear that and always gave it back, even if it was hers.

A lover had once asked if she'd ever resented Anthony for living when their mum had died giving birth to him. She hadn't spoken to that woman again. Waking up on Christmas morning to find that her mummy was dead, her new brother was critically ill in hospital, and that Santa hadn't been and wouldn't come again, had set off two things. Her hatred of Christmas, and her love for her brother.

'You're angry with me.' She spoke before he could.

'You could have compromised everything.' Sean wasn't looking at her. Ever since he was little, this is what he did when he was upset. 'I could be removed from the case, or even disciplined.'

'But this isn't me investigating,' she lied. 'I knew Veronica. I taught her at St Mary's. I felt I had to do something.'

A look of worry crossed Sean's face. Edie felt the urge to smooth his brow like when he was a boy. To her, he still was. That was one of the things about being older than most: people were kids till they got to sixty.

'You taught her?'

'For two years. She was fantastic at maths.'

'And what happened?'

'She got corking results, and I sent her off into the world, apparently to be a fertility expert. Admittedly one who may have had some problems.'

'What problems?'

'Lesley alluded to her having influential friends. I got the impression that something controversial at the clinic was smoothed over. See what I can do when I get involved?'

Sean turned and walked off, quickly. Edie had to hurry to keep up. She tried to ignore the pain in her shins, knee and feet. 'Please. I can't stand it when you're mad at me.'

'Then don't go against what I ask.'

'Stop, please.'

Sean slowed to a halt and looked up to the sky. He'd yet to look her in the eye.

'Maybe you're looking at this the wrong way,' Edie said. 'I don't have to be overtly involved, but I can get into places, go incognito, be the invisible woman. No one will know we're related.' Shaking out her Alexander McQueen scarf, she put it over her head and then slumped into her shoulders. 'If anyone notices me, they'll think I'm an old dear out for a spot of air before going home to nap in front of *Escape to the Sun*.'

'An old dear in a skull headscarf?'

'You millennials have no idea what makes a pre-Boomer tick. You know what they call us? The Silent Generation.'

'You? Silent?'

'Silent and invisible. As I said, no one notices a crone. It's why I'm so good at pickpocketing.' She waved her fingers at him.

'Tell me you're joking, Aunt Edie.'

'I'm joking.' She winked at him, but Sean didn't laugh. She could usually always make him laugh.

'I have everything I need. I have all the resources of the police at my disposal. I don't need you.' His tone was flat, his mouth too.

She'd never seen him this angry, not with her. She felt sick. 'I can do things official investigators can't.'

Sean's laugh was as sarcastic as he got. 'Yeah? Like what?'

'Okay, well, how about Lesley telling me that Veronica had an affair.'

'Who with?'

'The headmaster from St Mary's School. The one we saw yesterday.'

Her nephew stopped still.

Edie showed him a picture from the *Dorset Echo* of Dr Edward Berkeley at a school event in 2010, his hand on

Veronica Princeton's waist. 'She dug this out for me. After all, I was a family friend.'

'I would have found that out.' Sean didn't sound sure, though.

'But would you have known that I taught Veronica?'

Sean resumed walking in silence.

'Where are you off to now?' she asked.

'The woods.'

She left it a whole second before saying, 'Can I come?'

And he left not one millisecond before replying, 'No.'

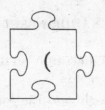

Twenty-Two

The jiffy bag lay on Edie's YOU ARE NOT WELCOME mat, waiting for her like Peggotty, Fezziwig and Mr Bumble, who appeared in the doorway, tails twitching.

As she stepped into the porch, her heart juddered, out of time with itself. She placed a hand on her chest. The cardiologist had told her to do more exercise, eat fewer pastries, etc., etc., but he hadn't mentioned avoiding murder investigations, so she must be fine to continue.

Edie tore open the package, not even pausing to put gloves on. The jigsaws were for her, and she wasn't going to give them to the police. Sean had made it clear there was no point.

She looked at the letter first. Same paper, same typed font.

```
Ms O'Sullivan,
   Another corner piece. Another death
for me to place, unless you can roll
out this scroll and solve the clues.
Not that you have managed so far.
Shame. And you must suffer such shame.
   Rest In Pieces
```

'Oh, fuck off,' Edie said. Fezziwig flicked his ears back.

She hurried through into the lounge and placed the pieces on her tray with the others. She could tell at a glance that few of them fitted together, but that one of the new arrivals would intersect with the one she'd kept back from Sean. The edges, and the outline of a body, matched each other perfectly.

Taking a picture of each piece, she zoomed in on them in turn, taking in every detail. That was the key to jigsaw puzzles: keeping a mental note of where you've placed each piece, rather than looking only for the one that fits. Jigsaws require a mind that can hold the whole picture as well as the pieces. And the murderer was charging her with putting it all together. But why? And was that what they really wanted?

The right-hand corner piece was a section of carpet, or a rug, with gold fringing. One piece had black and white tiles with holly, two pieces featured sea waves, and two joining pieces featured a stack of books – Dickens, Austen, Shakespeare – the big 'uns. One more piece had the word 'warehouse' written on it in a fancy font. Given that the word 'scroll' was used in the letter, it could be a library, maybe big enough to be considered a warehouse. Or maybe some kind of book factory on an industrial estate, producing volume after volume. That would be a good place to commit murder.

Feeling the thrill of getting to grips with a puzzle, of slipping into a flow state, Edie got out her phone and started looking for book-based warehouses in the area.

The nearest printing press was in Poole, called House of Books.

It looked like she was off to Poole.

'Take a look at these,' Sean said, passing DC Ama Phillips his phone. 'They're the latest jigsaw pieces, found in Veronica Princeton's hair.'

Ama shivered and Sean switched the heating up to full blast. He'd just picked her up from the station and had already phoned Michaels to set her onto the Weymouth Runners angle. Both Carl and Veronica were connected to the club, and he needed to keep his distance, just as he did from running. Liam would have to be interviewed, and by someone else.

Sean's Spotify was set to the playlist he'd made for Edie. It ranged from Elvis to Aphex Twin, with plenty of seventies and eighties alternative jostling in the middle. Her taste in music had always fascinated him. She'd been a forty-five-year-old punk, a mid-fifties raver, always an outsider.

'What's this?' Ama asked, when Captain Beefheart came on. He was about to change it when she added, 'Keep it on. I like it.'

She stared at the phone screen and the photo of the jigsaw pieces found in Veronica Princeton's hair. Sean had already studied them. Two showed a crumpled newspaper cutting, two contained more black and white tiles spattered with blood, and two, including a corner piece, looked like part of a tasselled rug.

'Anything come to you?' Sean asked.

'Whoever is sending them doesn't want us to have all the pieces. They like having the power to drip-feed information that couldn't possibly lead to a result.'

'Sounds astute.'

'Whoever they are, I bet they're scrutinising everything we do. They want to see us try to find them, and fail.' Ama had studied criminal psychology at university before joining the police. Profilers were not in vogue, or in budget, but Sean liked to hear her thoughts.

'There must be a deeper motive driving them.'

Ama nodded. 'It'll become obvious, but only at the end, when they've won. Because that's what they need to do at all costs: win.'

Usually, talking with Ama reassured Sean. Now, though, it made him realise that Rest In Pieces didn't just want to win: they wanted Edie to lose.

'I'll tell you one thing that surprises me, though.'

'Go on.'

'There was a message with the jigsaw box and the initial pieces, but not one since.'

Sean's brow crinkled. 'They've set the challenge – what more needs to be said?'

'I don't know. But someone who gives themselves a title – a moniker – like Rest In Pieces, wants people to know them. They want to be heard.'

'So, you think there'll be more letters?'

Ama's look of worry mirrored his own. 'Or there have already been some, and we've missed them.'

Sean parked on the outskirts of the woods, near cars

belonging to other officers. Even from here, he could hear the search team calling out to each other as they moved through the undergrowth.

'We both need to stay behind the cordon,' Sean said to Ama as she began to march towards the sounds.

He hadn't been in these woods for years. Edie and Sky had brought him to the adventure playground at its heart, and then, as a teenager, he'd discovered under a yew tree that the human heart was itself an adventure playground, without any soft landing if you fell.

Today, though, the woods were full of SOCOs, searching through bushes and taking pictures of paths. One officer in uniform stood by the cordon. As Sean got closer, he saw that the PC was Zola Harker from Weymouth station.

'Zola!' Sean approached her, stepping over a branch that covered the path. He remembered what Carl Latimer had said about tripping over something similar. Staring up at the tree, Sean saw from where the branch had fallen. That could be what had happened to Carl. It was equally possible, though, that someone had placed the obstacle in his path. Someone who must have known his running route.

Zola came over with her familiar lope. 'I was hoping you'd come.' Her face was full of the eagerness of a uniformed officer who wished to become a plain-clothes detective.

Sean had felt that same enthusiasm, and tried to encourage it when he saw it in others. 'What can you tell me?'

Zola pointed to the tree at the centre of the cordon, around which the search revolved. 'That's where Carl

Latimer fell.' She then motioned towards a large branch nearby. 'And that's where he tripped; you can see the scuff marks. But no sign of where the branch came from – there's no tear in the tree, so it was probably taken from somewhere else. Same with what we think is the weapon. It was found covered over with leaves, remnants of blood still on it.'

'And that's gone to forensics?'

Zola nodded.

'I suppose all evidence of footprints or other tracks has gone?'

'The scene wasn't properly manned – the cordon just acted as a red flag to some youngsters last night. Even if it hadn't rained, any evidence would have been destroyed.'

Sean saw the remains of a fire, along with cans of Red Bull and cider. His cheek twitched in annoyance. If the DCI had listened to him yesterday, this wouldn't have happened.

'Make sure no one else gets near it.'

Zola nodded. 'Yes, Inspector.'

Walking off, Sean tried to get a sense of where Carl had been running. Paths intersected and weaved through the trees, worn down by joggers and dog walkers who probably all trod the same route every day. It wouldn't take much to get to know someone's routine. People made themselves into jigsaw pieces. They made their lives fit together in the same way every day.

Something hit the trunk of a tree to his right. As he turned, someone tapped him on the shoulder. He spun round.

Helena was standing there, grinning. 'Just wanted to show you how easy it is to jump out at someone out here.'

'Well, you did that. Well done. What are you doing here? I thought you were off for the whole day?'

'When I heard the site needed SOCOs, I couldn't resist. I'm not letting someone else take all the glory.'

'Because SOCOs are bathed in glory so often.'

'You're very sarky today. You're turning into your Aunt Edie.' She didn't seem to think that was a good thing.

'Don't,' Sean said. 'I'm not in the mood. Anything else you want to show me?'

'There is, actually.'

Helena led him off down a path, stopping eventually in a clearing with three trees in the centre. On one of the branches hung a soaking wet hoodie, drooping like a grey ghost.

'I thought it was someone hanging there at first, scared me stupid. But then I saw it was just a hoodie. It's out of the search zone but I thought it was worth mentioning.'

'Oh, Helena. It was definitely worth mentioning.'

On the front of the hoodie was the slogan 'Weymouth Runners', and, when Sean got close enough to read it, on the inside was a label that said, 'ST MARY'S SCHOOL'.

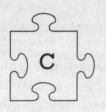

Twenty-Three

'Dr Berkeley?' Sean stood in the doorway of the study, watching the headmaster stare out towards the dark sea.

Edward Berkeley turned to face him. 'DI Brand-O'Sullivan. You were here yesterday, correct?'

'Good of you to see me, headmaster.'

Berkeley smiled. 'You're not part of the school, Inspector, you don't have to call me that.'

'I like your study.' Sean wandered around, taking in the shelves of academic texts and files. He thought of Edie, who, whenever she went into a study, had to turn it into the anagram 'dusty'. This study, though, was pristine, with not one mote of dust in the air. On top of the fireplace was a photo in a frame. 'She looks like a lovely woman.'

'Lorelei. My late wife.'

'My condolences.'

'It was a long time ago. Or at least it seems it. We never forget though, do we?' He blinked a few times, then sauntered to his desk, stopping to pull out an armchair for Sean. 'Now, how can I help you? Is there news about Carl? From what I hear, he's recovering well.'

'Yes, he should be out of hospital soon. In connection to Mr Latimer, I was wondering if you recognise this hooded top?' Sean showed him a picture of the hoodie found in the woods.

Dr Berkeley frowned. 'I feel I've seen it at some point, but I can't remember where.'

'Carl Latimer didn't wear it at the school?'

The headmaster shook his head. 'Games teachers have to wear the St Mary's games uniform. Dark blue tracksuit, with the school's name on it. He may have worn it while running outside of work hours, I suppose. But I didn't see him then.'

'Why would it have the school's name inside?'

'I don't . . .' Dr Berkeley stopped talking and inclined his head, then walked over to a cupboard. Taking out a photo album, he flicked through to a middle page and brought it over to Sean. 'There it is. I knew I'd seen it somewhere. It's the old St Mary's uniform. Before my time.'

The photos showed tweens and teens in grey uniforms, some smiling, some surly. In one picture a sports team stood lined up, all wearing grey hoodies. 'When was this?'

'Ten, fifteen years ago maybe? Or perhaps even longer.'

'I also have some questions about another case,' Sean said, writing notes.

Berkeley glanced at the clock. 'I hope it won't take long.'

'It may do, I'm afraid. The body of a woman, Dr Veronica Princeton, was discovered in the early hours of this morning.'

Edward Berkeley grew still. His mouth seemed to be trying to find the edges of words. His face creased with pain, and he closed his eyes; when he opened them, they were wet.

'I believe you knew Dr Princeton.'

Berkeley nodded and gazed down at the blotting paper on his desk. The ink spots reminded Sean of blood spatter patterns. That's what being in the police did to him.

It was three minutes before Berkeley spoke, and when he did it was haltingly. 'I met Dr Princeton at a number of Rotary Club do's. We were both committed members of the community.'

'Of course.' Sean glanced towards the slightly open door, then got up and closed it. 'But we both know that your relationship was more than that of peers and colleagues.' He paused. 'Dr Berkeley?'

The headmaster looked up.

'I think I lost you there for a moment.'

'To be honest,' Berkeley said, 'I was wondering how to talk about what happened between me and Veronica.'

'How would you describe your relationship?'

Berkeley took off his glasses and rubbed his eyes. 'That's not easy.'

'If you could try?'

'I'd say it was a love affair. By the end, Veronica considered it a mistake.'

'When did it begin?'

'2000, I think. Another long time ago.'

Sean's pen scratched across the rough paper of his notebook as he took down the details, causing Berkeley to wince at the sound. In another interview he'd keep using it, but he felt for the man, and searched his pockets for a biro to use instead.

'Strange to think it's approaching a quarter of a century. She was going through a difficult time with her husband and there I was.' The headmaster opened his arms wide. 'She enjoyed sneaking around, booking into hotels for afternoons together. She craved excitement.'

'And you didn't?'

'I craved love, adoration, attention. The usual.'

'Were you married at the time?' Sean looked over to the picture of Berkeley's wife.

'I'm not proud of what I did. I could say I didn't get those things at home, but I don't think that would be fair.'

'And how long did the affair last?'

'Till the mid-2000s, on and off.'

'What happened?'

'Lorelei, my wife, found out in 2002, and she didn't take it at all . . .' The headmaster stared into the distance as if replaying the moment. 'She didn't take it well. Especially when I said I wanted to leave her for Veronica. She was already going through a lot of difficulties at work with her awful boss, and it tipped it her over the edge, caused her to . . .'

'She killed herself?' Sean tried but couldn't keep the recrimination out of his voice.

'I don't blame you for blaming me. I didn't behave well. But when Lorelei died, I could hardly function. Veronica and I clung to each other in grief. We hung on for a few years, I suppose to try and convince ourselves it had all been for the sake of something, but in the end, we broke up.'

'What about her husband – did he know about your relationship?'

The headmaster shrugged. 'If he did, he never mentioned it to her, or to me at the Rotary Club.'

'Interesting.' Sean knew couples who accepted each other's infidelities. Some of them didn't want to know the details, while others very much did. There was no way, though, that he was secure enough to cope with that. The idea of Liam with someone else made Sean want to vomit.

'So, it was an amicable break-up?'

'It petered out, so yes. Neither of us felt the same about each other after what happened.'

'And yet you still seem very affected by her death. Do you still have feelings for her?'

'Fondness, or even indifference, after a break-up is always a target. Exceptions occur, of course. Sometimes love remains, despite the relationship changing status from active to invalid.'

Sean nodded, thinking of his own past relationships and which category they fit into. And then he thought about Edie. Love for Sky was etched into her bones.

'You look like you understand.'

'I do. But I was also thinking of someone else for whom it definitely is true.'

'The love I had with Veronica is like a tattoo. It doesn't grow out, however much I might want it to.'

Sean thought of the tattoos he and Liam had got when they married. And what it would be like to be told that his husband had died.

'When were you last in touch with Veronica?'

142

'I bumped into her at council lunches, Rotary do's, etc., but otherwise it was no contact. We considered it kinder to our hearts.'

'What were you doing from last night until early this morning?'

Berkeley blinked. 'I was here until eight, then I dropped some Christmas treats off for my mum and stayed with her until she went to bed, then I went home too. And I was back at work by half seven.'

'And is there anyone to confirm that you were at your house? A partner, or other family members?'

Berkeley hesitated, then shook his head. 'My daughter lives in North Yorkshire so I hardly ever get to see her. And I haven't had a partner in a long time. A neighbour may have seen me, I suppose, but that's not going to help you be certain I stayed in one place.'

'Where does your mother live?'

'Montague Place, an assisted living block in Swanage.'

Sean wrote down the address. 'Did Veronica Princeton have any enemies when you were close?'

'Not that I know of. We made a pledge not to talk about work, or our home lives, but I think she'd have told me if there was a problem.'

'What *did* you talk about, if you remember?'

Berkeley was blushing. 'I remember everything. Hopes, dreams, politics, literature, pillow talk. After a long day teaching and running a school for me, though not this one at the time, and looking after people's expectations for her, as both a fertility expert and a councillor, thinking only about ourselves was refreshing.'

'What about Carl Latimer – any connection between him and Dr Princeton?'

'Other than me, you mean?' Berkeley gave an awkward laugh. 'Wait, I thought you said these were separate cases?'

'Just being thorough. If Carl Latimer *was* attacked, then it pays to be aware if these events are related.'

'Very much like how I teach history. Everything connects. It's good to also bear in mind, though, that life doesn't intersect in the same way. Much of it is random. We must be aware of what we each bring of our past to history.'

'Could you answer my question, Dr Berkeley?' Sean's voice was edged with irritation.

'I can't see how they'd know each other, but then I haven't spoken to Veronica for years.'

'For the record, can you tell us where you were the night that Mr Latimer was attacked?'

'When was that? Day before last?'

'Yes, two nights ago.'

'Then same as last night. Marking here at the school, then I popped in to see Mum, then home. Not much help for you!' He was blushing again, and fiddling with his pen.

Sean looked back through his notebook. He didn't know whether to ask his next question; after all, the press had, miraculously, yet to get the information. 'I know this is an odd question but—'

'None of your enquiries could be odder than those I get from the kids.'

'What are your feelings on jigsaws?'

'Jigsaws? I take it back. That *is* a strange question.'

Sean smiled a little and bowed.

'I haven't completed a jigsaw in many years. Actually, tell a lie: Mrs Challis brought some to a staff social and timed us.'

'So, you take no particular interest in them?'

'I have no particular feelings towards jigsaws at all.'

Sean closed his notebook. 'That's it for now.'

Dr Berkeley stood awkwardly, rubbing his slight stubble as he walked the detective to the door. 'Does this have to be made public? Our affair, I mean?'

'I can't promise that it won't come out, but discretion will be applied at all times.'

Mrs Challis was in the room next door to Berkeley's office when Sean passed.

'This won't be tolerated,' she was saying, in a voice that made Sean feel as if he'd been naughty. 'You are *this far away* from being dismantled.'

Sean popped his head around the door. 'Is everything okay, Mrs Challis?'

Mrs Challis was wagging her finger at a large printer which was spitting out paper. 'This contraption will not behave.' She gave it a swift kick. 'No matter what I do, it won't print more than one copy at a time.' Mrs Challis handed him a schedule of events for the 'St Mary's Staff Festive Luncheon Party'.

'Maybe you could leave it to reflect on what it's done, while I interview you,' Sean said.

Mrs Challis gave the printer a long, hard stare and one last warning wag of her index finger, then ushered him through into her office. It was surprisingly cosy and comfortable. She had made her own nest, with an armchair and blankets, a stuffed plush cat and a fan heater. There was even a pair of fluffy slippers.

On the shelves were crossword primers and books of facts that he'd also seen on Edie's shelves. And there was his great-aunt's latest cryptic crossword laid out ready to complete, presumably once Mrs Challis had finished arguing with rogue machinery.

She settled into her armchair and pointed at a hard dining room chair in the corner.

'Who normally sits here?' Sean asked.

'Staff on their breaks, usually,' Mrs Challis replied. 'They think I'm some kind of camp counsellor when I am very much not. I keep the chair uncomfy to make them leave.'

'Edie would approve.'

'I can well believe it. Now, Inspector, I presume you want to know where I was on the night Carl was attacked, along with my whereabouts last night.' She reached into a drawer and pulled out a stack of printed pages, presumably from when the printer had been feeling more amenable. It was a spreadsheet of every hour of each of the two nights, right down to what she had eaten for dinner, the programmes she had watched and when she had gone to the toilet. But, like Lesley, Dr Berkeley and Dr Newman, there was no one who could corroborate.

'Thank you for being so . . . thorough. How did you know that Veronica Princeton had died?'

'A school receptionist knows all.'

'I need a bit more than that.'

'Fine. It was on a Weymouth Town Facebook group. Circling helicopters and murder get top billing.'

'What can you tell me about Carl Latimer?'

'Officially, as in present in the school records?'

'Is there an *unofficial* account? One that's not in the records?'

'There might well be.'

'You wouldn't happen to have a print-out of that vers—'

Mrs Challis reached into her drawer and pulled out a file. 'Of course I do. It doesn't make pleasant reading.'

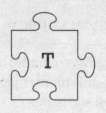

Twenty-Four

House of Books was at the far reaches of an industrial estate that was edged by the sea.

'Can you wait for me?' Edie asked the taxi driver.

The trip had already cost her a fortune, so she might as well go all-in. And she didn't know yet where else she might need to go. That was the beauty of puzzles: they took you in unexpected directions.

The driver nodded, looking at the clock. 'Fine by me.'

Edie wrapped her skull scarf around her neck to keep out the cold hands of the wind. The water had taken on the pink streaks of the darkening winter sky. The briny air made her think of the cockles she'd once pinned in nearby Poole Harbour. Surely the salt couldn't be good for the books.

The receptionist grinned at Edie when she entered. She had blue hair, pink-rimmed glasses and tattooed hands. Edie approved. 'I love what you're wearing! Is that vintage Westwood?'

'If Vivienne is vintage, what does that make me?' Edie smiled despite herself.

'An OG? In pagan terms you'd be a crone.' The young woman had the open face and triple moon pendant of someone who regarded the 'C' word, 'crone', with honour and respect, quite rightly.

'Yes. I'm an OG crone.'

'Are you an author?' She looked down at a diary on her desk. 'Because I wasn't expecting a signing today.'

'No,' said Edie, though she liked the thought. 'But I was wondering if you could help me? I've got a puzzle I need to solve.'

The young woman leaned forward. 'I love puzzles!'

'What's your name?' Edie asked.

'Merribeth.'

'Merribeth, do you recognise this rug?' She showed the young woman the jigsaw piece.

Merribeth reached out, taking it before Edie could move it out of reach. She looked closely at the image, then shook her head. 'Sorry. Never seen it before. It'd be too dangerous to keep a rug or carpet on the factory floor.'

'It's not in the breakroom, or where the authors sign books?'

'No. Why did you think it might be here?'

Edie looked at the young woman, this maiden, and decided that, appropriately for maritime Poole,, she liked the cut of her jib. Enough to share more, anyway. 'I've got to find where this is. I think a crime may take place there.'

'Oh, brilliant,' Merribeth said, blinking.

Edie shook out the jigsaw piece with 'warehouse' written on it. The letters swooped and curled. 'Although, looking at it again, the font doesn't seem like one a warehouse would use, even one for books.'

Merribeth's teeth were moon-white and gleaming as she smiled. 'That's because it's not for a warehouse – it's a bookshop. I haven't been in ages, but I used to go every Saturday when I was a teenager. Every Poole goth still does.'

'Thank you. Don't stop being you, Merribeth. You're excellent.'

Merribeth blinked again.

'Is it far, this bookshop?' Edie was thinking of the taxi driver and the ever-tocking clock.

'Poole High Street, in the Old Town. Harbour end.' Merribeth tapped on her keyboard, then turned her monitor around to show Edie.

The same fancy font as on the jigsaw piece was on the screen, with one extra, crucial, letter – 'Aware House'.

Pauline Figes' face was ruddy, eyes red and hair wet as she came out of Weymouth Swimming Pool and Fitness Centre. Across her forehead was a thick band where her swimming cap had been. She was followed by the smell of chlorine and discarded verruca plasters.

Sean could tell that Michaels was trying not to look smug that her plan to 'run into' Pauline had worked. She'd divined that Pauline posted her lap times on Instagram after every swim, between five and seven each weekday. Her resting 'I-told-you-so' face won through. She shared that facility, and several others now he came to think of it, with Edie.

Sean didn't know why they couldn't just go to Pauline's

place of work, or her home, but Michaels' reasoning was that catching her in her zen zone would help. 'The endorphins will make her more philanthropic,' she'd said, making him think that she was also part of the fit cult. Isla called them dolphins – 'get those dolphins rising to the surface! They'll help you swim through anything!' Now that they were here, Sean, in his guise as a benevolent DI, was allowing Michaels to test her theory by leading the questioning.

'Pauline Figes? I'm Detective Sergeant Michaels, and this is Detective Inspector Brand-O'Sullivan.'

Pauline did a double take at the sight of Sean. 'You're Liam's hubby, aren't you? I've seen your wedding pictures! Is this about Carl?'

'It is,' Sean said. 'Among other enquiries.' He nodded at Michaels to continue.

'We're trying to find out what happened to Mr Latimer, and we thought the Running Club might be able to help.'

Pauline's bloodshot eyes shone. She really was on an endorphin high. 'That's what we're here for. To help the community. And we're always up for new members,' she said to Michaels.

'Watch out, Michaels, the Runners are coming for you,' Sean said, grinning at Pauline.

Pauline gave him a little punch on the shoulder. 'Liam told us you were a wag.'

A wag? Sean would rather Liam had described him in almost any other way. A *wag*?

'Go on then,' Michaels said, picking up on the tone of the conversation. 'Convert me to running, Pauline!'

'We're a very friendly bunch, with people of all levels of experience and fitness. It's great fun.'

'I don't know if I'm fit enough,' Michaels said, which was ridiculous. She'd be able to outrun him easily.

'Nonsense. Our oldest runner is ninety-five, although I do worry every time he goes out that he'll die and we'll be in the papers!'

'That wouldn't be great for recruitment,' Michaels said. 'Especially after what happened to Carl.'

'Don't let that put you off! The idiot was running alone at night in the woods. We've told him time and time again not to.'

'Do you always tell each where you're going?' Michaels asked.

Pauline nodded, with a touch of her own resting smug face. 'We do, for security reasons. Each of us is connected via a running app so we always know where we are in case of emergencies.'

'Is that how it was discovered that Carl had been injured?' Michaels asked, knowing full well none of the runners had found him.

Pauline no longer looked as smug. 'Carl's a little different, as he asks us not to track him.'

'Why?' Sean asked, though reading through Mrs Challis' file before they came had given him some clue.

'He often . . . er . . . visits friends.'

'I see.'

'Mainly, though, we run together, and meet up for fundraising half-marathons etc.'

'Any particular charity that you support?' Sean asked.

'We've all got some pet causes. And not just for animals.' She laughed at her joke and looked across expectantly at Michaels.

Michaels turned up her smile. 'And what's *your* pet cause?'

Pauline's face was shadow-striped. 'I support charities for women who have been let down by the medical profession.'

'A worthy cause,' Sean said, thinking of Edie's mum.

'We don't go after the NHS, though.'

'So, you target private health companies?' Michaels asked. 'I don't blame you. All that money, and what do you get for it?'

'You come away with less than you went in with.' Pauline's hand went briefly to her stomach.

Sean felt so much empathy for her it was as if her pain was contagious. 'I know this is sensitive, but have you been treated at the Family Ties Fertility Clinic?'

Pauline's eyes were considerably less shiny now. They lowered to the ground and she nodded.

'We've received some information that one of the admins on the Facebook group is sending hate messages to the clinic.'

'Oh no,' she said, face full of alarm. 'No one in the group would do anything like that.'

'I've seen them,' Sean said. 'Full of hate speech and misogyny. And death threats.'

'Well, we don't support that.'

'In which case,' Michaels pressed, 'you won't mind giving us a list of all the admins and information on how they log in.'

'But you won't be able to tell who it is, will you?' Pauline's tone was increasingly taut. 'Because there are ten admins and we all have the same log in.'

Michaels' tone grew steely. 'We'll find out who sent the messages, and we'd rather you gave us this information than us having to make a formal request. That wouldn't reflect well on you, should anything go to court.'

Sean contrasted her words with a silken tone. 'Did you send those messages, Pauline? Because something bad happened to you at the clinic?'

'I didn't send anything. And I don't want to talk about the clinic.' Tears were welling. So many tears in this job.

'I understand the pain of involuntary childlessness,' Sean said. 'There are organisations who can help that I could put you in touch with, if you want?'

'How could you possibly understand?' Pauline spat.

But he did. A wave of the pain that had been suppressed by hope since meeting Juniper came back as he thought of the years he had longed to be a father.

'Why do you ask that?' Michaels asked Pauline, sharply.

Pauline jutted her jaw forward. 'He's not a woman, is he? He wouldn't know what it's like to keep trying for a baby and they never catch.'

Sean hated that old-fashioned term – 'catch', as if embryos were cricket fielders – but the fierce tears in Pauline's eyes stopped him saying anything.

'It's not just those with working wombs who long for children or have fertility issues.' Michaels' voice was strained with a pain that Sean hadn't seen in her before. So much goes on beneath the waterline.

'Why are you having a go at me?' Pauline snapped. Her endorphins had definitely swum away now. 'It's Lucy you should be talking to. She's the one who sent those messages.'

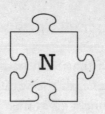

Twenty-Five

Poole High Street was a Jekyll and Hyde: on one side of the road, it was all charity shops, knock-off stalls and unrented spaces, while on the other, independent shops and restaurants were just a pedestrian crossing away. Edie's Fitbit buzzed as she got out of the taxi by the crossing, registering her pulse rate skyrocketing. It asked how she was feeling and gave several options. 'Excited,' she pressed in response. She felt more alive than she had in a very long time.

Aware House was at the posher end of the street, equal sniffing distance between Lush and the harbour. The olfactory cacophony was added to once the door of the bookshop tinkled closed. Nag Champa sticks burned in every nook, the air smoky and thickly scented.

'Can I help you?' a woman in wafty black broderie asked. She had Stevie Nicks hair and a patchouli aura. There was no sign that a murder had taken place here. Yet. Edie had made it in time. Maybe no one else would die.

Edie again showed the rug jigsaw piece, this time keeping it out of touching distance. 'I think you have this rug.'

The woman's smile was immediate. She opened her arms. 'You're the first one! Congratulations!'

Edie took a step back. 'What do you mean?'

'You're doing the charity scavenger hunt, right? You solve clues and collect things from certain places.' She bustled over to a black cabinet and opened the top drawer. 'I'm supposed to give you this.'

She handed over an envelope. Edie's heart was unmoored as she opened it and found another printed letter.

```
Ms O'Sullivan,
   For someone who sets the questions,
you are a very bad puzzler. You went
for the obvious route, and you know
very well that will lead to you
pencilling in the wrong answer. Still,
it's your time you're wasting. And that
of the next victim.
   R.I.P
```

Sean was late for his own briefing, having gone straight from the swimming pool to the gym before returning to the station. Isla had had to cancel their session, but she'd still sent him detailed instructions which he felt duty-bound to follow. His thighs screamed as he slowly went up the stairs. By the time he'd got through the door into the stuffy room and sat down in the swingy chair, he was already apologising to the team.

'It's alright, sir,' Michaels said. 'We waited for you.' Her tone was one of superiority and disdain.

Sean knew that Edie, his boss, and most people maybe, would say, 'I should bloody think so.' He just said, 'Thank you.' Edie had often told him he was too nice, and that it would get him into trouble one day.

'Right, let's catch up. Michaels did a great job in prompting Pauline Figes to point the finger at Lucy Pringle as the author of the threatening messages to Veronica Princeton.'

There was a ripple of reluctant applause. Few liked Michaels.

Sean went on. 'I'd like you to bring Lucy Pringle in for questioning, Michaels.'

Michaels inclined her head. 'Is that before or after I interview your husband?'

Silence in the room.

Sean broke it, keeping his voice as light as possible. 'Before, thank you, seeing as the only reason to talk to him is that he's part of the running group. We have a lead on Mrs Pringle.'

'We should also interview your great-aunt as a matter of urgency,' Michaels continued. 'She received the first pieces, after all. It's worrying that she hasn't been formally interviewed yet. You can't do it, of course.'

'Naturally. I'm sure you'll do a great job,' Sean replied. And he was equally sure that Edie would do a job on Michaels.

He looked at Ama. 'DC Phillips, could you go through the client list we received from Family Ties and cross-reference it with members of the running club and the school. Those are our three areas of interest.'

'How did it go at the school, guv?' Phillips asked.

'The hoodie's part of an old St Mary's uniform, so it's possible there's a historic connection between the school and R.I.P. And while Berkeley doesn't have an alibi for either attack, he doesn't seem bothered. He admitted to the relationship with Veronica Princeton but said it ended a long time ago, and he seemed genuinely sad that she was dead.'

'Doesn't mean he didn't kill her,' Michaels said.

'Very true. Could you, Michaels, look into number plate recognition for his alleged journey times? He seems devoted to his mother, who's in an assisted living facility in Swanage, and there must be *some* CCTV cameras working in the area. We may be on the Jurassic Coast but we're not that fossilised.'

Michaels nodded. She was tapping her foot while stroking the file on her lap as if it contained precious news.

Not as important, he bet, as the file he'd obtained from Sandra Challis. 'We also need to interview Carl Latimer again about possible offences that weren't reported to the police. The school receptionist, Mrs Challis, gave me a document which suggests that when he was a teenager he was suspended for making – and distributing to friends – home videos and photos of himself and various girls of the same age, using his dad's cameras. Basically, revenge porn before it was a crime. That may well be a misdemeanour when a minor, and it would have been twenty-odd years ago, so possibly not relevant, but the intricacy of this jigsaw means there's a planning brain behind it. Every detail needs attention.'

'Someone getting revenge for revenge porn, maybe?' Ama suggested.

'I'll get the IT department to look through his computer and social media,' Michaels said. Her knee was now jolting the underside of the table.

'Thanks, Michaels. And you look like you've got something from when you and Ama investigated Veronica Princeton's activities last night?'

Michaels stood and strode to the front of the room; an unnecessary move.

'Veronica Princeton did indeed go out in town last night. She had a meal with friends at the Thai restaurant in the harbour and left drunk, by the looks of the CCTV footage. Two of her friends then went home, and she stayed out with the remaining two, Helen Baker and India Wang. All doctors on the lash.'

'Have you talked with them both?' Sean asked.

Michaels looked indignant. 'Of course. Ama talked with the two who went home early, and I targeted Baker and Wang.'

Sean noted the use of 'targeted', as if she saw herself as an assassin rather than an assessor.

'Both say that Veronica was on good form, which seems to be doctor code for off her face, and that they went into various bars and clubs. She waved them off in a taxi and said she was waiting for another.'

'Did they have a code?' Phillips asked. When everyone

looked blankly at her, she added, 'A text saying that she was back and safe.'

'Baker said they agreed to message when they'd got home safely, but both she and Wang fell asleep on getting back.'

'Some friends.' Phillips was shaking her head.

'Why should they be responsible for their friend?' Sean said. 'Her death was entirely the fault of the killer. What about after that? Any CCTV?'

'The last we have is her standing at the taxi rank. She seemed to look at her watch, hesitate, then walk away.'

'Nothing near Pocket Lane or Crescent Street? Of either her or a potential killer?'

'Not much of that area is covered, and very little of the seafront that goes up to it. What *is* there, isn't working.'

'Of course it isn't.' And it wasn't as if that was privileged knowledge. The station always got complaints from residents and businesses about non-functional CCTV.

'Has anything else come up?'

Phillips looked up and hesitated.

Sean recognised in her his own tendency to not come forward, thinking he wasn't important. 'Anything at all, big or small.'

'When I was chatting with the two women who went home early, Rachel and Yrsa, they said that Veronica kept looking at her smart watch, as if waiting for a message.'

'Maybe she was checking her step count or calories?' Michaels countered. Perhaps to offset the fact that she hadn't gained that information herself.

'Or she got a message and went to meet her killer?' Phillips' voice was quiet but steady. 'I've asked for Dr Princeton's phone records, but they haven't come through yet. Should be here in an hour or so.'

'Great work. Anyone else?'

'Nothing back from forensics yet, obviously.' Michaels said this defensively, as if he'd accused her of being at fault.

'It's possible we won't get anything now till after Christmas.' The season slowed everything down, from diets to forensics.

'What about me?' Phillips' eagerness was excruciating. Maybe Edie was right about his own niceness and naivety. 'What else can I do?'

'Talk to any member of the Weymouth Runners that you can contact.'

Phillips looked at him expectantly, asking for more with her eyes.

'Honestly, you don't need any more tasks. There are hundreds on their Facebook group, including our own SOCO Helena. It'll take you ages to contact them all and get their alibis to corroborate, or otherwise.'

'I like having things to do. It distracts me.'

Sean made a mental note to ask her what she needed distracting from. She'd learn eventually not to take on too much. 'Then, you could look into how the box and jigsaw were made – if there's somewhere locally or online. It may well all be made with a home 3D printer, but it won't hurt to look into it.'

Phillips nodded, with a bit too much glee. 'What about

solving the jigsaw side of things, sir?' She was looking at the print-out of the jigsaw pieces that had been pinned to the board. 'What are we supposed to be looking for?'

Maybe he shouldn't have excluded Edie. If this were another, similar case, he'd get her in as an expert.

But she was too involved.

'You're right, Ama. We need to prioritise the puzzle.'

'You can handle it, guv,' Michaels said.

Sean had no idea if she was being sarcastic or not.

'After all, your aunt must have taught you how to solve puzzles. Let's see how good a teacher she really is.'

P

Twenty-Six

The taxi driver talked all the way back to Weymouth, but Edie didn't hear a word. She was staring out of the window, burning with shame and anger. Like the snow, her thoughts wouldn't settle. She had been bested by Rest In Pieces, a killer with a terrible pun of a name.

They were right, whoever they were. She had gone with her first reaction to the clues and used flimsy evidence to back it up. She'd assumed she knew best. And that had cost her an extortionate amount of taxi money, much of the day, and her pride.

When she got home, it was dark. She made the universal sign of 'wanker' back at the illuminated Santa climbing Lucy Pringle's pebbledash and went inside. She felt every one of her eighty years, and more, as she slowly climbed the stairs to her bedroom, trying, as always, to ignore the locked-up dining room.

The cats lay against her on the bed, settling in for a quality nap. She needed a snooze too, but her brain wouldn't rest. It turned over the jigsaw pieces and every piece of information she both knew and didn't know.

When she'd questioned the owner of Aware House about who'd given her the envelope, the woman had said,

164

'A man called me from the charity, and then the winner's letter was pushed through the letterbox overnight.' She got quite tearful. 'They made it sound like a good thing.'

After a restless hour, Edie eased herself up with a groan, then went down to the lounge. Fezziwig followed, miaowing.

Edie had seen a lot of crime programmes; she knew the importance of visualising connections. She had an old roll of wallpaper from when she'd last redecorated (the useful side of being a hoarder) – she could use that as a base for a makeshift evidence map, the kind with red string to represent links and firing synapses. But there were no free walls. She tried to roll it out on the floor, but there wasn't room among the stacks of books. The kitchen was a mess, too. And upstairs. There was only one room with enough space.

Edie stood outside the dining room, hand trembling on the handle.

She couldn't go in.

The dust alone would set off her tear glands.

No. She couldn't go in there.

Not alone.

Riga knocked on the front door fifteen minutes later, and Edie hurried to answer it.

Her friend leaned over her stick, taking deep, raspy breaths.

Edie put her arm round Riga's bony shoulders. 'What are you doing? I told you I was coming to get you!'

'You can't say you're going to unlock "The Room" and expect me to wait like a good girl for you to pick me up.

What if I died in the meantime? I had to leave immediately. Also, I didn't want you to miss this.'

She pointed over the road. Lucy Pringle was walking down her drive with a uniformed officer towards a police car. The flashing lights on her house showed her progress in a strange multi-coloured strobe effect.

'What's going on?'

'No idea. But the road WhatsApp is pinging every second.'

Lucy stopped at the car and looked towards Edie and Riga. She waved, as if this was a perfectly normal evening for her. 'You are coming to my party on the 23rd, aren't you? Drinkies and nibblies?'

The officer placed a hand on Lucy's shoulder, and she waved again before ducking into the back seat.

They watched as Lucy was driven away.

'Taken away by the police and she can still do small talk,' Riga marvelled. 'It's almost admirable.'

'I'm more appalled by "drinkies and nibblies".'

'You'll go though, right?

'Now this has happened, I'll have to.'

'You and everyone else.' Edie's other next-door neighbours, Ryan and Julia Raymond, were standing in their porch in matching kimonos, having watched the whole thing. The road's curtains would be restless until Lucy returned.

In Edie's hallway, she and Riga stood in front of the dining room door that had represented so much for so long. Too long, most people would think. But that door was a dam, and she could drown once it was opened.

Edie's heart pounded. 'I can't do it.'

'You have to, otherwise I'll have come over for nothing. You can't bring me one step nearer to death through exertion and then cancel the main event. Anyway, you need to do this. You've been locked up for too long.'

Riga was right. Edie felt with shaking hands for the key on top of the door frame and placed it in the lock. Then she turned it.

It was as if the door opened by itself, even though Edie knew that she was pushing it. The smell of damp hit her first. Neither the room nor her time within it had been aired in decades. The word 'must' came into her head, but she couldn't work out if it was describing the room's atmosphere or the modal verb compelling her to do something.

Taking a deep, dusty breath, she walked inside. Everything was as it had been left. Sky's workstation, empty. Edie's easel, with the half-started still life. The vase of flowers on the table was now reduced to dried sticks, its petals desiccated on the floor. The armchairs round the fire still held the indents of their arses. And, in the corner, the silver necklace Sky had wanted to give her as a present lay tarnished on the floor.

Memories had always leaked through the sides of the door, but now they flooded over her. So many difficult times and tears – not just the leaving, but so many arguments caused by Edie. And then, right at the end, like hope at the bottom of Pandora's jar, a small, sweet memory.

They'd been in front of the fire, one Christmas Eve.

'I know you don't want presents,' Sky had said. 'And I

understand that completely. But I wanted to gift you something.'

Edie had started to object, but then Sky handed her a packet of bubble gum.

'My mum told me that the best presents are great experiences that you can remember. And you've always been impressed by how I can blow bubbles. So, I thought I'd teach you.'

It was the best present Edie had ever been given. Her first ten attempts resulted in flat gum, fart sounds and giggles, but then it had started to work. Initially, her bubbles were the size of Rudolph's nose. Sky clapped and suggested Edie leave it there, but it wasn't enough. Edie needed to master the skill. By bedtime, she could blow a bubble to rival the size of Santa's sack. Their midnight sex tasted of cherry cola gum.

'You've gone again.' Riga placed a hand on Edie's shoulder. 'Are you okay?'

'I think so,' Edie said, dazed. 'All those memories.' She'd expected it to be worse than it actually was. Perhaps seeing Sky again had already blown open the doors of her heart and this was just stepping through them.

'I'm not losing you to Ghosts of Christmas Past; we have an investigation room to construct.'

Half an hour later, the dusty mirror had been removed from the fireplace wall and the blank side of the spare wallpaper Blu-Tacked up. Peggoty and Fezziwig were still sniffing the room with suspicion. Mr Bumble, however, was already asleep on an armchair, stretched out on his back, armpits displayed.

Riga was sitting in the other chair, drinking Campari and watching as Edie wrote the names of known and potential victims on the wall. In lieu of red string, connections between them were signified by Riga's green garden twine.

'Not exactly *CSI: Miami*,' Edie said. 'But then, we are in Weymouth.' She knew the police would be investigating angles that she, frustratingly, knew nothing about, and finding things through official routes, so she'd have to use whatever she could – and that meant solving the clues the police didn't have.

Edie began to stick the jigsaw pieces onto the wall. 'Solving crime may be like solving crosswords, but it's also like putting together a jigsaw. Get the known areas in place first, establish its boundary lines, and then go for the details.'

'It's a wonder they don't have crossword setters and jigsaw doers in every police station.'

'Dissectologists,' Edie corrected.

'What?'

'That's what accomplished jigsaw fiends are called. And crossword setters are known as compilers, especially in the US.'

'So, you can put things together and take them apart.'

'Absolutely. Although I prefer the word "enigmatologist". Makes me sound mysterious.'

Riga's laugh was so loud that Mr Bumble almost stirred awake. 'You are the least mysterious person I know. Everything you think comes out of your mouth.'

'You'd think so, wouldn't you. But there must be a reason why I was chosen, and that's a mystery.'

'Maybe they're a fellow enigmatologist who wants your recognition?'

Edie thought of Mrs Challis, solving her puzzles. 'Perhaps.' She walked back and forth in front of the unlit fireplace, looking at the wall. Peggoty and Fezziwig paced with her, curling their tails like the ends of Poirot's moustache.

'Do you have any hidden secrets that could be surfacing?'

Edie had already opened one door full of memories; she didn't want another. 'Nothing worth mentioning.'

'Then to get notoriety through press coverage? Fame seeking. Some murderers like that. Get a famous puzzler to—'

'I'm hardly famous.'

'A *well-known* puzzler to engage with the crime, yet be unable to solve it. That's quite the ego boost.'

'Maybe we'll come back to "why me". Let's look at the jigsaw itself. I like to get the corners set first, and I suspect our killer does the same.' Edie pointed at the top left-hand corner. 'Carl Latimer forms one corner. And then Veronica Princeton is on the bottom left. I bet the intended next victim is alluded to here.' She held up the most recent corner piece, showing the gold-tasselled rug or carpet. 'And the murderer managed to trick me.' She filled Riga in on her humiliation at the hands of Rest In Pieces.

'So, you're dealing with a fuckwit.' Riga's distaste was clear in the graceful furl of her lip.

'If the killer follows the form to date, then the fourth victim will be hinted at in the top right-hand corner once an attack has taken place on the third, represented on the bottom right. The killer is working anti-clockwise.'

'And then?'

'Then they'll move on to whoever is in the middle.'

'Whoever it is, they're wearing the watch you gave to your brother, nephew and great-nephew.'

'Yes.' Edie didn't want to think about it too much for fear that she'd freeze.

'Show me the jigsaw pieces that came with the most recent corner,' Riga said.

Edie handed over her phone with the enlarged images on the screen.

Riga tapped the pieces featuring the classic books. 'You know what these make me think of? The terrible blocks of fake books that are put on bedside tables and book-shelves in furniture stores.'

Edie looked at it, feeling stupid for the second time that day. 'You're right. With the carpet there, and "ware-house", we could be looking for a home furnishing store.' Something snagged in her brain. She looked again at the message which had come with those pieces.

'"Roll out this scroll".'

She looked at the wallpaper curled up against the skirting board. It looked like a scroll, or a roll, of carpet. 'Maybe we should be looking for a carpet warehouse specifically?'

'But where to start? Do we even know if the killer is only going to act in this area, or Dorset more generally?'

'We hardly know anything.' Edie didn't want to jump to conclusions this time. Sometimes a jigsaw piece looked like it fitted when it didn't. She couldn't waste time forcing things into place.

'I think that's how they want us to stay. Several pieces behind at all times.'

'They're not playing fair,' Edie said. Part of the enigmatologists' code involved being oblique as you like, but always giving enough information to solve a puzzle. But then, how was murder fair?

'Let's get on,' Riga said, stifling a yawn.

'How about we look at the middle. So far, we have the black and white tiles, the partial outline of a body, holly leaves everywhere, and all that seems to be surrounded by sea.'

'How come the jigsaw has so many things on it?' Riga said, squinting at the wall. 'I thought they were broken up pictures of one thing.'

'They often are. But in the last ten years or so, more complex jigsaws have come on the market.' Edie went through into the living room and came back with three Wasgjj boxes, each of which had a mystery to solve once the thousand pieces were in place. 'It's not just placing the pieces, it's how you put together the information once you have the picture.'

'At least these help by having a picture on the box to follow. Our jigsaw-maker hasn't given us any help at all.'

'Oh, there are plenty with blank boxes and just a word, if you know where to go.' A puzzle speakeasy. God, that would be a great night out. 'There are even jigsaws where the picture on the box is the mirror image of the one you have to make. And some are even from another person's point of view.'

Riga rubbed her temples. 'People do this for fun?' Her head kept dropping, her eyes closing.

'You should go home. I'll walk you over.'

Their journey over Edie's lawn to Riga's drive was slow and difficult, with Riga's stick frame sagging into Edie's arms. They were silent, with not even the return of Lucy Pringle prompting comment.

Edie had thought she'd be relieved when they got through Riga's front door, but instead her heart sank. A brown padded envelope was waiting on the mat, addressed to her. A charity Christmas card was inside. Taped to the front were another three jigsaw pieces: one showed an ocean wave, another showed a portrait of an old git she vaguely recognised, and the last showed more of Sean's watch.

Inside the card was another printed message.

```
What does your precious Sean look up
to? It will crash down around him, and
he will crash down too, never to get
up, unless you solve this jigsaw soon.
  Happy Christmas, Ms O'Sullivan.
  Rest In Pieces
```

She turned to Riga to discuss it, but her friend's eyes were shut. She'd show it to her tomorrow.

After helping Riga get ready for bed, Edie left, looking up and down the street as she hurried back to her house.

She was under surveillance, she was sure of it. R.I.P. knew not to deliver to Edie's house while she and Riga were there. Riga had said the twitchy-curtained WhatsApp group hadn't seen who had made the first delivery, but Edie couldn't help wondering if anybody had.

The door to the dining room was still open when she got home. She closed it, yet still felt like she was inside. Maybe she shouldn't have followed her instincts to enter. Now she'd woken up the ghosts. So many memories repeated on her. She'd had a chilblain, once. Sky had knelt at Edie's feet on the rug in front of the drawing room fire and applied witch-hazelled cotton balls to her toes.

She looked again at the Christmas card. What did Sean look up to?

He always glanced up to the sky.

Sky.

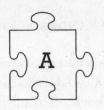

Twenty-Seven

When Sean got home, Liam was lying on the bed, fully dressed, watching something on his laptop. Sean wanted nothing more than to curl up in bed next to him in their own nest and not get out for days.

Liam snapped the laptop closed. Guilt shone on his face.

'Oh, yeah?' Sean asked, trying to be the light-hearted man that Liam had married. 'What were you watching?'

Liam slowly opened the laptop again. The screen glowed like the unseen inside of the briefcase in the forties noir they'd watched last week. It showed a frozen Sandi Toksvig in a Santa hat.

Love lifted Sean's lips. 'I can't believe you're watching Christmas *QI* without me.'

'I missed you, so I put our friends on. If it helps, it's one we've seen before.'

'It does help. I forgive you.' Sean sat on the edge of the bed and slumped his head into his hands.

Liam stroked his back. 'That bad?'

'It's been a long and difficult day.'

'Come here.'

Sean's limbs felt leaden as he peeled off his clothes and

lumbered under the covers. He snuggled into Liam's shoulder. Only then did he feel he was really home. 'I had to tell Edie to back off from the investigation.'

'It's the right thing to do, for everyone's sake. How did she take it?'

'Quite well, I suppose, in her own way.'

'Every time you say "in her own way" or make another excuse for Edie, it just makes her sound like more of an arsehole.'

'She's had a difficult life. So many people around her have died, and so she puts up walls. She thinks everyone will leave her.' Sean thought of the sharp corners of Edie's jigsaws, and the black and white boxes and rules of her crosswords. After a life of chaos, she'd built boundaries around her that puzzled others but kept her safe. 'She's really not as hard to please as she tries to make out.'

Liam's laugh was sardonic. 'She does a very good job at pretending.'

'Let's not talk about Edie. Let's talk about Juniper.'

'Or we could just cuddle? I've got an hour or so before I go out.'

'Again? Where are you going tonight?'

'It's Christmas, I've got another client do. Got to show my face.'

Sean tried to bury his jealousy. 'Well, you do have a gorgeous face.' It was true. Liam's face and body were Michelangelo-perfect.

Liam grinned. 'I know. And I won't be back late tonight. At least, I don't think so.'

Sean heard Michaels in his head, wondering about

Liam's alibi. Trying to keep a prickle of suspicion out of his voice, he said, 'By the way, looks like one of my team will need to talk to you tomorrow.'

Liam froze. 'What?'

'It's about Carl. They're covering the whole running group, pretty much.'

'Don't suppose you could interview me?'

Sean shook his head. 'I wish I could.'

'Shame, I'd've liked to see you in detective mode.'

'It'll be fine, I'm sure of it. You've got alibis, after all.'

Liam didn't answer, just hunkered back down in the bed and pressed play. They watched Sandi in a silence that seemed stuffed with secrets.

The killer looked up to the solstice sky, hoping the snow wouldn't settle. They were in their car, but the engine wasn't running so no one would be alerted to their presence. Not that anyone would pay attention to a car parked here. It was known as the most festive collection of streets in the area: people came from all over Weymouth and the Purbecks to drive infuriatingly slowly down the roads, taking pictures of the Christmas decorations that lit up the houses and lawns, fences and street signs. Some were beautiful, elegant even, with tiny twinkling lights. Others less so.

A local newspaper had claimed you could see this particular street from space, but the killer thought that was hyperbole. A scientific inaccuracy catering to local pride. Besides, what alien or astronaut would be impressed looking down at a road of shimmering trees and flashing reindeer?

One of the large, detached houses had been transformed into a gingerbread cottage, with lit candy canes and giant lollipops against the walls, and thousands of lights shimmering to look like snow on the roof. A blow-up Nativity scene sat on one side of the lawn, with Joseph doubled over as if he was at the end of an inn crawl. On the other side, grotesquely-sized gingerbread figures – father, mother and daughter – waved. It was a parody of family that made the killer want to fuse the whole street into darkness. In the middle of a path was a huge sign saying 'PLEASE DONATE TO POOLE NEONATAL UNIT!' The grass was covered with coppers thrown from slow-moving cars.

Linus Cramer, the next victim, stood on his doorstep, smiling at the reaction to his masterwork.

The killer had been watching Linus for weeks, getting to know where he went and when. Everyone had their own pattern, and it would soon be time for Linus to fit into the killer's.

The front door opened, and a little girl ran out. She bounded up to Linus and jumped into his arms. Her little hand extended into the snowflakes falling around them, delight on her face.

Linus nuzzled into her, holding her close. A real family man.

The killer imagined Linus' daughter's face when she was told that her daddy was dead, and looked down at the jigsaw piece in their trembling palm. The killer didn't know if they had the hands, let alone the heart, to kill again. The strength it had taken to kill Veronica was extreme, and they would need even more for Linus. Maybe they'd done enough already. Played their part in the whole, and the rest of the pieces could be scattered into the sea and left to drown.

But they had to keep going. Otherwise, the picture wouldn't be complete.

They looked back towards the house. Linus' daughter was waving at the cars as coins fell like scattered stars on the shadowed lawn. And tomorrow her sky would fall.

Twenty-Eight

December 22nd

'Just one more rep,' Isla said, as Sean strained into the Cable Chest Fly, arms outstretched in sacrifice to a great bod. 'Just think about wearing revealing tops come August.' She was sitting on the seat of the chest press, opposite Sean. It was early morning. Sean was trying not to think of Liam coming home at midnight with alcohol breath.

'Easy for you to say.' He hated Chest and Arms Day just as much as Leg Day, and moreover was convinced that it couldn't be good to exercise before the sun had got up. 'You're not the one in pain. You're just telling me what to do.'

Isla laughed. 'I'm your instructor, so I'm instructing.'

Sean took deep breaths, hoping the crackle on his lungs from the last chest infection wasn't anything to worry about. 'I'm not a fan of summer. But I get your point.'

'You'll be walking around in vest and shorts on holiday.' Isla looked to a 'motivational' picture of a hot couple and a sunset on the wall. 'Are you going to Crete again this year?'

'Depends what happens with the adoption.' He came off the machine, chest complaining.

'Ha!' Isla pointed to the kettlebells. 'Twenty reps. Then I've got your motivation right there. You'll need a strong core, back, shoulders and arms to carry a child around everywhere.'

This was true. He had seen the strained look on parents' faces as they picked up tired or stubborn kids.

'What do you want to be, a bad dad with a dad bod, or a father who can carry and protect his child?'

Sean, though, really wouldn't mind if he and Liam were good dads with dad bods. He was, if all went well, about to be a dad who had a bod, and that was all he really wanted. And then he pictured himself carrying Juniper, maybe even a little baby, across a beach on holiday, walking without care or strain on the shifting sand and into the sea. The child giggling, waving a bucket.

Nina, the woman from the last bootcamp, came over to them.

'Be with you in ten,' Isla said. 'Get yourself warmed up.'

Nina grinned at Sean. 'Hope she's putting you through it!' She headed over to the recumbent bikes and, after a quick stretch, slowly started to pedal.

'She's keen,' Sean said.

'She's new. Give it a few weeks and she won't be as enthusiastic. Now, back to it!'

Sean stood in the centre of the black mat and started swinging the kettle bell. Nineteen reps to go.

An hour later, he was only halfway up the stairs to his

office when Phillips rushed down to meet him. She over-shot and grabbed onto his arm, spilling his coffee.

'Sorry, guv.' She dabbed at the steps with a tissue. 'I wanted to tell you what I'd found.' When she stood, her eyes were bloodshot and a little wild.

'What time did you get in, Ama?'

'I haven't exactly gone home, sir.'

'Phillips!'

'I got excited when I checked ANPR for Berkeley's car and it was logged not far from Godlingston Woods on the night Carl Latimer was attacked.'

'Is that on the way back from his mum's place?'

'Yes, but wouldn't he use the visit to his mum as an excuse to be there at the time?'

'True.'

'There doesn't seem to be anything linking the hoodie to anyone, but I did find out where the jigsaw box was made. There's a white embossed seahorse on the corner of the lid, which led to a manufacturer in Wareham that makes bespoke boxes. They're not answering the phone—'

'It's not even half eight, Ama. Not everyone has been up all night.'

'I thought I'd go to Wareham after popping into St Mary's to see if they can identify who ordered it.'

'You don't think you've already done enough today?'

'Nah. Sleep is overrated.'

In his early twenties, Sean could stay up for what felt like days on end without chemical assistance. He missed it. 'Sleep is essential for us to make considered judgements and not lose track of the facts. Leave early today, and that's an order.' Maybe he'd be good at being a dad after all.

'Not sure the DCI would like that. He was well chuffed when he came in at six and I was trawling through CCTV.'

Sean could well imagine DCI Leyland approving of people burning the midnight oil, right up until they burnt out. 'I thought Michaels had already done that?'

Ama turned away, a little guiltily. 'When I found out about Edward Berkeley parking near the woods, I thought I'd look specifically for him, just in case.' She met his eyes again, beaming. 'And I found an image, just a quick glimpse, of him walking towards Esplanade.'

'Fantastic work, Ama. Can you send me the clearest image of his face?' Sean wondered how Michaels had missed it the first time, but he also knew how difficult and draining CCTV trawling could be. It was easy, especially when tired, for a detail to slip through. He wouldn't have enough to charge Berkeley, though. It was circumstantial and easily explained. And there was nothing in Berkeley's personality to suggest that he was a master puzzler who wanted to play games. Sean had been wrong before, though. It was one of the downsides of having faith in human nature.

'No problem. You sure I shouldn't just crack on with the list of things to do this afternoon?'

'Nope. Go home and rest after you've been to the manufacturer. Okay?'

Ama nodded and ran back up the stairs, as excited as a new police puppy. Sean had never seen anyone so thrilled about going to Wareham. He wondered when he had started to feel old. Somewhere between twenty-five years old, and three days ago. Edie would laugh at him and say he was still a baby compared to her. Everyone was a baby to their parent until the very end.

In his office, Sean began looking up shops and warehouses in Dorset that sold carpets and rugs. Not even that distracted him from imagining Michaels questioning Liam, and then Edie. He wasn't sure who he felt most sorry for. And if looking for the right carpet from a fraction of a jigsaw piece was an impossible task, at least he believed in Christmas miracles.

Twenty-Nine

'You know how to live, Riga,' Edie said, as the waiter brought a silver salver of cinnamon brioche, two flutes of champagne and pots of tea and coffee to their table.

They were in the bay window of the Royal Harbour Hotel, looking out onto the harbour's jostling masts and jeering gulls. The snow might have stopped for now, but the fish-belly sky promised more to come. Edie regarded the water with unease and turned her chair away.

'I see it as knowing how to die.' Riga poured a swirl of single cream into her cup of coffee. She had applied her make-up as meticulously as ever, but it couldn't hide the dark shadows under her eyes. And she was walking even more slowly than usual. 'Death will come soon. I may as well greet it with decorum.' She raised her pinkie finger and wiggled it. Riga's stark beauty had always stunned Edie. Not that she'd ever told Riga in all their years of friendship. As she'd aged, Riga had become even more arresting. Cliff-edge cheekbones, undercliff eroded with time; her clavicles deep harbour walls; moss-green eyes contrasting with her steel bob.

'I wish you wouldn't talk about dying.'

'Everyone should talk about death, no matter how

young or old. It's our only friend, always there, whatever we do to ignore it.'

'Like a stalker.'

'It's a fine line between friend and foe.' Riga blinked at her, slowly. She was unable to wink, but her blinks were like those of a cat who was pleased to have commanded attention.

Death, like war and Christmas, was always on its way.

'What's wrong?' Riga asked.

'Why do you ask?'

'Because you've torn the bread into pieces. You'd never normally decimate a pastry without eating it.'

Edie looked down. Both her plate and the tablecloth were strewn with bits of spiced brioche. 'It's the card put through your door, addressed to me. What do you make of it?' Edie took the latest Christmas card from the killer out of her bag and handed it to Riga.

'I was wondering when you'd show me.' Riga read the card, tutting as she did so, then handed it back and returned to her coffee.

'Is that all you've got?

'They are threatening you and your family; I don't want to give them the attention they're looking for.'

The killer did seem strangely needy, like a child having a meltdown. Edie had always admired Sean's tantrums as a toddler. They were honest, and she had to admit that thumping the floor seemed a much healthier way of dealing with things than sweeping feelings under the carpet, like she did.

'What do you think he's like, this killer of yours?' Riga asked.

'What makes you think it's a man?'

'Very few murderers are women. We don't have the time.'

Edie was silent for a few minutes while she wondered how to say her next words, then blurted out, 'What if I told you that Sky was back in town?'

'Your Sky?'

'Is there another?' Although she hadn't been Edie's in a very long time.

'Why would that make me change my mind about the gender of the murderer?'

'Read the card again.'

Riga went through it slowly, eyes narrowed. 'You can't think that refers to her?'

'It might do. Sean always admired Sky; she was a big part of his early life. Until she left and never got back in contact, of course.' But then Edie had told her not to. Something she had kept from Sean.

'Also, whenever I anger or annoy him, he looks to the sky in despair.'

'Is that really what you think of when you read this? That Sky is back to punish you by killing people?'

'I know it's not likely. But I didn't treat her well.' The song 'Always On My Mind' played in Edie's head. It made her cry whenever she heard it.

Riga's laugh made several hotel guests turn around from their posh breakfasts. 'How many people do you piss off every single day?'

'Sure. I'm an arsehole. But not enough for one for them to commit murder, surely?'

'You annoy me sufficiently to make me want to kill you all the time, and I love you.' Riga took a sip of coffee, smiling.

'Not the same thing. I keep thinking of all the things that I might have done.'

'And there are too many to narrow down?' Riga's grin had a malevolent edge. She was enjoying this far too much.

'You're not helping.'

Riga stared at Edie, shaking her head. 'You don't see it, do you?'

'See what?'

'Read the card again.'

Edie once again went through the words. She looked up, blank as an unwritten card.

Riga rolled her eyes. 'What, or rather who, else could Sean possibly look up to?'

'Liam? His colleagues? His friends?'

Riga leaned forward and grabbed Edie's hand. 'For someone so clever, you don't see what's right in front of you. It's you. He looks up to you, always has done.'

'*I* come crashing down?'

'Maybe it's someone you humiliated, and now they're trying to do the same to you.'

Edie's breath was punched out of her, as though she'd run into the winter sea. 'Ouch.'

'And if you really want my advice—'

'I do.'

'Then you should take the game to them. Whoever it is, they're goading you. So far, R.I.P. has overseen events. Make things happen on your terms and your timetable.'

Riga was right. It was time to take control. Edie nibbled a new brioche and dipped it in her tea.

'And while I have you in a vaguely receptive mood, go and talk to Sky. Find out why she's really here.'

Edie gave a grudging grunt in reply.

'Now that's sorted, let's get back to more important things. Like planning the food for my funeral.'

Edie shook her head. 'The things you do for fun, Riga.'

'Says the woman who does jigsaws.'

'You won't even be around to eat the food at your wake.'

'I never eat anyway.'

'Before we get onto funeral meals,' Edie said, 'have a look at this extra piece I got last night.' She showed Riga the photo she'd taken of the old portrait of a moon-faced man in a big hat.

'Don't show me such sexy pictures in public, Edie,' Riga said, sardonic as ever. 'Who is this dish?'

'It took me too long to work it out last night, but I knew I'd seen the painting and his face. It's Bishop Berkeley.'

'Religious fella?'

'Somewhat. Eighteenth-century Anglo-Irish philosopher who advanced the theory of immaterialism.'

'Don't like the sound of him. I love material things. I love material.'

'Don't we all.'

189

'But why give you a jigsaw piece with his face on it?'

'Either I'm to approach the case with a sense that nothing exists, or I should look closely at Dr Berkeley, the current headmaster at St Mary's.'

'I've met him,' Riga said, watching people pass by their window. 'Edward Berkeley. He was in one of my reading groups.'

'What did you think of him?'

'He makes good literary insights and bad flapjacks.'

'You can't have everything, huh? Can I ask you one more thing?' Edie said, quietly.

'Ask away. Although if you're asking me to marry you, then I warn you, I don't have much money.'

Edie hoped she didn't blush, or if she did, that Riga would put it down to the champagne. 'How do you say that so easily?'

'Say what?'

Edie squirmed like a fish in a seagull's beak. 'You said you sometimes want to kill me even though you . . . you feel a certain way about me.'

'Say "I love you" to someone? It's easy. You should try it sometime. Just put your lips together and go for it.'

Thirty

'You've reached Liam at Dorset Blooms, designer florists. Please—'

Sean hung up. It was the fifth time he'd got Liam's answerphone in the last hour. Michaels hadn't left to interview him yet so it couldn't be that. Perhaps he was busy making the displays for a festive wedding tomorrow. But Sean's husband usually answered, however busy he was. Maybe Sean took that too much for granted.

Catching up with the rest of the team, he'd learned that the post-mortem on Veronica Princeton had confirmed her cause of death.

'Veronica Princeton,' Michaels had reported with solemnity, 'was most likely stunned by the blow to her head, falling to the floor where she injured her arm. The killer then strangled her, face on. There were white fibres under her nails which have been sent off for analysis.'

'What time did she die?' Sean asked.

'Between three and four am.'

There had been silence for a moment, and Sean had wondered whether Michaels, too, was thinking of Veronica

Princeton lying, dead but still alone, in the alleyway until she was found hours later.

'How did it go with Lucy Pringle last night?'

'She was very amenable. Invited the whole station round for drinks today and promised to drop off mince pies on Christmas Eve. She didn't, however, have an alibi to offer for either night, and she's also linked to St Mary's. Two of her children attend the upper school, and she's a parent governor.'

'From what I've heard, parent governors are fierce.'

'She did admit to sending the threatening messages to Veronica Princeton.' Michaels read from Pringle's prepared statement: 'A number of us fell foul of poor practice at her clinic. She didn't have up-to-date storage facilities and, when we lost our eggs or embryos as a result, the whole thing was swept under the carpet. She was a councillor and got her and her husband's friends in the press to hush it up. I wanted her to know how much hurt she had caused.'

'Did you charge her with harassment?'

'With the DCI's go-ahead.' Michaels had paused, thinking. 'Interesting that Lucy Pringle should say "carpet", isn't it?' Without waiting for a response, she left, to talk first with Liam and then with Edie.

It certainly was interesting. And, after finding more stores selling carpets or rugs than he could visit in a week, Sean had been glad to walk away from his desk and get into the car. He couldn't see how to make progress. All the information was too scattered. Edie always said that the brain needed a break from thinking to fill in the gaps.

Even though he was still angry with her, it was fading. He hadn't answered her messages all day. He should at least send a text to warn her that she would be questioned.

I'm afraid you'll have a visit from Michaels today. I can't apologise enough, she is a lot, but we need a statement. Sorry!

He wondered what else to say, in the end going with

Keep safe, I love you.

He was about to do the least Edie-like thing possible: go shopping for a Christmas tree.

The Christmas tree farm was off the A31, not far from Monkey World, another of his favourite places (he sponsored a gibbon called Robin Goodfellow). From a wooden hut near the car park, next to the cashpoint, the sound of a resident Santa's 'Ho ho ho's boomed over the frozen ground.

A blast of warm Christmas spirit started to thaw Sean's frozen brain. The smell of pine was definitely better than the station stink of Gregg's sausage rolls and armpits.

Whittling his choice of trees down, he chose a friendly-looking fir with branches that called for a hug and a top that would tickle their ceiling. While he was wrestling the tree onto the roof of the car, his phone dinged.

Michaels had emailed:

DI Brand-O'Sullivan,

I have interviewed Liam Brand-O'Sullivan and now
need to speak with you as a matter of urgency.

DS Michaels

Short and sour. Much like Michaels herself. He called
her back immediately.

'What's happened?' he asked, as soon as she answered.
'What did Liam say? Is he okay?'

'He's fine. Other than the fact that he has no alibi for
either night, but then few of the running group have.
What is it about runners that they're always alone?'

'Not sure that's fair. Wait, he was out with suppliers
and colleagues. Why is there no one to corroborate?'

'People saw him arrive, but that's about it on both
occasions. There's no evidence of him drinking with
people or having conversations. Pretty strange for a busi-
ness event.'

'He doesn't like them at all. Maybe that's why he usually
turns up then gives an Irish goodbye.'

But then where did he go when he didn't come home?
What was he doing? The creeping, chilling thought that
he didn't truly know Liam settled in Sean's heart.

'Perhaps he shouldn't offer them as alibis, then.'

'If you haven't done anything wrong, you don't expect
to need an alibi.'

'If I may say so, sir,' – Michaels' tone was supercilious
and he could just picture her face looking all prim and
smug – 'that's a bit naive.'

'You may not say so.'

'Are *you* able to give him an alibi, sir?'

The impulse to lie, to cover everything over and make it appear okay, was so strong. 'I don't know. I was already asleep when he came in, both nights.'

'That's a shame, for his sake.' He could tell she was trying to keep her voice neutral, and failing.

'Most of the runners haven't got alibis, and neither does Lesley Maupert for that matter, a woman less likely to kill than anyone I've met, so why did you want to talk to me about Liam so urgently?'

'Oh, it wasn't about your husband. DCI Leyland told me that Phillips has gone over my head and looked at the CCTV again without informing me.'

Sean repressed a sigh. 'Phillips should have run it past one of us, yes. But she also found something that you missed, something that I wasn't going to bring up with you as I know how tricky CCTV can be.'

'There's still no saying that the CCTV she found is any use.' So, Michaels had been thinking about herself and her mistake, not about the victim. Sean was glad they weren't on videocall as it was impossible to keep his face looking professional.

'Let's move on, shall we? Have you talked with my great-aunt?'

'She wasn't at home and isn't answering her phone.'

He didn't need Michaels' face to be on his screen to picture what it looked like. Sean found himself bristling at her brusque tone and had one of his rare surges of impishness. 'Well, in the meantime I've got an important job for you, Michaels. Look into all stores across Dorset and beyond that sell carpets, rugs, tapestries etc. that could match the one on the jigsaw piece.'

'Isn't that an impossible task?'

'Thanks, Michaels. Appreciate it. Excellent work.' Sean hung up, feeling a guilty bubble of pleasure. Maybe he had more Edie-ishness in him than he'd thought.

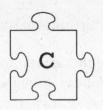

Thirty-One

Edie's phone kept ringing, but she was buggered if she was going to answer. She *made* phone calls; she didn't take them. Besides, Sean's warning text had put her off going home or answering calls. She was too busy for police nonsense. She was taking Riga's advice and making things happen.

The taxi dropped her off at the entrance to St Mary's and a wave of memories came back. One she weighted deep, deep down – there were some things she still couldn't face – but she let the others flow over her. She'd thought she was drowning in the past when she'd come with Sean, but arriving alone triggered something else, as if she had stepped into the ghost of herself. She used to walk through these doors, always slightly later than she should, trying to avoid Mrs Parker, the Mrs Challis of her day.

Now Sandra Challis was seated on her swivel chair throne, telling a Strident School Mum off for daring to take their kid to Disneyland Paris during term time. 'The fine is £60 per parent. You will receive an invoice shortly. Now, if you'll excuse me, I have vital business to attend to.' She then picked up a copy of the paper, glancing at Edie and winking.

Strident School Mum tapped on the glass barrier. 'It's not easy to go on holiday during school breaks. There's the cost of it for one, then there's having to apply for holiday at the same time as everyone else at work. Plus—'

'I happen to know, Mrs Pond,' Mrs Challis interrupted, 'that you took your child out of education in order to meet up with your boyfriend in Paris.'

Strident School Mum's fillered lips hung open. 'How do you know that?'

'I suggest you pay up, Mrs Pond.' Mrs Challis turned to Edie. 'How can I help you, Edie?' She beamed.

Strident School Mum Pond stared at the receptionist in shock. It was as if she expected Mrs Challis' cheeks to creak from unexpected smiling in the facial area. She shuffled away, looking back over her shoulder.

Edie met Mrs Challis' eyes. 'You're not going to like this. I need to speak to Dr Berkeley.'

Mrs Challis winced. 'You're right, I don't like it. I've already seen off a pugnacious, plain-clothed police officer this morning.'

Edie guessed that it had been Michaels. Sean had talked to her about both Michaels and Ama Phillips, and no way could naive Ama be called pugnacious. 'If it's who I think it was, then plain-clothed is an understatement.'

'Not like us.'

Mrs Challis looked at Edie's green trouser suit and purple shirt, then proudly down at her own paisley dress.

'Panache is your middle name, Sandra.'

Mrs Challis grinned. 'I didn't like her at all.'

Definitely Michaels. Sean had said she possessed a remarkable ability to get people to loathe her within seconds of their meeting. It would serve her well once she got to commissioner rank.

'I don't blame you. And I wouldn't blame you for barring my entry either, but I do need to chat with the headmaster.'

Mrs Challis winced again and shook her head. 'I'm sorry, I can't. He's really stressed. Never seen him so worried.' She looked down the corridor, frowning. Her hand went to her heart, perhaps showing her true feelings for the headmaster.

'What's making him so worried, do you think?'

'The police sniffing around, Carl Latimer attacked, now Veronica Princeton murdered.' She grimaced as if the fertility clinician's name caused her physical pain to say. 'Plus, we've had a rumour that Ofsted will be in during the first week of term.'

'Ouch.'

'Quite.'

'From what I've heard,' Edie leaned in, hoping she was doing gossiping right, 'Veronica Princeton was quite something.'

'I only moved here five years ago so I didn't know her when they were together, but I've seen the results. He's still messed up. Won't go near a committed relationship.' Her chin quivered.

'I won't mention her to him, don't worry. I just wanted to ask him a philosophy question, for a possible crossword clue.' Edie hoped that would assuage Mrs Challis' guard-dog instincts.

The other woman looked torn, but then resolutely shook her head.

Edie would have to play her trump card. 'To sweeten the deal, I was wondering if you'd like to set the Across questions for this week's Quick Crossword. I can then have the fun challenge of completing the Down clues, following your lead.'

Mrs Challis' eyes glinted. 'You're trying to bribe me.'

'I am.'

'And you think it'll work?'

Edie pushed a crossword sheet through the envelope gap in the glass. The black squares were already filled in, the rest empty boxes.

Mrs Challis stroked the paper as if it were the soft skin of a Parisian lover. She glanced towards the door and the corridor leading to Dr Berkeley's office. Then she nodded,

'Go on through. He's got half an hour before another meeting.' Her voice dropped to a guilty whisper. 'Tell him you slipped past while I was disciplining a parent.'

Edie tried not to laugh at the image that came into her head. Instead, she nodded, her face serious. 'And now, Sandra, we shall both fill in the blanks.'

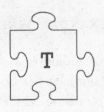

Thirty-Two

When Edie strode into Edward Berkeley's study – *dusty* – he was staring at a framed photo and it took him a moment to realise she was there. He placed the photo back in front of him. From what Edie could tell from this distance, it was a picture of a woman; she presumed it was his wife. 'I'm sorry, I wasn't aware we had a meeting, Mrs . . .'

'O'Sullivan,' Edie said. 'And it's Ms. Or Miss. I'll even accept Madam, if I must, as that confers a certain amount of respect, devastating as it is when a French waiter first calls you it, but not Mrs. I never married.' Yet she wished she had, with a fervour that had only grown since she'd opened the locked room.

'I'm sorry, I should have remembered your name. You were here the day we heard about our Games teacher?'

'I was. A nasty business.'

'I must warn you that I can't talk long; it's the last day of term so there are year-end performances to sit through. If I'd known you wanted a chat, I'd have had Mrs Challis book you a proper slot. In fact, I'm surprised you got past her. She's usually very protective.'

'Don't blame Sandra. She was chastising an unchaste parent. I slipped in without her noticing.'

He smiled as if picturing Sandra in full flight. 'How can I help you, Ms O'Sullivan?'

Edie took in every detail of the room as if it were one of her jigsaws or puzzles. It was the study – not at all dusty, in fact – of a meticulous man. His books were flush at the front of the bookshelves, not one out of place. Their subjects ranged from art history to chemistry and philosophy, with a section on education that included books he'd written himself. Impressive. Best of all, there was not one Christmas decoration in the whole room.

'As you are an educated man, I was wondering if you could tell me more about this gentleman.' She took the jigsaw piece out of her handbag and showed it to him.

He raised one eyebrow, but otherwise showed no reaction. 'Ah, the great Bishop Berkeley. He who subsumed matter under mind. And please, take a chair. If you perceive it to exist, that is.' He laughed at his own philosophical joke.

Edie sat. 'Is he any relation of yours?'

Berkeley laughed again. 'Unfortunately not. At least, I don't think so. What kudos it would bring if he were.'

'I don't know what circles you are part of in which that would be considered a boon, but I want to join them.'

'An esteemed cruciverbalist such as yourself would always be welcome at my reading group. Your thoughts on words must be fascinating.'

'I thought you didn't know who I was.'

Berkeley coloured. 'I fear I was being coy, disingenuous even. I know who you are. Mrs Challis and I have been fans of your work for some time. I just didn't want to "fanboy" at you, as I believe they call it these days.'

'Don't worry about that. I could do with some adoration. It's been a trying time.'

'Hasn't it just.' Berkeley glanced again at the jigsaw piece. 'Is your enquiry into Bishop Berkeley related to one of your crosswords? I'd appreciate a spoiler. I could pretend I got the answer myself and Mrs Challis would be amazed.'

'I wasn't planning to, but I could. Philosophy *is* one of my favourite themes to set.'

'I know. And is the bishop one of your favourite thinkers?'

'No. Not that I'm bashing him.'

The headmaster laughed, this time at *her* philosophical joke. 'I should think not.' He paused in thought. 'You're welcome to borrow any of my books on him, but let's see if I can remember something. Irish, born near Kilkenny—'

'Like my mum.'

'In the late seventeenth century.'

'Unlike my mum.'

'He's known for Berkeley's Puzzle, among other things, in which he could not fit together all his beliefs. Then he twigged that one of these beliefs could be discarded, and the whole picture came together.'

'Like getting rid of a stray jigsaw piece from another puzzle,' Edie said. This couldn't be a coincidence. Or maybe it was another red herring, intended as misdirection.

'That's the second time in the last few days that jigsaws have been mentioned in here.'

Edie was rather enjoying talking with the headmaster, and she rewarded him with the truth. 'I received this jigsaw piece in relation to the death of Dr Princeton and the attack on Carl Latimer. Do you think it's telling me to look in your direction?'

Dr Berkeley blinked as if trying to take in the information. 'But why me?'

'It's your school; Mr Latimer is one of your staff. And this is a delicate matter but I'm less likely to tread lightly than stomp gracelessly: there is the fact that you were sleeping with Veronica Princeton.'

Berkeley winced and looked towards the photo.

'Is that your wife?'

He nodded. 'My Lorelei.'

Edie leaned forward in her chair to get a closer look. 'She's smiling, yet she also looks sad. Did she know then about you and Dr Princeton?'

'At the time that photo was taken, she had suspicions. She asked me outright, and I denied it, told her she was being paranoid. She later found out she was right.'

'The usual shitty gaslighting.'

Berkeley's face crumpled. 'I wasn't a good husband. And, when she died, I wasn't a good man, either. But it's not that simple. Things never are. Have you never cheated on someone, Ms O'Sullivan?'

Edie thought of the first letter from Rest In Pieces, accusing her of cheating. 'I've never been accused of being unfaithful.'

Berkeley's smile was rueful. 'From that careful reply, I infer you did not hold a relationship in good faith.' When Edie didn't reply, he added. 'I should've guessed that a crossword setter would be good at using words to avoid saying what they really mean.'

'What can I say? You know that internet thing, Am I The Asshole? Well, I don't need to ask. Because I am most definitely, at all times, the asshole.'

'The police suspect that I might be an arsehole, too. They've asked me to go to the station and undergo formal questioning as I don't have an alibi. My car was spotted in the vague vicinity of the woods where Carl Latimer was found – which was, in fact, where I said I was – and they'll have no doubt found something else to quibble over. All of which is circumstantial, and none of which points to a motive.' He paused. 'And the thing is, I *do* have an alibi.'

'Tell them then!'

'I can't. I've promised. I'm trying to be a better man, and to keep people's secrets.'

'Even if you're arrested?'

'Wouldn't you do far more for someone you loved?'

Thirty-Three

'I haven't finished the crossword yet!' Mrs Challis said, when Edie emerged from the headmaster's study. Her face was flushed, her normally helmet-smooth hair at all angles. She had the Bradford Crossword Solver's Dictionary open next to her.

'How long do you need?' Edie asked.

Mrs Challis glanced at the partially filled-in crossword, then at her clock. 'Fifteen minutes?' She handed Edie a visitor's lanyard. 'Have a look around. It's lunchtime, so you won't be disturbing any lessons. Not that any learning takes place on the last day of term.'

Before Edie could thank her, Mrs Challis was back at work on the Across clues, looking to the heavens as if begging crossword legend Araucaria, aka the Rev. John Galbraith Graham, for inspiration. Funny how most crossword setters are either former teachers or vicars.

Edie slipped past a queue of kids with five-pound notes in their hands to take a peek into the dining hall. The noise inside made her wish she'd brought earplugs. She'd forgotten how loud and ebullient teenagers could be. All that energy inside needing an outlet, like the sugar-powered sprouts in potatoes. Talking of which, the smell of buttery mash and disintegrating vegetables almost overtook that of the huge traybake cake that could probably be used as one of the crash mats in the gym.

The dark panelled walls still featured oil portraits of headmasters and mistresses of the past hundred years. A few more had been added since she was last in here. The one of Edward Berkeley hung at the end. He looked almost handsome. The painter, or maybe his own vanity, had urged him to take off his little round glasses, showing off his eyes. In this flattering depiction, Berkeley had the look of Sean's favourite actor, Cillian Murphy, rather than the headmaster's in-person collage of odd angles. It was amazing the little lies art could apply.

That reminded Edie of the art room, where she'd spent much of her time when she'd first joined the school. Part of her wanted to go and see how it had changed; the other part roared to stay away.

But still she went out through the doors and across the courtyard to the Art and Design building. The glass-walled extension to the side of the school had looked strikingly modern thirty years ago, but now looked more like an unwashed suburban conservatory. Green gunk covered the sloping glass roof. Like so many of its students, it needed a good wash.

Despite the decay, memories came. She was walking through it at once now and in the past. The windows were still covered with awkward attempts at life drawing. The foyer remained the place where the brave A-Level art students who attempted sculpture could show off their baked bean can monstrosities.

She peered through the window of one of her old class-rooms. Before abandoning art altogether, she'd been one of the GCSE Art teachers, alongside her A Level Maths and English responsibilities. Geometric painting had been her speciality, although she'd also chipped in with pottery and lino cutting. She'd revelled in helping students find their artistic voice; to discover a palate, and a palette, that was entirely theirs. She'd been a medium for them to find their media, guiding them towards one area or another as the spirit took her. Time didn't matter; she'd be there till all hours, painting alongside her students. Until Sky took off and the clock stopped on Edie's art for good, and for bad.

Through the window, right now, Edie could see a lone student taking pots out of a kiln. Her back was turned, but she seemed to be holding the pots up to the light, inspecting each one for cracks.

Watching her, Edie remembered coming into the pottery the night of that terrible day in January and lying on the floor, sobbing. She'd been through fire and hadn't made the grade. She didn't need to inspect herself for hairline cracks; she knew they were there.

The next day, the headmistress agreed that Edie should leave St Mary's with immediate effect. No goodbyes, no last meal. Everything was to be smoothed over, as if that were possible.

Edie became a supply teacher, sticking to maths, history, science and music, and only the facts of those subjects, not the slippery business of creativity.

Now, as the young woman placed her intact pots in front of a selection of enamel glazes, Edie envied her.

But the time for art was over. She had Sean's future to ensure, not hers.

Sandra Challis had had long enough now. Edie stopped in the courtyard and watched a frog hide under a rock. She knew how it felt. 'You can't give into that urge, you know,' she told it. 'Hiding doesn't help. You know how to jump. So, jump.'

The frog burped.

'Charming.'

Back in reception, Mrs Challis was waiting for her. 'I've finished.' She passed the crossword paper through the gap in the glass. She had a knowing smirk and a twinkle that Edie recognised in herself. Mrs Challis was trying to out-puzzle her.

'I look forward to taking you on.'

'If you ever need an accomplice' – she pointed to the half-finished crossword – 'let me know. Till then, I'll get back to telling off parents and planning the bloody staff lunch party tomorrow.'

'They don't deserve you, Sandra.'

'Don't I know it. They'll learn, one of these days.' She looked down at her pen and tapped it on the table. When she glanced up, her eyes were shining and full of hope. 'I was wondering if you'd like to come to the party?'

Edie felt her usual flare-up of fear and panic at the thought of socialising. 'I'd love to. But I don't know what I'm up to yet.' Sandra looked pained. Edie felt like she'd accidentally stepped on a cat's tail. 'But thank you. I will come if at all possible.' Edie turned to go, then stopped.

'I was wondering, how *did* you know that School Mum was meeting her fancy man in Paris?'

Mrs Challis tapped the side of her nose. 'Receptionists know everything.'

'In which case, is there anything you think *I* should know, that maybe you've picked up from police queries, or through your own omniscient receptionist means?'

'I don't want to get myself, or anyone else, in trouble.'

'It's just me, Sandra. The Down to your Across. We have to be a team to get the answers.'

Sandra beamed. Recognition at last. Checking that there was no one in the corridor, she went into her office and set something printing in another room. She then popped in to collect the pages, before handing them, in a ring binder, to Edie. 'You're lucky. I have bent the printer to my will.'

'Thank you.'

'Now I must get Edward's lunch ready. He likes things just so. As do I.' When Sandra said his first name, she glowed.

'Can I give you some advice, Sandra?'

'Of course!'

'If there's something you're not saying, or not doing, to save face or avoid shame, then just get on and do it. Make a commitment. Do the right and best thing. I believe Dr Berkeley, or Edward as you just called him, will thank you for it.'

In the taxi, Edie had a strong urge to change direction, to tell the driver that she wanted to go home. She'd already had a long day and wanted to retreat like a toad to the comfort of her hiding zones – armchair, cats, Sol, jigsaw. But jigsaws couldn't console her now, not until she'd solved the one in front of her.

And she had something else to confront.

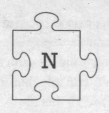

Thirty-Four

Everyone in Weymouth seemed to be at the Christmas market, and in annoyingly good cheer. Bastards. Edie had to elbow her way through a crowd of people all hoping to pay far too much for some wine that had been punched with a pomander like a medieval mace.

The whiff of the stall-holders' desperation as they competed for dwindling amounts of festive credit mixed with that of hot chocolate and sausage. The smell got everywhere. Having already chewed the mint out of her gum but not possessing any more strips, Edie did her usual trick of spitting it into the lace hankie up her sleeve. She bought a bag of humbugs and sucked on two at once. Anything to get the taste of Christmas out of her palate.

It was also because she knew Sky liked the taste of mint. Her heart was running ahead of her as she turned into Cove Street and the row of tents where Sky worked. She went through everything she wanted to say, hoping it would come out okay.

But Sky wasn't at her jewellery stall. A young man in one of those annoying hippy jester hats was there instead. His wispy beard was disconcertingly pubic.

'Where's Sky?' Edie's tone was even more brusque than she had intended.

The young man took a step back and looked up at the clouds. He looked confused for a second, then took on the 'oh dear, it's an old dear' look of patronising youth. 'It's above us.'

Edie sighed. 'Not *the* sky, you ridiculous child. Sky. The woman whose jewellery you're selling.'

'Oh, right.' His eyes had the far-off glaze of recent hash-taking. 'She's rehearsing.'

'For what?'

'The carol concert tomorrow. She's joined her old choir. Do you want to leave a message?'

Edie shook her head. She was too busy remembering how she and Sky used to sing together in the Purbeck Singers. It was where they'd met, two altos sitting together, then lying together. Their voices matched and so did they. Jigsaw pieces.

'Do you want to buy anything? Cos I get a cut if you do.'

'Don't tempt me,' Edie said, thinking of the sharp lino cutting tool she'd picked up from the art department. Just in case.

It took ten minutes for her to get to the church where the Purbeck Singers still rehearsed and sang, but another ten before she could actually bring herself to enter. St Mary Magdalen's was down the hill from St Mary's School. She had sung to its rafters with Sky and then, after Sky had left, taught a few supply lessons in its crypt. The building would be as full of memories as it was incense smoke.

She stood in the entrance, by the open door. Above it,

the stained-glass window was dulled by the lack of light. The sound, though, was too beautiful to walk away from. Layers of tones and melodies drifted out. It wasn't one of the joyful, strident carols but '*O Magnum Mysterium*'. A melancholy plain chant take on the Matins of Christmas from the Roman Breviary. She thought she could hear Sky's voice at the centre of it all.

Edie walked past the fundraising pillar for obtaining money to redo the crypt, its levels like notches on a bedpost, and into the nave. The singing reverberated through her chest as she sat down in a pew with a good view of the choir in the chancel. Sky was to one side, with the altos. She was sharing a songbook with a silver-haired woman and smiling. Edie used to share Sky's songbook. She used to call her 'my songbird'.

Above Edie, the ceiling climbed in wishbone arches. Below her, she knew, was the crypt. She had encouraged her students to sit on the broken floor and draw the dust-sheet-draped Reformation-reclaimed statues kept down there like trapped angels. She'd often dispensed sage advice, which was far beyond her pay grade. The crypt and its contents had needed salvation for a very long time. *Join the queue*, she thought.

Pages were flicked as the choir found their next song. There were at least fifty of them, in rows and vocal range clusters, but all she saw was Sky, as they began John Tavener's 'The Lamb'.

They'd sung that at the last concert they'd performed in together. Edie's eyes stung from saline and frankincense tears. It was as if twenty plus years hadn't happened.

This couldn't continue. Riga was right, and so was Sean – she had to move on. She'd go up at the end and talk with Sky. Say things she should have said decades ago. Ask painful questions; receive heart-breaking answers.

In the back of her brain, though, suspicions whispered and writhed. Sky had turned up in Weymouth the very week that these events had started. What if she was R.I.P.?

But that made no sense. The Sky that she had known had never held a grudge. The phrase 'wouldn't hurt a fly' could have originated from observing her. One summer, their kitchen had been abuzz with the bastards, so Edie had strung up flypapers. When Sky got home from her studio she'd been devastated and had spent the next hour trying to free the surviving flies from their sticky graves. As for the timing of her return, unlike in crossword setting, coincidences happened all the time and meant nothing. Maybe Sky had her own reasons for being back.

The song's last notes hung in the prayer-thick air.

'Wonderful!' the choir leader called out. 'Wouldn't change a thing. Now take a break before we do the second half.'

Stress chemicals surged. Edie stood, but that was as far as she got. She was paralysed between choices. She could run away through the main doors, or she could move towards her past, maybe even her future.

Sky came down from the chancel and went over to the trestle table in the transept, just as she always used to do during the break. Tea and coffee were being served from familiar huge urns into the same mould-green cups that Edie had once drunk from.

Edie thought of Riga's disapproving face if she were to be told that Edie had run away again, and she took a deep breath. Then she walked up the aisle, towards Sky.

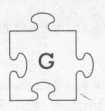

Thirty-Five

Sean was in Leyland's office, hoping that the meeting wouldn't go on too long.

'How are you handling the case?' the DCI was saying.

'It's progressing, sir.'

'Must be difficult.' Leyland's tone was patronising, his eyes scornful. 'After all, this is a murder investigation, not your usual cases of finding a missing teenager or a cat with a lost collar. And you've had to make sure your great-great-aunt, or mother, or whatever weird dynamic you two have, isn't involved. I assume that is still the situation?'

Sean fought to control his anger. 'I'm leaving Edie to Michaels.' On Leyland's desk were a nostril trimmer and several scattered short hairs. Sean hoped that it had smarted.

'So, what *have* you been doing?'

'We're going as quickly as we can; we're aware there's a race against the clock, sir. The note said that four people would be dead by Christmas Eve.'

'Speaking of which, Della Ingrit has been bugging me even more than usual. I want to be able to tell the press that we have key suspects. Can we?'

'It's early days, sir.'

'Yet you said there was "a race against the clock".'

'We do have potential suspects. Such as Lucy Pringle, who we've charged with harassing Veronica Princeton, and Dr Edward Berkeley, the headmaster of St Mary's, who's coming in for a formal interview in an hour. And we've just heard that Dr Newman was also spotted on CCTV on Esplanade on the night of his wife's death.'

'I hope you're not suggesting Edward and Samuel planned this together.'

'I hadn't even thought of it, sir.' But he should have. All possibilities should be considered open until they were closed down.

'Talking to Edward feels like a waste of everyone's time.' Leyland was shaking his head. 'I know him very well. Pillar of the local community.'

Of course he was, and therefore untouchable.

'He's also well regarded in the international educational community,' Sean said, 'both as an academic and a head-master. I've been looking through some of his books. But even pillars can fall.'

Leyland ignored this. 'On a similar note of caution, I've heard that you're investigating Dr Princeton's fertility clinic regarding unsubstantiated allegations from an online critic. Have you not heard the expression, "Don't Feed the Trolls"?'

'I thought the point was for us to investigate allegations and see if they have any grounds?'

'Don't be facetious, Sean. Dr Princeton was also a well-loved community figure. As a councillor she supported the police, and her clinic not only raised a lot of money for the station, but enabled my brother and sister-in-law to have a longed-for child. So, let's wait for the forensics on the jigsaw pieces, box and hoodie, along with any DNA found at the murder scene, before maligning a dead woman's professional reputation and causing harm to her husband. He's very upset, as you can imagine. Losing his wife and then hearing slanderous rumours about her.'

Sean wondered how Leyland knew Dr Princeton's husband. Through golf, maybe. Or perhaps the whispers about Leyland's affiliation to a certain town centre Lodge were true. If Edie were here, she'd bring it up and get slung out, enjoying every second. It was a wonder that she'd ever been employed anywhere.

Leyland stroked his smooth face. 'Thinking about it, we should feed Lucy Pringle to Della. That would be a good story: online troll comes out from under her bridge and possibly kills a community angel.'

'I think we should keep as much information to ourselves as possible.'

'I disagree. These jigsaw pieces are in the national interest.' Leyland's eyes gleamed. He paused in thought, then continued. 'Leave the headmaster, Inspector. Concentrate on the salient areas of investigation. You must learn to prioritise and lead, otherwise you'll never make it to DCI.'

Sean understood a veiled threat when he heard one.

'Do you understand what I'm saying?' Leyland lifted his trimmed eyebrows, clearly waiting for an answer.

'I get it.'

'Now, next steps?'

'There are so many open tabs, with only Andrew Thomas, Isla Mackey, Liz Foundry and five others in the running club having rock-solid alibis; the rest have no witnesses to their whereabouts. Even our own Helena Rice doesn't have an alibi.'

'I hope you're not going after her?'

'There's no evidence, so no. I was more thinking of changing direction and concentrating on solving the puzzle, including finding the location of the black and white tiles in the picture.'

Leyland tutted. 'There you go again. Misdirecting resources.'

'The tiles are clearly the centrepiece of whatever the killer has planned.'

'Or maybe it's a needle in a haystack situation. Or, should I say, a needle in a manger!' He paused for Sean to insert a laugh.

Sean did not laugh.

Leyland's jaw flexed. 'Don't make a habit of time-wasting, like you making poor Michaels, with all her abilities, look for carpets. It was a very close-run thing between you two. Don't make me regret choosing you.'

'No, sir.'

'What else are you going to do?'

Sean swallowed the words that came first. 'You don't need to micro-manage me, sir. I am running the case.'

'Are you, though? Because I think you're struggling.' Leyland's face was full of fake concern. 'Maybe it's because your aunt was the one who was sent the jigsaw.

We should circle back to that. It's clouding your judgement.'

'It's not.' He didn't think so, at least.

'She hasn't responded to any of Michaels' calls or emails, and she was not present at her house on either visit.'

Sean should never have told Edie that she'd be interviewed. 'If we could get back to the case? As you think the press would be into the jigsaw angle, do you think there's anyone in the force, or an outside resource, who could help us with the clues?'

'We don't have funds for other forces or sources.' Leyland smiled, pleased with his phrase.

'I believe that there is more of this case to come, and I want to get ahead of whoever is behind it.'

'And you'd better.' Leyland placed his hands in a prayer position. 'I'll be rooting for you to succeed, for your sake.'

The threat was now abundantly clear.

It took every bit of restraint Sean had not to tell Leyland to fuck off. It looked like Edie's blood punked in his veins after all.

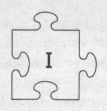

Thirty-Six

Sky looked down at Edie, and Edie up to Sky. Neither spoke. Edie hadn't known her heart could beat so fast or so hard. Around them, the laughter and gossip and teacup chinks faded to a hum.

'It's good to see you,' Edie said, at last.

'You too.' Sky's eyes were so soft, so fond. 'I won't offer you tea. I know it won't be to your liking.'

'I'll have a biscuit, though.'

Sky handed her a plate of stale Rich Teas, then looked across to the row of side chapels that flanked the south side of the church. 'Would you like to talk in private?'

Edie nodded, and followed her ex into the small chapel dedicated to St Brigid. Among the trellis work, statuary and displays of white lilies, they stood alone, only a person's breadth and their own breath between them.

'This is your favourite, right?'

'You remembered.' Edie might have expected, if she'd thought about it, Sky to recall how she liked her tea, but less so her preferred chapel or saint. But then, no matter how hard she'd tried, she'd never forgotten anything about Sky.

'I remember everything.'

Edie looked down, trying to hide the emotions she knew would be naked on her face. Beneath their feet were ledger stones with the names of honoured former clergy and parishioners. They were standing on the past, perhaps on the brink of a future.

'How are you doing, Edie?' Sky asked. 'And by that, I mean how you're *really* doing. I know you hate small talk so maybe we should skip to the big stuff.' Sky had changed slightly, it seemed. Trust her to get even better with age.

'I have no idea how to answer that.'

'Then what are you up to now?' The way she said it made it sound as if she was asking if Edie wanted to leave with her. She must have realised this as she added, 'With your life.'

'Not much has changed for me.' Edie didn't need to add 'since you left' but it was there between them.

'That can't be true.'

'I'm still in the same house . . .' Their house. 'I still have cats, different ones, obviously. The bigger shift, I suppose, is that I put together crosswords for local and national papers.'

'That's amazing!' Sky seemed genuinely surprised and thrilled. Edie felt a holly stab of hurt. Sky would already know that if she'd maintained even the slightest interest in Edie. Although, Edie knew, she was being illogical and hypocritical – she'd avoided discovering anything about Sky's new life. She'd wanted time to remain stuck, like a fly to flypaper.

Sky was smiling encouragingly at Edie, waiting.

'And Sean is doing well. A detective inspector at the

local station, married, and hoping to adopt with his husband.'

Sky clapped her hands together in delight. Her eyes were tear-brimmed. 'Wonderful!'

Edie knew she should ask about Sky's life now, but she felt skinned just being in her presence. No need to add salt.

But she had to say something. It was why she was here. 'When I saw you at the Christmas market, I skittered like a kitten. But I wanted to say to you . . .' She paused, trying to keep it together. 'That I'm sorry.'

'For what? I'm the one who left.'

Edie stared at the floor. She thought of all the things she'd got wrong in her life, from their relationship to her failures with the jigsaw. And, most importantly, she thought of the reasons why she'd got them wrong. 'For not stopping to think. But mostly for not listening. I should have understood how you felt, asked more, talked things through. Helped you be what you wanted, as you did for me.' She couldn't stop emotion from choking her voice.

'It's okay,' Sky said, simple as that. 'You did as much as you possibly could.'

'It wasn't enough.'

'Not for me, but that's okay. It wasn't right for us to be together at that point.'

Edie looked up. Did that mean it was the right time for them now? Hope made her heart beat. 'And now?'

'Now . . .' Sky smiled, leaning back to look through the entrance to the chapel. 'Now I've got my own jewellery business, and I'm married to a wonderful woman, Roberta, the one I was singing next to.'

Edie's heart seemed to stop as she recalled the silver-haired woman sharing the song sheet.

Sky, though, carried on. 'We have two kids, adults now. When Roberta's mother died, and she wanted to get away from her home town, I suggested we come here.'

Edie had a thousand recriminations and bitter responses running through her head, each one intended to hurt. But that wouldn't be playing fair. Sky had hardly been cryptic. She'd spelled out what she wanted the theme of her life to be. Edie hadn't listened. And now Sky had got all she'd wanted, just not with Edie. 'If I was doing small talk,' she said, when the words would come, 'then I'd say I was happy for you, but I'm not. I'm ripped apart. Even after so long.'

Sky closed her eyes. 'I'm sorry. I have regrets, too. But remorse should be a way of moving on, not a trap to keep you back.'

Remorse = *some err.*

Roberta, Sky's wife, popped her head round the side chapel's latticed wooden partition. She looked with curiosity at Edie, then turned to Sky. 'We're starting up again soon.'

'You carry on. I'll be with you in a minute, love. Just saying goodbye to Edie.'

Roberta's mouth formed an 'O'. Her eyebrows were high circumflexes of surprise. 'Ah. Of course.' She went off, still looking over her shoulder.

'She's beautiful,' Edie said.

'And a whizz at crosswords. I'll tell her to look out for yours.'

The choir started again, with 'Away in a Manger'. The singing was soft as a lullaby, yet carried round the church.

'Is it strange for you too, being back here?' Sky asked. 'There's only one other person from when we sang, Stella Acres, and she said you stopped coming a long time ago.'

'I didn't want to sing about Christmas, or anything else.'

'How do you feel about this time of year now?'

Edie looked to the white lilies, with their symbolism of rebirth. Sky was right, remorse was a way of staying stuck. Edie had erred. She knew that. And maybe now, it was time that she stopped stopping and embraced Christmas present rather than hating Christmases past. 'I'm thinking of entering a new relationship with it.'

Thirty-Seven

Sean, to Michaels' clear annoyance, and Leyland's if he found out, took Ama in with him to interview the headmaster. In his rucksack he had a copy of the book Dr Berkeley had written when he was an academic: *Towards a Pedagogy of Achievement and Fulfilment*.

They were in Interview Room 2, which somehow always smelled of fish and chips. Sean had once tried to determine why, suspecting that it was the preferred snack spot of a station night shifter, but it remained a mystery.

Next to Berkeley sat Shay Chichester, the smartly dressed smart alec of a solicitor who often made life difficult for the Weymouth Constabulary.

'Good to see you again, Dr Berkeley,' Sean said, after he'd given the official spiel about the interview being recorded on tape and that Berkeley was free to leave at any point.

'What's the time?' Berkeley asked. 'I don't have a watch on. I like yours, DI Brand-O'Sullivan. Looks old, too.'

Sean checked his watch reflexively, then placed the rucksack on the table. 'Nearly twenty past three. Do you have somewhere more important to be?'

'Like everyone else, I'm sure, I've got Christmas shopping

to finish. Mrs Challis has also charged me with picking up food and drink for the staff lunch tomorrow following our half-inset day. I would appreciate an expedited chat.'

'We won't keep you long. Well, no longer than it takes.' Sean got the book out of his bag. 'I've been enjoying reading this. It's fascinating.'

'Feel free to tell my publishers. I could do with it having a reprint.'

'You seem to believe in bringing coaching methods into teaching. Setting goals, achieving dreams. Is that a philosophy you shared with Dr Princeton, along with her bed?'

'Is that kind of language necessary?' the solicitor asked.

Dr Berkeley's smile was calm. 'Following dreams is a philosophy shared by many educators and health facilitators. I'm sure even police officers have dreams.'

DC Phillips laughed, then tried to smother it with a cough.

'I have plenty,' Sean replied, 'but I don't write about them. In your textbook you mention that one should aim for everything one wants. But what if you don't get it?'

Berkeley swallowed. 'In my opinion, the trick, when a particular goal faces an insurmountable obstacle, is to change this dream to something achievable. My mantra for students is: change your aim, change your game, change your name, if you have to.'

'Not so easy for some.'

'Are you asking for personal reasons? I know that you and your husband are following your dream to adopt. I think that's absolutely wonderful. Having kids brings such perspective and motivation.'

Sean stared at him, startled. 'How did you know about my home life?'

'My receptionist, Mrs Challis, gets on very well with your great-aunt Edie. And I can see why. Edie came to see me at lunchtime, and and we got on really well too. She's quite something.'

Sean didn't know how to reply.

'Didn't she tell you she'd visited? She showed me a jigsaw piece featuring a philosopher's face, thinking I might be able to help. I'm not sure I was any use though.'

Sean felt Ama's questioning eyes on him and didn't blame her. What was Edie doing?

'Perhaps,' he said, trying to regain control, 'we should concentrate on what you were doing in Weymouth town centre on the night Veronica Princeton was killed.'

'I stopped on my way back from seeing my mother to get some chips – from the place on the seafront that sells them in buckets with a free spade, I can't resist it! – and take some cash out.' He leaned forward, bending low to the table and adding in a conspiratorial whisper, 'Even though I've had years of assemblies, I'm not a morning person, so I had to do it then.'

'And why would you need cash so urgently?'

'I like our teachers and support staff to get a present from the school, and I'm putting my own money into getting the gifts. The governors don't like it when we use school funds for teachers. Heaven help us if we look after our staff. So, Mrs C. needed a roll of twenties to get Aldi's best whisky and chocolates.'

'The chip shop will confirm this?'

Dr Berkeley nodded, then blushed. 'I'm more of a regular than I'd like. In fact, the smell in here makes me want to stop off on the way home.'

Just then the door swung open, slamming against the scuffed wall. Leyland stood in the doorway, Michaels next to him. She was grinning.

'Here you are, Edward!' Leyland strode into the room.

Dr Berkeley stood up, smiling. He held out his hand and Leyland shook it. 'Julian! I wasn't expecting to see you today!'

'I'm here for two reasons – to ensure that DI Brand-O'Sullivan is treating you right.' Leyland glared at Sean, who shrank in his seat.

'We've been having a very pleasant chat about chips,' Berkeley said, 'and the importance of having a goal.'

'I thought your goal was to beat me on the green one day.' Leyland laughed.

'Everyone needs a dream.' Berkeley gave a half-smile.

'Maybe you'd achieve it if you ate fewer chips!' Leyland thwacked him on the back.

'What are you talking about?' Berkeley bit back. 'I'm wearing the same size trousers as when I was twenty. Unlike you.'

Sean hated manbantz. 'And what is the second reason, sir?'

'To let you know that a firm alibi has been established for Dr Berkeley on both occasions. So, he is absolutely free to go.'

'She actually did it!' Dr Berkeley said. His voice was hushed and, looking at him, Sean could see the headmaster was as surprised as he was himself. 'She came forward!'

'Yes, Mrs Sandra Challis has given us a detailed account of your evenings, and very stimulating they seem too, Edward.'

'But why did you both lie?' Sean asked, as the already flimsy case flew away from him. Two people falling in love, crossing words and lives should not make him feel desperate. But now he had nothing, and another day was getting closer.

'We've been seeing each other for a while. But Sandra didn't want the school gossip mill grinding away. She thought it would diminish her authority.'

'Kids don't care about who people sleep with,' Sean said.

'She meant the parents. They're much harder to deal with than the children.'

'Now, you go and do your Christmas shopping, Edward. We won't bother you again.' Leyland stood back to let Berkeley through and winked. He was such a winker.

Thirty-Eight

Carl Latimer hadn't been home long, but he was already bored. Mrs Bleniou, from the flat below, had left him with a flask of coffee and a keto-tastic breakfast of cheese, olives and meat. She'd also left a can of lager within touching distance, but she hadn't thought to bring him the remote.

He was stuck here, unable to move, until she returned. His cracked rib was agony and his broken elbow throbbed. The painkillers the hospital had sent him home with were shit. He'd ask his dealer to come round but he didn't want to be seen in this state, his shattered leg in its huge cast elevated by a pile of cushions. His ex-girlfriend had left them in the flat when she'd run out on him, and at least now they were finally coming in useful. He was comfortable, but stranded. No music, no TV, no porn, no running. For an active man like him, it was torture.

Still, at least he didn't have to teach gawky teens how to kick a ball. And Mrs Bleniou would be back before long. She'd gone shopping to get more supplies.

She was loving having the door unlocked so she could pop in at any time to look after him. She'd never been in his flat before, hard as she'd tried, and used to leave him meals by his door. Her plates were all brown and had tin foil hats like they were conspiracy nuts. Her food wasn't bad, actually. He might even develop a taste for Greek food, that'd show his ex. She'd said he'd never grow up, but here he was, eating olives.

At least Mrs Bleniou had opened the lounge windows. The sofa, with its high back – which had cost him an arm and a leg, not a phrase he liked any more – faced the window that looked out over Weymouth. He could watch the snow trying to fall and see whether he was right about the woman over the road nicking stuff from his bins.

A car pulled up just out of sight. It didn't sound like Mrs Bleniou's Fiat, and she'd hardly been gone half an hour. He heard the door open, then slam. Probably a delivery driver, trying to earn a bit of Christmas cash.

The buzzer went for the communal front door, and someone let whoever it was in. Footsteps echoed on the staircase, coming up to the first floor. Maybe the parcel was for him; a present from the school. Fruit basket. Bottle of whisky. He'd get the bloke to bring it in and pass him the remote control.

His front door opened, and someone walked into his flat. He tried to turn to see who it was, but couldn't raise himself up. 'Just leave it on the table, mate.' The delivery driver smelled of cologne, probably to cover the stink of sweat that also emanated from him, like the kind Carl had when he was anxious. Must be hard to get deliveries done in the time allowed, especially this time of year. But you shouldn't take on jobs if you couldn't do them.

The delivery driver didn't answer. Or leave.

Unease coursed through Carl. 'Hello? I said just leave it on the table.'

The driver came closer, footsteps sounding on the laminate.

Carl again tried to push himself up, but he had no strength. For a second, he caught a glimpse of the driver, but they were wearing a baseball cap and face mask, and holding a hammer. Adrenaline screamed at him to run, but he couldn't even get off the sofa. The hammer fell, splitting Carl's head. As blood dripped into his eyes, he saw one of his ex-girlfriend's cushions looming. Suddenly the 'Prosecco O'Clock' cushion was pressed against his face.

'Why?' Carl asked. But the fabric smothered his words, and he never heard the answer.

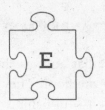

Thirty-Nine

The killer bent over, ear close to Latimer's mouth. Carl's lungs were hushed, and he'd stopped kicking his one good leg and flailing his one good arm three minutes ago. But they had to be sure. The killer held their breath as if to match Carl's. There was nothing. He was dead at last.

The killer thought of taking a picture of Carl lying there, looking pathetic, but they were better than that. Not much better, but these gradations were important.

They looked around the large apartment, with its three blenders in the kitchen and the vats of protein shake lined up around the counters. Over the glass mantelpiece hung a large, gilt-framed picture of Latimer. Carl would have stared into it as if it were a mirror. The killer wanted to spit at the dead man's portrait, or even the dead man himself, but that would leave evidence. They had done enough; kept their unspoken promise to Latimer that revenge would be taken for what he had done.

But the killer felt waves of nausea and tiredness. And they still hadn't finished. One more must die tonight, another kind of runner exposed.

The killer left the flat and, as they closed the door, a tinsel wreath fell to the floor. They walked away, leaving another piece of their soul behind.

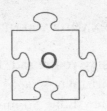

Forty

The taxi driver kept glancing at Edie in the rear-view mirror on the way from the church back to her house. 'You alright, love?'

Edie was *not* alright. She was so un-alright that she nodded instead of snapping at him.

'If you say so.'

She couldn't stop crying, tears dropping without sobs to accompany them, just rain falling. When Sean was three or so, he used to come to her if he was upset or having a meltdown and say, 'Help me stop crying.' She had always distracted him with anagrams. 'If you change around "tears" you get "stare" or "taser". If you muddle up "sobs" you get "boss", which, if you think about it, means that there's power in vulnerability.' She hadn't believed it but had hoped it would help.

'But I can't read, Mummy Edie. I don't know my letters.' Sean had blinked at her, but the tears had stopped, jewelling his long lashes.

'That will change, Seanie darling. Everything does, in the end. Whether you like it or not.'

When the car pulled up outside her house Edie went to pay the driver, but he pushed her hand away. 'This one's on me. I'm sorry you're sad. Bless you. I hope you have a very nice Christmas.'

Such kindness threw Edie. So much so that she didn't know what to say. He drove off before she could thank him.

Across the cul-de-sac, the ever-present Lucy Pringle was cutting holly from a bush. She was listening to something on her headphones and smiling triumphantly, as if she hadn't been subject to a police charge, as Riga had informed Edie. Edie hated being the receiver of second hand news. She really must get on the WhatsApp group.

In her porch she looked through the junk mail and Christmas cards, but there was nothing more from Rest In Pieces. At least that meant no one else was dead.

Her house felt strangely empty, despite the mess. She put the kettle on and tried to ignore her sense of loneliness by solving the crossword clues that Mrs Challis had started. As the kettle whistled and all three cats weaved around her chair, her phone rang. It was Sean.

'I'm so glad you called.' She gripped the phone as if it were his hand.

'My DCI has told me I'm permitted to tell you that Carl Latimer was found dead twenty minutes ago.'

'What do you mean? Were there complications from his injuries?'

'Complications due to him being murdered.' Sean had never sounded so cold or curt. Or so hurtful.

'Sarcasm doesn't suit you. I just want to know what's happened.'

'I'm on my way over there now, to find out more. All we know is that someone finished off what they'd started.'

'You can pick me up on your way and tell me about it. I can stay in the car if it's easier.'

'I'm only phoning to inform you that DS Michaels will be with you in a minute or so, to ask the questions she's been trying to put to you, along with several more serious ones.'

'I've already told you about finding the box.'

'But you didn't tell me about paying a visit to Edward Berkeley, or about a new jigsaw piece that you've received.' The fury in his voice pierced her Sky-raw heart. 'What else have you been hiding from me? No, don't answer that. Tell my colleague.'

'I don't know if I can take this today.' She paused. 'I saw Sky again, Seanie.'

He inhaled sharply at hearing his now-rare pet name. 'I am DI Brand-O'Sullivan to you at the moment. You've potentially hindered a police investigation and could well be charged, possibly also for tampering with and withholding evidence.'

'I don't think it's that serious. If I could just see you to expl—'

'I can't, Edie. You're an active part of the investigation. And, even if you weren't, I don't want to see you right now.'

'You're making it sound like it's my fault. I wasn't the one who left a jigsaw at my door.'

His quick intake of breath, as if suppressing what he really wanted to say, was a lino cut to her heart.

'If you've got something to say, Sean, just say it. I can take it.'

'I should have given the whole case over the minute you called me, but I thought it just might bring us closer. That having something you actually cared about – though God knows how, since you don't care about anything else – might mean we could connect.' His sardonic laugh ripped her apart.

Edie took the jigsaw pieces with his watch on out of her pocket. 'Please, Sean. You don't know why I'm doing this. I haven't told you everything.'

He laughed again. 'No shit, Edie. Just like always, you keep a little bit of yourself back.'

'It's not that. Not this time. Please believe me, Sean, love?'

'Don't "love" me.'

And her beloved Sean hung up.

Forty-One

'And here we have our ready-to-roll collection.' Linus Cramer was leading his last customer of the day around the carpet hall of his furniture warehouse, just outside Poole. 'Very popular this time of year. Halfway between a rug and a full carpet. You can just pop them down on your living or dining room floor and you're all ready for a party. Covers a multitude of sins.' Linus glanced at the client to check they weren't offended. So many were these days.

The customer, though, turned to look at the detail on a paisley pattern.

'There's also, if you prefer, the option to "rent-a-rug" over ten days of the season; that way you get to try it out, or just return it when the rellies have left. Am I right?' Linus didn't stop to get an answer. He was on autopilot, already thinking of getting home, shutting the door. Beatrice would run at him, shouting, 'Daddy!', and he'd kiss her, and then his wife. They'd open a bottle of champagne to celebrate their biggest turnover day of the year so far. He loved Christmas, and not just because so many people ordered new flooring to impress festive guests.

'I need one with tassels. Gold ones. I saw some on your website.'

'You'll be looking for our deluxe ready-to-roll. And may I say what an excellent selection that is. One of our best—'

'How absorbent is it?'

Shaken out of his spiel, Linus said, 'That's not a question we're often asked. I suppose, with the thicker lining, they could probably absorb a bottle of wine before it saturated through. Although it wouldn't then be eligible for the rental scheme, obviously.'

'I won't need to return it.'

'Sounds like you're going to have quite the party! Can I come?!' Linus gave one of his hearty laughs – those usually pleased the punters. He waggled his eyebrows in a way that suggested the customer might be having some kind of orgy.

But this one didn't even look at him. Never mind. Linus didn't care if the customer was happy, or who they were, as long as they bought something.

'Right. May I suggest you get the thickest wool and backing on the market, and in a dark red, perhaps. Any spillages will be soaked up and disappear in no time.' Linus strode down the rows of rolled carpets that were laid out like winter hay bales. 'This one would be perfect.'

The customer inspected the carpet, flicking a finger through the gold tassels as if they were harp strings. 'I'll take it. Today.'

Linus managed to stop himself whooping. It was the

most expensive carpet he sold. He was going to buy the finest fizz he could get in the Esso garage.

As he looked in the drawer by the till for the parcel tape, the customer seemed to relax. Linus knew what it was like to be charged with a task and, once it was completed, to surface and come back into the world. 'I don't suppose you have cash, do you? Only the machine is acting up.'

The customer took a wodge of notes out of their wallet and handed them over. Linus could tell by the thickness alone that it was the correct amount. Happy days.

'Is it only you here? You seem a bit light-staffed.'

'It was the staff lunch today, for all our branches. The others were too squiffy to sell anything afterwards, so I sent them home.' If truth be told, he'd fired one of them, and given another a warning. Who gets pissed at their first work Christmas do? Not that it mattered. He had enough staff to get through the January sales, then he was off to the Seychelles, using money he'd stuffed under the carpet for many years. 'I, however, am as absorbent as this beast.' He slapped the rump of the carpet roll. 'And someone needs to keep the wheels on the track.'

'Absolutely. Someone has to get the job done.'

With the notes safely in the till and the receipt printed, Linus felt it was a job very well done.

'I've pulled my car up to the back entrance,' the customer said. 'Could you help me get the carpet in? Don't think I can manage by myself.'

'It'd be my pleasure. Let's get the party started.'

As Linus led the way to the back door, he started

thinking about having friends round on Christmas Eve. They could sing carols, watch a movie in his home cinema. He'd got a popcorn machine that actually worked, unlike his last one, and a wine fridge under the seats, not to mention—

A hard thwack at the back of his skull put a stop to these thoughts. Linus slumped, his head burning as he hit the concrete floor. Jigsaw pieces fell over his body like snow. The red carpet rolled out in front of him as red blood flowed into his eyes. Then all that red faded irrevocably to black.

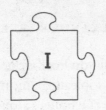

Forty-Two

'I'm coming round,' Riga said when Edie phoned her. 'I'll act as your solicitor.'

Edie was pacing her hallway, waiting for the detective sergeant to arrive. 'I don't need a solicitor. And *you're* not a lawyer.'

Riga sighed. 'No, I said I'd *act* as one. I'll rummage in my wardrobe for a briefcase. It'll be fun. Like amateur dramatics, but less shagging other people's wives. I'm not sure I have the energy for that fleet foible today.'

'It's a bit more serious than that, Riga.' Peggoty was pacing alongside Edie, looking up with what could be construed as concern.

'Nah. They'll go away within half an hour. All you have to do is tell them that a single jigsaw piece was put through your door, and you wanted to know who it was, so you asked an educated man.'

'That makes me sound pathetic. And it's not true. I've had a lot more pieces than that.'

'You've got even more, if the rustle of the envelope I found in my porch earlier is anything to go by.'

Edie stopped, right in front of the now-unlocked dining room. 'What? Why didn't you tell me?'

'I was waiting till you got back. Now you're back.'

'I shouldn't even look at them, just give the unopened envelope straight to the police, along with the pieces they don't know about.'

'I mean, *sure*, you *should* do that, but—'

'But what if the threat was real, warning me about handing them in? I'd be putting—'

'You'd be putting Sean in danger. *And* yourself. Besides, do you have any reason to think that the police are solving the clues?'

'None at all.'

'Then I'd say it was clear. You tell her nothing.'

'You're my enabler as ever.' She paused. With crosswords there was always another way of looking at things. 'I wonder if this is an opportunity to find out what the police know and we don't.'

'Turn the tables on her.'

'Exactly. You will remember to bring the new jigsaw pieces, won't you?'

''Course I will. I want to see them, too. You're lucky I haven't already.'

A car pulled into the driveway, engine stopping. 'She's here.'

'I'll be over in a few minutes, or, well, as long as it takes my legs to move to grace you with my moral support and acting skills.'

Sean felt as winded and sore as the time he'd been knocked over by a car while riding his bike. He'd argued with Edie so few times in his life that, when it happened, it was devastating. He knew through therapy that this was because he had attachment issues – something he'd have to watch out for if he were to be a good parent. But that was a big if. His own parents and brother had died when he was too small to know or remember them, no matter how hard he searched in his dreams.

Sean's chest closed up even more. He couldn't have a panic attack. Not now. He was scrabbling in his desk drawer for an inhaler when Ama knocked on the door and entered. 'Are you alright, sir?'

Sean took two puffs on the blue inhaler. 'I just had to tell off Edie.' A wheeze whistled through his voice.

'*And* inform her of Michaels' imminent arrival. Not a great day for her.' Ama's eyes were sparkly with humour. When she succeeded in getting a small laugh out of him, she grinned. 'You're off to Latimer's flat, right?'

Sean nodded. 'Helena's already there, apparently. I want you to come with me to interview all the neighbours while events are still fresh, check out any bell cameras etc. It'll be a door-to-door slog, I'm afraid.'

Ama's eyes shone. 'That's what I'm here for. I also wanted to let you know that I've found a connection between Carl Latimer and Veronica Princeton. I saw a Facebook photo from last Christmas of her standing close to him, her hand on his chest.'

'Well done, but keep digging. We need more.'

'And I've got more, sir. I'd just finished cross-referencing the information we gleaned about Carl Latimer from the receptionist with the files IT recovered from his computer when I heard that he'd died. None of it's good.'

'So, Mrs Challis was right about the complaints made about him?'

'Two fourteen-year-old girls reported to the headmistress of St Mary's at the time that Latimer, just shy of sixteen, took intimate photos and videos of them without their knowledge or consent, and sent them to friends. His dad was a war photographer and encouraged him to experiment with his camera equipment and dark room.' Ama took a breath. 'And there is, apparently, more recent footage, going right up to the present day, some of which has been shared and uploaded on porn sites.'

'Revenge porn.'

'Yeah, but even calling it that kind of suggests there could be a reason for posting it.'

'True. Are any of the victims recognisable?'

Ama paused. 'It's difficult to tell. Maybe. Can I get back to you on it?'

'Is it someone you know?'

Ama bit her lip. 'I'd rather not say until I'm certain. It's someone connected to the case.'

He burned with curiosity, but knew he had to trust her. 'Look into it, but take care of yourself. This is horrible work, and IT are trained to handle it; well, handle it better, anyway.'

'Thanks, sir.'

'What about the head at the time?'

Ama again checked her notes. 'A Mrs Singer. It looks like, other than suspending him for a week, she swept the complaints away. No evidence of what happened to the two girls.'

Sean remembered Edie talking about Mrs Singer a few years ago. It had been a strange conversation, so it stood out among their many.

It was just after he'd been accepted as a DC. They'd been having fried egg sandwiches at the Lookout Café by the bowling green on the seafront. Edie had complained about the number of steps up to its terrace, and had complained even more about the wind, the seagulls, the view. As usual, she'd sat facing away from the sea, occasionally looking over her shoulder as if afraid it was coming for her.

'You loathe the sea almost as much as you do Christmas,' Sean had said. 'I just don't get it.'

'You know why I can't stand Christmas.'

'And I understand that, although I wish you'd lighten up on it. You did when Sky was around.'

'I lightened up *a little*, and that was a big mistake. I let my guard down.'

'But why the sea?'

'You know the saying "worse things happen at sea"?'

'Of course.'

'Well, they do. And I don't want to talk about it.'

They'd been silent for a few moments. Edie dunked a succession of tea bags into her takeaway cup, staring at the houses up on the ridge. 'Mrs Singer couldn't swim, either. But she never sank, not like I did.'

'Who's Mrs Singer?'

Edie turned back to him, eyes refocusing as if she'd

been drowning in the past. 'The headmistress at St Mary's when I taught there, and for some time after.' Then she'd abruptly stood and walked off, leaving him, her sandwich and the conversation on the terrace.

Sean's desk phone rang. It was Carly from reception. 'Just had a call from your husband, Inspector. I asked if he wanted to wait to be put through, but he said he had to get going. The social worker has arranged a pre-Christmas meeting with your potential adoptee.'

Sean stood, excitement building. 'Where and when?'

'Lodmoor Country Park. At the café. As soon as you can make it.'

'Okay, thanks, Carly.'

Sean shoved his things into his rucksack, gripping the phone under his chin. 'Oh, and if Liam calls back, tell him I'm on my way.'

He looped the bag over his shoulder.

'What about the crime scene?' Ama asked, as Sean pushed open his office door.

'Go there straight away and tell them I'll be a bit late. You'll be my proxy till then. You're ready.'

Ama beamed.

Maybe Sean *was* ready to be a dad. Time to find out.

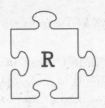

Forty-Three

'So, you've had no further correspondence from Rest In Pieces?' Michaels was sitting on Edie's sofa, side-eyeing Mr Bumble on his cushion close by.

'Other than what I found on my mat, I have had nothing from them through my door.' Edie congratulated herself for not lying; not exactly, anyway. It was a good job Sean wasn't here – he'd notice her twisting words. He'd had enough practice.

In the far corner, sitting regally in an armchair and sipping one of her own herbal elixirs, Riga snorted.

'This isn't funny, Ms Novack. If you interrupt again, I'll have to insist you leave.'

'I'll be as quiet as Christmas.' Riga was playing with Michaels like Peggoty did with mice.

'But Christmas is noisy,' replied Michaels, frowning.

'Not if you spend it alone.' Riga looked upwards, placing the back of her hand to her forehead in dramatic despair.

'Right. Yes.' Michaels turned back to Edie, then started as she realised that Mr Bumble had crept up to sit right next to her. He stared at her with his unnerving grey eyes. 'And why did you not inform DI Brand-O'Sullivan, or another officer, as soon as you saw this additional piece?'

Edie shrugged. 'I didn't think it was relevant.'

Michaels wrote this down slowly, shaking her head in disbelief. 'Carl Latimer has died, Ms O'Sullivan. Other lives are in danger. Nothing is irrelevant.'

'I am well aware that others are at risk, Sergeant Michaels.'

'You appear as oblivious to other people as you were when I was at school.' Michaels' jaw clenched.

'I taught you?!' Edie peered at Michaels, but had not one flicker of recognition.

'Only for one lesson. In my last year. But you made an impression.'

It was a shame that Michaels hadn't made one on Edie. 'Shall we get on with the interview? Once this is over, I can get on with my life and you can go and search through CCTV or whatever.'

Michaels bristled, and Mr Bumble lumbered onto her lap. Edie knew the cat's attention didn't infer that Michaels was a good person. On the contrary, cats loved a twat.

'Did *he* tell you about that?'

Both Edie and Riga sat a little straighter. Edie had inadvertently hit a nerve. Michaels was needled. Perhaps Edie could get her to crack. 'Sean would never divulge that. But then he didn't need to tell me; it's common knowledge.'

'It was only a frame or two. Really easy to miss. If Phillips hadn't been so keen to prove me wrong, she'd never have spotted Berkeley, or Newman.'

Edie shook her head with sorrow. 'You have my

sympathy. I know what it's like to have bad eyesight.' She didn't, never had.

'It's one thing to have bad eyesight, another to be asked not to see. I see more than—' Michaels' words dried up as she realised what she was saying.

'Don't stop, Sergeant,' Riga said. 'Please. You were just getting interesting.'

Blizzards were rare in Dorset, so rare that Sean had never driven through one before. It was making navigating the winding roads far harder than usual. He turned the heating as high as it would go. He had goosebumps, but it wasn't just from the cold. He was going to see Juniper!

It would be the very best Christmas present ever if things went their way. Deep down, he believed they would. No matter how much this case had caused his certainties to slide, he had to believe that good things still happened. That people were inherently good and that was what made the world connect, not nepo babies, contacts and corruption.

Lodmoor Country Park was beautiful during the day, with its many RSPB-protected acres and space for circuses and other events, as well as, importantly, a pub and other attractions. He had no idea, though, why Sunny had suggested it for their meeting today; it was already dark. You'd never know, what with it being December 22nd, that the sun was on its long way back to dominance. Light means an awful lot more when you're faced with the lack of it.

ALEXANDRA BENEDICT

Maybe there was a special event for kids, Santa coming inexplicably early to give an out-of-date selection pack to children in care. Sean would have to watch himself, otherwise he'd become as cynical as Edie. It would be hard to be sceptical though, when he saw Juniper happy.

Arriving at the familiar entrance, he stopped in the first car park and got out into the swirling snow, wondering what Juniper would make of it. He pictured her holding out a mittened hand and laughing as the flakes landed there and melted.

Sean turned around, trying to see where they could be. There were no lights on in the café over the way, and no other cars parked up.

Maybe, with the café closed, they were meeting by the pirate mini golf. That was probably floodlit. Although he wasn't sure putting in the snow was a great plan. He bet not even Leyland did that, preferring to drink in the clubhouse.

He dialled Liam's number, but there was hardly any reception.

Just then, headlights blared as a vehicle drove into the car park. Maybe it was Liam, or Sunny. Maybe they'd been delayed by the snow.

The car accelerated towards him.

Sean stood still for a moment, confused, then turned and ran. He sprinted for the grass hill, but the car was quicker. It roared up behind him.

Sean tried to leap to one side, but the car was already smashing into him, knocking him to the ground.

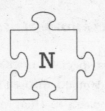

Forty-Four

The killer grabbed Sean's wrist. The detective was unconscious from the fall, but a pulse still beat in his veins. Given the force of the collision, he'd most likely have a broken hip. Maybe a broken leg and ribs, too. The killer could see little blood, but internal bleeding was a possibility. The inspector needed medical attention, but he wasn't going to get it.

The killer could hardly feel their fingers as they tried to knot the rope around Sean's wrists. They were numb, trembling and fumbling, but not just from the cold. Every second that the killer failed to secure Sean took them closer to a car turning up. The killer had come here often when it was dark. They wouldn't again.

They were flailing and they knew it. Their plan had been brilliant. Everything had fit together so well. But that was when it had been a hypothesis. Now they were confronted with the reality of murder. Cramer's death had been the worst yet. It was incredibly hard to achieve, both physically and mentally. And there was no sense of satisfaction at reaching the desired goal.

Murder was messy, ugly and sickening. They should never have started this, but they hadn't had a choice. And they didn't have one now. Cramer's blood was caked in their hair and had soaked into the skin on their arms. The smell of it lingered in their nostrils, going deeper inside them every time they breathed. The taste of death lined their mouth.

Feeling bile rise, the killer vomited on the side of the hill. It burned through the snow. They were getting careless, but finding it harder to care.

When DI Brand-O'Sullivan's ropes were tight, the killer heaved him into the back of the car, and covered both Sean and Cramer's body with tarpaulin. Breathing heavily in the front seat, they went through the rest of the plan, deciding how to break it down to make it manageable. Jigsawing it.

They had to go back to Godlingston Woods, with all the risks inherent in carrying a carpet containing a corpse into a copse where joggers jogged and doggers dogged.

Then they would take DI Brand-O'Sullivan to the place where all the pieces would finally be put together.

Only then would they be able to get ready for Christmas.

'Get them out, then,' Edie said when Michaels had gone. She stood over Riga, holding her jigsaw tray.

'I *beg* your pardon.' Riga placed her hands on her hips in mock indignation.

'You know full well I meant the jigsaw pieces.'

Riga grinned and tipped up the envelope that she'd kept in her handbag.

Edie took them through into the dining room and looked at each under her magnifying glass.

One was the last corner piece, from the top right. Edie realised with a chill that if the killer was following their pattern then the third victim, bottom right, was already dead, or about to be so. She had failed again.

'The corner piece is the Aesculapian Rod.'

'The what?' Riga had followed her in and was now sitting at the table. Every now and then, she poked at the dying fire.

'The staff of Asclepius, a wooden stick with a snake wound round it. It's used, especially in the US, to symbolise medicine, as Asclepius was the god of healing.'

'Healing seems the very opposite of killing.'

'Unless someone considers themselves to be healing through murder, either themselves or someone else?'

'That's a warped view of the world.'

'The thing is,' Edie continued, 'the symbol can be confused with that of the caduceus, the staff carried by Hermes or Mercury, so an emblem of messenger gods. I've used the two-way interpretation in crosswords sometimes.'

'So, what does it mean here?'

'Could be a medical matter – Drs Newman and Princeton. Or, if it's a messenger, it could be a reporter, or writer, or the jigsaw setter themselves. It depends on the wider context.' Edie scanned the other jigsaw pieces. More tiles, more holly, more of the corpse outline, more waves. Three pieces were interlocking, and showed a carpet beater next to a corset.

More carpets. Edie had a flash of hope that these were additional clues for the third murder, and that she still had a chance to prevent it.

She carried the pieces over to the fireplace wall with its partially completed jigsaw. Her joy at discovering that one slotted into a previously received black-tiled piece was shot down by it clearly being part of the top right-hand set of clues. These were, if the killer was following their own MO, clues for a fourth victim.

'Potential murder weapons, maybe?' Riga suggested. 'Someone will be beaten with a corset?'

Edie didn't want to think about anyone dying, and distracted herself with the many anagrams Riga's phrase contained. *Beaten corset = a better scone. Beaten corset = carbon settee. Beaten corset = . . .*

'Beacon Street!'

'What?'

'That's an anagram of "beaten" and "corset"!'

Edie grabbed her phone and googled. 'There's a Beacon Street in Swanage.' She switched to street view on Google Maps and virtually walked along the row of shops and residential houses. 'Guess what's on that road?'

Riga shook her head. 'No idea.'

'Beacon Street Medical Centre. With the anagram, which the killer knows I like from my crosswords, and the Aesculapian Rod, I think that's where the killer is telling me to go.' Edie grabbed her bag and opened her taxi app. 'Do you want to come with me?'

Riga held up her hand. 'It'll be closed by now. And what if,' she countered, 'it's another false lead from the puzzle setter? Could there be something else behind your first impulse?'

Riga was right. This wasn't the time to dash off again without thinking. Or listening.

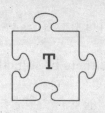

Forty-Five

Sean was bobbing on the sea, he was sure of it. Flotsam. He was a piece of driftwood from a wreck, floating. Jostled one way and another, tossed like a branch on water. But why would he be in the sea? And why would it be so warm, or so hard to breathe?

Sean fought for his thoughts, trying to steady them.

He hung on to what he knew. He couldn't see. Or feel his arms or legs, or anything really. But why?

He'd been trying to get to Liam. The meeting with Juniper.

But they hadn't been there. Someone else had come. A car.

A spike of adrenaline pulled him back into his body. His head pulsed with pain.

The car had driven into him. He'd fallen, his face hitting the snow. He remembered nothing after that.

By the way he was being jolted, the purring sensation beneath him . . . he was in a car. Maybe the one that had hit him.

Sean tried to move, but his back screamed and his limbs were stuck. Possibly tied up, possibly broken. He didn't know if his eyes were open or closed; either way he couldn't see anything.

The car turned a corner and he rolled against something, sending a searing pain through his hips. His fingers could flare, very slightly, and he was able to touch what felt like tough fabric. Carpet, with tassels.

Panic seized his lungs as he thought of the jigsaw piece. Was he the third victim?

He tried to open his mouth to gulp for air, but his lips were taped shut. He told himself to be calm, to breathe through his nose, all the things he had done since he was a child to ward off asthma and panic attacks. Occasionally it worked, but not this time. As he tried to raise his head, something shifted over him. He was covered by it. Plastic sheeting. A makeshift shroud.

Sean bucked in pain. Cortisol coursed through his body. He now knew exactly how he was tied: hands, feet, two ropes placed across his middle and upper chest. He thought of all the times in the gym, at circuit training or doing squats on a clifftop when he'd held back. Only now did he regret it.

His lungs burned as he struggled, twisting and writhing as much as the bonds would allow. He didn't care if the killer heard. There was no point playing dead if you died in the process.

The car stopped. One of the doors opened, then slammed.

Sean's heart matched the beat of the car ticking and tutting, counting down the seconds before the boot opened with a whoosh of cold air. It smelled of snow-topped pine and grave dirt. An owl cried out, but he couldn't reply.

The plastic covering was taken off with a crunch, the tape over Sean's mouth ripped away. The eye covering stayed.

'Please,' Sean tried to say through his raw, ragged throat. 'I . . . can't . . . breathe.'

An inhaler was placed in his mouth. The button was depressed with a hiss, and Sean took two huffs of the powdery steroid. But before he even knew what he was going to say next, something soft and sweet-smelling was placed over his mouth and nose.

Chloroform.

He knew that he wouldn't pass out immediately – that was a myth – but within five minutes his already weak respiratory system would come under attack as he slowly shut down.

A syringe was placed between his lips, and a dribble of salty water was injected into his mouth. He knew the taste. He'd described it to countless halls full of teenagers, warning them about the dangers of GHB.

Sean felt the warm, boozy ooze of the party drug combine with the ether's siren song, calling him to slip back below the surface of consciousness. At least he wouldn't be able to think and feel down there.

Nevertheless, he tried to stay awake, blinking against the blindfold. He had to think, to stay alert. Why would the killer fend off an asthma attack while making sure that he passed out? And for how long would they keep Sean alive?

The car dipped. He could hear the killer struggle with something, then the roll of carpet was dragged away. It thumped onto soft ground. It sounded heavier than Sean had expected.

The tarpaulin was thrown back on top of him. The heavy roll of carpet was dragged away across the earth. The car boot slammed shut.

Sean couldn't bear to stay awake any longer. The pain in his head was nothing compared to the pain in his heart. He was alone. When the tide dragged him down, he was glad.

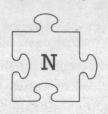

Forty-Six

December 23rd

Sean woke as a door slammed behind him. He couldn't move, and yet he was moving. He was being dragged along a cold, hard floor. He heard rustling and thought of Helena in her SOCO suit, coming to help him, then realised it was the tarpaulin, with him wrapped up inside. He was being transported, in a heavy-duty pupa, like a present. But by whom?

His captor was tired, taking frequent breaks and halting breaths. They smelled of earth. Sean didn't want to think about what had happened in the woods.

He tried to stay calm, keep his breathing as steady as the pain would allow. Hyperventilating would finish him before the killer had a chance to.

The dragging stopped and a key rattled in a lock. The door took forever to open, as if it had been sealed shut for a long time. At last, it creaked and gave way.

Sean waited, expecting to be dragged into whatever room this was. Instead, his captor dropped Sean's legs, sending jolts of pain through his body. Then he felt hands on his shoulders and heard the deep breath of his captor.

A second later, he was shoved, hard, and he was falling again into dark nothing. Just before the blackness took him back, a church bell tolled once, just for him.

Edie woke to the bat of a cat's paw. She opened her eyes to find Peggoty purring, paw raised for another swipe.

'Okay, okay. Breakfast will soon be served.' Edie sat up, feeling more tired than she had in a long time. It had been a restless night as her brain tried to turn around the pieces of the jigsaw to see what she was missing.

It was still dark outside, but it was in fact seven thirty. She'd slept through her alarm. No wonder Peggoty had become impatient.

The doorbell rang just as Edie reached the bottom of the stairs. She opened the door to find Liam on the doorstep. He was shifting from foot to foot, his eyes red. Stubble showed through the light snow on his jaw. She had never seen him unshaven before.

'What is it, Liam? What's wrong?'

'Tell me he's with you.'

'Who, Sean?'

'Of course, Sean!'

'I haven't seen him for a day or so.'

'Never mind.' Liam turned, arms folded, head down, heading back to his car.

Fear crashed into Edie's heart. Something had happened to Sean, she knew it.

She stepped onto the drive in her slippers and dressing

gown, aware of the blinds being raised like hemlines around the street, the curtains drawn back. She flipped birds to whoever was watching. Called out, 'Wait. Liam, please. Come inside.'

They sat at her kitchen table, cups of tea in their hands. 'I called him all night,' Liam said, 'but it went straight through to his answerphone. I thought it was to get back at me for not phoning him—'

'Sean would never do that. He's not petty. Unlike you.'

Liam sighed and rubbed his eyes. 'Can we not fight, Edie? If we could just have a truce while we find Sean?'

'Fine.'

'Is it "fine" though? Because I don't think you've ever even said "come in" to me before today, and that was only because Sean is missing.'

'Now that's a lie.'

'The few times I came over it was always, "I suppose you best come in, then".'

'What more of an invitation do you need?'

'Being welcomed would be nice.'

'A million pounds would be nice, but we can only dream of such things.'

Liam put his mug down and made to leave. 'There's no point if—'

A tide of tiredness swept over her. 'I said "fine", and I meant it. We can go back to sniping when he's safe. Have you tried the station?'

Liam glared at her. 'Of course I have. Do you think I'm stupid, for God's s—'

'A truce, remember?'

He breathed out slowly. 'Ama said he was supposed to meet her at a crime scene but never turned up. Last she saw of him, he was off to meet me at Lodmoor Country Park.'

'And he didn't show?'

'I wasn't even there. Never was. Someone phoned the station pretending to be me, asking him to meet me there so we could see Juniper before Christmas.' A hairline crack appeared in Liam's voice, as if he were a pot that hadn't survived firing.

Edie froze in place. Fezziwig, on the chair next to her, looked up to see why her hand had stopped its stroking.

'So, he was tricked. And possibly kidnapped.'

Neither spoke for a moment.

'What are we going to do?' Liam sounded small, defeated.

'Well, we have to find him, don't we?'

'We?' he said, perfect eyebrows raised.

'Fuck, yeah. Come on.'

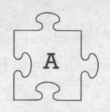

Forty-Seven

Ama Phillips was already in Lodmoor Country Park car park when Edie and Liam arrived. She was talking to a man in a rustly onesie, who was standing by a bent bollard. Sean's car was parked on the other side. Not that you could see it now in the driving snow.

Edie strode towards them, snow biting at her cheeks. 'So, what do we know, then?'

The onesie man looked at her in confusion. 'I'm Scene of Crime Officer Mark Ulver. I'm afraid I don't know your rank, ma'am.'

'This is Edie O'Sullivan,' Ama said. 'Sean's great-aunt, and his mum.'

Ulver looked away, embarrassed. 'Sorry, I thought you were a commissioner I hadn't met or something.'

'She's definitely something.' Liam was now standing next to Edie.

'Liam!' A big-haired woman in a crime scene onesie bounded in and hugged Edie's kinda son-in-law.

'Helena, this is Edie, Sean's—'

'Oh, no introduction needed.'

'Don't tell me,' Edie said. 'I taught you and I was a terrible teacher.'

Helena's laugh carried across the car park. She put her hand over her mouth, remembering why they were there. 'I'm so sorry. About Sean.'

'Don't say it like he's dead. We don't know what's happened to him yet.' Edie softened her voice. 'Look, Sean will kill me for doing this when I find him, but I'm going to be a fucking pain unless you accept my help, and give me yours.'

'I'm not sure . . .' Ama said, looking to Helena for guidance.

'It's your call,' Helena said, 'but I think we should do everything we can to find him. I don't want to know specifics, that's all. If I'm asked by Leyland, I'll say I haven't seen you. And *I* will tell *Ama* that it looks from the gravel marks, at least those which could be seen under the snow, as well as the impact on this bollard and Sean's rucksack being found nearby, that there was, if not a chase, then a collision. But I didn't tell *you* that, Edie.'

'Any idea what car it was?'

Helena pointed to a piece of metal on the ground by the bollard. 'A fender came off, and from a quick search, it's from a black Ford.'

'Get Michaels to look into that,' Edie said to Ama. 'I need you to come to my house. It's time I showed you something.'

Ama hesitated for a moment, then nodded and walked a few metres away to contact Michaels.

'It's good to see you bossing other people around, not just me and Sean,' Liam said.

'Is that a dig or a compliment?'

'Take it as the latter, for the sake of the truce.'

Ama came back, worry etched on her face. 'Michaels just told me a body's been found in Godlingston Woods, in a piece of rolled-up carpet.'

'Not Sean, please, not Sean.' Edie gripped Liam's arm. He grabbed her hand and squeezed it tightly.

'No, it looks to be a man called Linus Cramer, the owner-manager of a furniture warehouse company that also sells carpets. He was found below where the hoodie was hung, so it's unlikely to be a coincidence. Michaels is off there now with the DCI and has asked if you'll go immediately, Helena.'

Helena was already stepping out of her onesie.

'And we,' Ama said to Edie, 'need to find Sean and—'

'Prevent the last corner death.'

No amount of scrubbing would get the day or night off the killer's hands or mind. They could still hear Linus Cramer's last breath, as well as Sean's asthmatic gasps and cries of pain when he'd slid down the stone steps into the dark. These were ghosts that could not be dispersed with soap and water.

And yet here the killer was at work – filing, whistling, drinking tea. Pretending everything was normal. Things hadn't been normal in twenty-odd years, maybe more. Maybe they never had been, and all this effort had been for nothing.

They would never not be a murderer now. Wherever

they looked, it would be through a killer's eyes; whoever they loved, it would be with an assassin's heart. The killer had spent so long thinking about how to carry out their plan, but they'd never given any thought to what to do afterwards. Life would be a masque of death. They didn't think they could bear it.

And still they hadn't finished. Now that the detective inspector had been captured, and the bait set for the final pièce de résistance, there was only one more death to achieve.

But what if it wasn't the one originally intended? What if they went *off piece*?

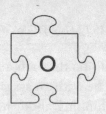

Forty-Eight

Ama stared at the investigation wall. 'You concealed all this evidence? All the jigsaw pieces and messages?'

Edie nodded blithely. She found Ama's shock to be at once sweet and concerning. Imagine getting into your twenties with that level of naivety. Edie almost envied it.

Ama continued. 'This is . . . impressive. It's a crime scene in itself, but impressive all the same.'

'When we've found Sean and caught the killer, you can lock me up, do whatever. But you need my brain to solve the puzzles the killer sent. Right?'

Ama nodded. 'Deal.'

Edie took the jigsaw piece with the watch on out of her pocket. The edges had been smoothed by her constantly turning it in her hand. 'This was in the original box. I didn't show it to Sean or anyone else. It's Sean's watch, and yes, I know that for sure. I gave it to him.'

Liam moved forward to take a look. 'It's true. That's Sean's.' He took out his phone and swiped to a photo of Sean wearing the watch.

Edie felt a pang. She missed him so much.

'In the jigsaw, though,' Ama said, 'the glass has been

broken, stuck at half eleven. Is that just before lunchtime? Or is it midnight, the deadline on the first card?'

Edie wondered if Ama too was regretting her use of the word 'dead'.

'Right,' she said. If her sleeves weren't so tight, with only enough room for a wodge of hankies, she'd roll them up to state that she meant business. 'Give me everything you know. Throw it all at me like snowballs. I can take it.'

'Where do I start?'

'First, I need to know what information you have about Carl Latimer being killed in his home, what the neighbours said etc.'

They all sat down round the dining table and Edie was surprised by how comforted she was at having people in her house. Ama opened her notebook and Edie nodded in approval at the clear, neat handwriting – perfect for filling out a crossword, unlike Mrs Challis' hand.

Reading from her notes, Ama described her interview with a tearful Mrs Bleniou. She had found Carl Latimer's body and phoned for an ambulance. She had also pleaded with Ama to take a moussaka with her. Not many neighbours had been in, and, of those who were, only one had been looking out of the window. He had seen a large black car park up, and another neighbour had let a delivery driver into the building.'

'Any description of the driver?'

'Just that they were wearing a baseball hat, hoodie and face mask. The neighbour was busy on the phone so didn't speak to them. Couldn't even say if it was a man or a woman.'

'People don't look at deliverers as real people,' Edie said. 'If they see them at all. They're like older women. What else?'

Ama flicked through to the next page in her notebook. 'I've been digging through Carl Latimer's hard drive with IT and I think that Lucy Pringle may have been one of his victims. I thought I recognised a picture of her sleeping, naked, so I compared the image to her St Mary's photo, and I believe it's her. She would have been around fifteen.'

'No,' Liam said, distraught. 'That's awful.'

'There are other photos of him touching her while she's asleep. It gives her a motive, and makes her connection to the case even stronger,' Ama said.

'But is it enough to kill?' Edie asked.

'One kind of revenge for another?' Liam suggested.

'There's also footage,' Ama continued, 'of Veronica Princeton and Carl Latimer having sex in the woods. It appears to be consensual, but she may not have agreed to him uploading the videos.'

'Did Dr Newman know about Carl and Veronica?' Liam asked.

'We don't know. But, possibly connected to this, there's another, potentially stronger, lead,' Ama said. 'Sean asked me to re-interview Dr Newman, given his lack of an alibi and the CCTV sighting of him in town on the night his wife died. But he's missing.'

'In what way?' Liam asked.

'He hasn't been seen near his house or at work for twenty-four hours.'

'What kind of car does he have?' Edie asked.

Ama checked her notes. 'A black sedan. Reasonably new.'

'He could have Sean in it right now.' Liam stood and paced the room.

'It's a possibility. We're searching ANPR, but it's important that you leave that to us. We need you to concentrate on ways you *can* help.'

'So, we stick to the jigsaw pieces,' Liam said. 'Edie's skills are in that area, after all.'

'How many pieces were left at Latimer's crime scene?' Edie asked Ama.

'Five. Four are the same as yours, but you had one extra, and so did we.' Ama flicked through her phone to find pictures of the jigsaw pieces. The unseen piece was a white tile with a gold goblet on it. 'Have you got any other leads?'

Edie felt strangely shy. 'I keep coming back to "beaten corset" being an anagram of "Beacon Street", and the symbol suggesting something medical. Someone at Beacon Street Medical Centre, maybe?'

Ama stepped out of the room to phone the medical centre, leaving Liam and Edie in silence.

'He'll be furious with you,' Liam said, at last. 'The one thing he can't stand is people keeping things from him.' He stared off into space as if he was stowing secrets of his own. 'I have to slope off in the evening to go out drinking 'cos I don't want him to see how worried I am.'

'About the adoption?'

Liam nodded and cradled his head. 'What if I'm a terrible dad? What if I can't love her properly? What if I change my mind and it's too late?'

Edie had an unnerving urge to hug him. 'Most parents, or any kind of carers, feel like that before the baby or child arrives. It's the unknown. The unfilled-in answer on the square.'

'Is that how you felt? When you had to take on Sean?'

Edie thought back to the day she had lost most of her relatives, yet gained a family. 'I was terrified. But the love I had for him made my heart coal. It gave me fire to cope. The same will happen for you two and Juniper.'

Liam smiled, then his face creased into worry again. 'Only Sean might not be here, and, even if he is, Sunny, her social worker, is already concerned about the danger he faces in his job. This could affect the whole adoption.'

Edie stood and put an arm round Liam's big shoulders. He started to sob, and she held him tighter.

'You're not very good at cuddles, are you, Aunt Edie?' Liam said, laughing and crying at the same time.

'Fuck off, Liam,' Edie replied, hugging him to her.

'We'll find him, won't we?' Liam sounded like a little boy. And he was. Not even forty, practically a baby. And why would she be so tough on a baby?

'We will, I promise,' Edie said.

Ama walked back into the room, her face flushed. 'The medical centre is sending me a full staff and patient list, but I asked about a few key players in the case, and I got some results.' She looked expectantly at Liam and Edie.

'Well, come on then,' they said together.

'Lesley Maupert was a nurse there until a couple of years ago when she was sacked for stealing opiates. Dr Berkeley was a patient, and so was his family: his wife until her death, and their daughter Bridget until she left home. Berkeley left the clinic last year, but the centre does have two current patients who are of interest: Lucy Pringle and Mrs Challis.'

Edie stood. 'We need to go to two Christmas parties.'

'Who are you?' Liam asked. 'And what have you done with our Aunt Edie?'

'Tonight we'll ask Lucy what she's up to, but first, a lunch do.' She pointed to the jigsaw piece that Ama had just shown her. 'What if that's not a goblet, but a Challis?'

Forty-Nine

St Mary's School was dark, apart from the central block containing the school hall and staff area. The party was visible through the long window on the other side of reception. Teachers were milling about, drinks in hands, but there was no sign of the headmaster.

From outside, the tableau showed mouths opening and closing, clown-wide laughs and frowns. Edie had the urge to paint it as Toulouse Lautrec would Montmartre.

'Leave the talking to me,' Ama said. 'Sandra Challis has an alibi and no motive, so we're looking for a clue that she could give us.'

'I assume Dr Berkeley is her alibi, and she's his?' Edie asked, delighted.

Ama nodded.

'I knew it! Well done, Sandra!'

'Even with an alibi,' Liam said, 'they could still have paid someone else to kill and kidnap.'

'Well, that's sunny as fuck, Liam.'

'Sunny!' Liam said, taking out his phone. 'I should tell her what's happening, and our social worker, too.'

'Isn't she worried about Sean being in danger? This could stop the adoption.'

'She also wants us to be honest. And she'll find out anyway. This is Weymouth.'

Leaving Liam to talk to the social workers, Edie and Ama walked into the party.

'Edie!' Sandra Challis ran over to them. She was wearing a flowing dress with a holly-leaf print. It looked like the holly leaves in the jigsaw.

'I like your dress, Sandra. Seasonal but spiky.'

Sandra curtsied. Her cheeks were berry red. She'd started the party early, perhaps. 'I'm so glad you came.'

'I've never been more flattered to be asked.'

Mrs Challis looked like she'd found a pound coin in a plum pudding and managed not to swallow it.

'This is DC Phillips.'

Mrs Challis' ingratiating smile dropped. 'I'm not sure police presence is appropriate for a staff party. No one will let their hair down.'

Edie and Ama looked at Sandra's hair. There was no way that hairsprayed helmet could ever be let down. 'My nephew, stroke son, stroke reason for wanting to be at this party, has been kidnapped, Sandra. It's a puzzle we have to solve. And you could help us.'

Mrs Challis' mouth dropped open, then she nodded. 'Let me get you a drink first. A good one, not the rubbish I bought the teachers.'

When she'd hurried off, Edie asked Ama, 'What should we be looking for?'

'If she is involved, we need to build a solid case, beyond circumstantial evidence; otherwise, as Sean always says, lawyers make ravines where fractures hide.'

Edie had heard Sean say the same thing about relationships. She thought of him trapped somewhere, maybe hurt and alone. Wearing his watch. Lying on black and white tiles. But where?

She needed a distraction, so she picked up a plate at the buffet table and began loading it with prawn sandwiches, smoked salmon and cream cheese rolls and chicken drumsticks.

Liam appeared, stared at her plate, and shook his head. 'How can you eat when Sean's missing?'

'If we're going to find him, we need resources, including food. Anyway, take some advice from a woman who's seen it all. Always take advantage of a buffet table. And go for the protein, get your money's worth.'

'But you didn't pay for it.' Ama was missing her deflection, and her point.

'Berkeley did, though. And I don't mind eating his money if it's tasty.'

Sandra Challis came over with their drinks, then went off again to find Dr Berkeley. Edie was about to make an excuse to go with her when she heard a voice over her shoulder.

'I didn't know you were coming, Edie!' It was Lucy Pringle, wearing a Santa hat and a sparkly, red-nosed Rudolph jumper with the message, *Merry Christmas, Deer!* 'It's the time of year when I go to several parties a day, including my own! Although,' Lucy leaned in, whispering, 'I will have much more of a spread. I'm off to Marks after this to pick up the bits and pieces I ordered.'

'Good to see you, Lucy.' Edie wasn't even lying. Because

THE CHRISTMAS JIGSAW MURDERS

this meant she could corner Lucy here and not attend her terrible party and eat her spread.

The bobble on Lucy's hat flashed, because of course it did. 'I'm amazed the mighty Mrs Challis let you in. I'm Chair of the Parent Governors and even I felt I had to slip past her reception desk without her seeing me!'

Edie took a bite of chicken. 'Sandra is a personal friend of mine.' She wiggled her eyebrows suggestively. 'We cross words together.'

Lucy faltered for a moment, then carried on. 'I know Liam, of course. But who's your other "friend"?' Lucy said 'friend' in a way that managed to be suggestive yet not suggest anything of any kind, other than prurience and prejudice. 'I think I recognise her.'

'This is DC Ama Phillips.'

Lucy didn't respond for a moment. A look of concern crinkled her face, and she necked the bad wine. 'I'll leave you to it, then. I've had enough of the police.'

Edie looked at Lucy, hard. She could in no way imagine that Lucy would be involved in either murder or kidnap. Yet she was part of the jigsaw. 'We'd like to talk to you, though.' Edie looked around the room, and pulled a reluctant Lucy into a corner, next to the trophy cabinet.

'My Sean has been, we think, kidnapped. Do you recognise these tiles?' Edie showed her a picture of one of the jigsaw pieces patterned with black and white squares.

'They're a bit like a place we went to in Scarborough,' Lucy said, squinting. 'And maybe the Ritz, although I only saw that on the telly.'

Edie turned away in case she screamed in Lucy's face, 'HELP ME!'.

'We also have some further concerns about your involvement with a case we're working on,' Ama said, taking over.

Lucy immediately started to sulk. 'I've already admitted to the messages.'

'We've discovered that you may have been a victim of Carl Latimer.' Ama's voice became so gentle that Edie felt strangely moved.

Lucy's eyes skittered about the room, filling with tears. 'How did you know?'

'We're looking into a number of complaints about him, historic and otherwise.'

'It won't be made public, will it?' Lucy looked so small and scared.

Edie stepped in. 'Absolutely not. That bastard will be investigated, but none of his survivors will be known. Isn't that right, DC Phillips?'

Ama nodded. 'We don't even need to take you to the station. There's a separate unit we use for more sensitive enquiries.'

Just then the headmaster walked into the staff room and a hush descended.

'Would you come with us?' Ama asked Lucy. 'Once we've finished here?'

Lucy looked over at the headmaster, then nodded. 'Once we're finished here, yes.'

Dr Berkeley came over to the buffet table, holding a large Christmas cake. Carefully, he placed it in the centre.

The Christmas cake was cloaked in white royal icing and topped with what looked like a Nativity scene.

The headmaster glanced over and saw Edie with Ama, Liam and Lucy. Closing his eyes, he murmured something under his breath, finishing with, 'Amen'.

Then, picking up a champagne flute in one hand, he tapped a cake knife against it.

'Thank you all so much for coming,' Dr Berkeley began. 'Not that I gave you a choice.' He paused for laughter. Mrs Challis obliged. 'I know you all want to be with your families at Christmas, as do I. There is nothing more I want to do than go home to them, and soon I'll let you go, or go off into the night together. I believe a group curry has been suggested. Don't worry, I won't be attending, so you can all relax without the boss watching. Now, though, I'd like to celebrate with you another way. This is my last Christmas at St Mary's, and in fact my last Christmas in Weymouth.'

Edie watched closely as the teachers turned to each other. Some looked shocked, some sad, others downright over-joyed. Many covered their reactions with their wine glasses.

Mrs Challis, though, was standing in the middle of the room, staring at Berkeley with wide eyes, her mouth open.

'This will come as a surprise to you all. Please, consider this my notice, parent governors. It has been a privilege to lead St Mary's these past years; the school has been like a family to me, and I will treasure the memories from now till my dying day.' He cut a slice of Christmas cake and raised it up, along with his charged glass. 'To families! The eternal bond.'

Others in the room also lifted their glasses, but no one joined in the toast. Everyone looked at each other, confused.

Then Berkeley took a big bite of cake and drained his glass. He closed his eyes. 'Delicious.'

Sandra hurried over, reaching for his hand.

Berkeley began to gasp for breath, holding his chest. Knocking the cake off the table, he fell to the floor, fitting and foaming at the mouth.

Ama shoved her phone into Edie's hand – it was already ringing 999 – then rushed to the headmaster. She checked his pulse and his breathing, then began chest compressions. His lungs expanded as she blew into his mouth, but his eyes were fixed on the snow-lined window.

A call handler answered.

'I need an ambulance at St Mary's School, Weymouth,' Edie shouted. 'A man is in respiratory failure.'

She looked up to see a crowd of educators standing around them, not knowing what to do. A few were even filming on their phones. Sometimes, people were worse than even Edie expected.

'Sending a quick response team now,' the call handler said. 'Please stay on the line and give me any information you have.'

'My name is Edie O'Sullivan and the headmaster, Edward Berkeley, is dying. He had some kind of fit and was frothing at the mouth.'

'Any signs of the cause?'

Edie made her way over to examine the buffet table, concentrating on Berkeley's champagne flute and cake remnants. Both smelled strongly of marzipan. 'It could be cyanide poisoning.'

Backing away from the smell, she stepped on something hard. The figures from the Christmas cake Nativity scene were scattered on the floor. Made of hand-cast pottery and delicately painted, the features had been sculpted with artistic finesse, but they weren't of Mary, Joseph and the baby Jesus. They showed a woman with long blonde hair, a tall man that looked just like Dr Berkeley and a young girl, three or four years old, holding both their hands.

She turned over one of the figures. On its base were the initials B.B.

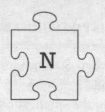

Fifty

Sean rose with reluctance to the surface, fear not allowing him to sleep any longer. He was lying on a hard floor, shivering in his tarpaulin cocoon, but he didn't know if it was because of the cold or the adrenaline that was screaming at him to RUN. He wished he could.

He tried to move, but not only was he tied up more tightly than he'd been before, the ropes cutting into his wrists, ankles and middle, but his leg, back and hip were agony. White-hot pain seared through him. If his leg was broken, and he suspected it might be, it would make escaping impossible.

The blindfold had slipped down, but it didn't make any difference. All he could see was thick darkness. He couldn't tell how long he'd been unconscious, or if it was day or night, Christmas Eve or Christmas Day.

It was as cold as if he were outside in the snow, yet he was inside. From the echoing sound when the tarpaulin rustled, he was in a large space with low ceilings. The air was spored with black mould. Something dripped, a few metres away.

A sound came from outside. Footsteps walked as if on shingle. Someone laughed. They seemed to be at street level, and he was below. In a cellar or a basement.

He tried to call out, but his tongue felt like carpet, and the sound stayed stuck behind his teeth. Tape covered his lips. It made him think of when he was away at college and Edie used to send him money in envelopes for his birthday, advertising the precious contents by sellotaping every inch of the flap.

If Edie were here now, she'd go into hyperdrive and sort this shit out. He'd seen her do it in crises. She went into a state of calm where she saw everything and did what was needed without fuss or even her usual spiky defence mechanisms.

And she would launch herself at his captor without even thinking of her own safety. But how would she know where he was?

At that moment, he heard something directly above him. It was muffled, and hard to make out, but it sounded like shouting. He realised then, in the dampening under-ground quiet, that there was a sound missing; something that, like Edie, was always there in the background. There was no delicate ticking. His watch had been taken, but he had no idea why.

Sean sobbed. He might no longer be blindfolded, but he was still in the dark.

'I don't understand.' Edie watched as Dr Berkeley's body was taken away in a private ambulance. In the distance, the sea held an orange tint. 'He wasn't alluded to in the clues as the fourth victim.'

'He used to go to the medical centre,' Liam offered.

'That's not enough. It shouldn't be him; it doesn't *feel* right. As a puzzle, it doesn't fit – it's like cramming an eight-letter word into a four-letter clue.'

They were standing outside St Mary's with the other attendees of the worst staff Christmas party in history. They'd already been here for over an hour, waiting for the initial investigations of the crime scene to conclude. Inside, SOCOs were doing their grisly thing, though not Helena – she must still be in the woods – while outside, a team of PCs were taking statements. Della Ingrit, of course, was already here, trying to interview staff members and parent governors. She had just talked to Lucy Pringle, who had returned to her mobile phone, and was now zeroing in on Sandra Challis. Sandra was sitting, rocking, on the cold ground, her dress soaked. Nobody, not even Edie, had been able to get her to stand up, so Edie had persuaded several people to give up their pashminas to wrap her up warmly.

All Sandra would say was, 'Why?'

Della Ingrit crouched down next to her, notepad in hand.

'Piss off home, Della,' Edie shouted over to her.

A few teachers shook their head at her in disgust.

'And you can fuck off as well.'

'That's not helping, Edie,' Liam said, quietly.

'It's helping *me*.'

It was getting dark again. Edie was glad of it for once. Shadows hid tears. Sean had been missing for almost twenty-four hours, but at least his body hadn't been found.

Ama trudged out of the double front doors, hair tumbling out of its band. She scraped it back and took a swig of water. 'My dad said I'd find being a detective hard, and I laughed it off. Until now.'

'Your dad'll be proud when you tell him what you've done,' Liam said. Edie thought, for the first time, what a good dad he would be.

Ama's laugh was sad and sardonic. 'He won't get the chance.'

'What's going on in there?' Edie asked, to change the subject. 'What have you found?'

Ama looked over to the other side of the car park where DCI Leyland was prowling.

Edie met her eye. 'Cone of silence, we never knew.'

'The overview is that he killed himself. There was a suicide note on his desk, along with a key. The key didn't fit either the school safe or the one in his office, so we'll be checking his house next. 'When he was examined, Berkeley had a corner jigsaw piece in his pocket, with his name written on it, in his own handwriting. No picture, clearly done on the fly, and not part of the set that you've been receiving.'

'Anything that points to where Sean is?' Liam asked.

'Nothing. I'm so sorry. But we're still looking.'

'What did the note say?' Edie asked.

'Just, "I'm sorry. I gave it all I had. Please, now, let it all stop. Let me be the piece that brings peace."'

'Stop what? The murders?' Liam asked.

'Presumably, yes – I think Dr Berkeley's now top of our suspect list.'

'But who is the intended recipient?' Edie mused.

'None of this helps us with Sean.' Liam started pacing. He was vibrating with anxiety and the need to do *something*. Edie understood completely.

'When can we leave?' she asked Ama. 'I need to regroup. Look at the clues and see what I'm missing.'

'You two can't be thinking of going home. Get yourselves to the station,' Ama told Edie and Liam. 'You'll each need to give a full statement and it'll be far safer than trying to find Sean.'

'We've already given a mini statement to one of your boring mates.' Edie pointed to one of the PCs. 'And I'll be safest at home.'

'Safer than in a police station?' Liam asked. 'I think Sean would rather you went. I can drop you off on the way.'

'To be honest,' Edie said, yawning, 'I need to go to bed. I can hardly keep my eyes open. Wait, what do you mean on the way? Where are you going?'

Even in the twilight, Edie could see Liam blushing. 'I'm going to all our usual places, me and Sean's, to see if he's at any of them. After all, it's only the rucksack that really makes us think he's been taken.' There was a wild glaze to his eyes, an unreality.

'His car was there, Liam. With the key in the ignition. Plus, there's the threat to his life that came through my door. You're running away from reality, and I understand why. I've done it for years. But it won't bring Sean home.'

In that moment, Edie realised with a punched-heart finality that she was never getting Sky back.

'Whatever you do, just stay safe,' Ama said.

'What about you?' Edie asked.

'I'll finish up here, take Lucy Pringle for her interview about Carl Latimer, and then I'll see if I can get anything out of Mrs Challis. I can also trawl CCTV for anything to do with what happened to Sean. I'm known for picking up on small details. Like you, Edie.'

'Talking of which, the figures on the Christmas cake looked handmade, and they seemed to be of the Berkeleys, including their little girl. As if they were frozen in time decades ago.'

'What about it?' Ama's tired sigh said she'd had enough.

'They have the initials B.B. on the bottom, and I wondered if they could have been made by the daughter – wasn't she called Bridget?'

'Even if she did make them,' Ama said, 'she could have sent them to him from Yorkshire, or made them years ago. My dad used to put the same stupid decorations on his Christmas cake every year.'

'It's just, with what Berkeley said about family bonds . . .'

'I'll look into it. Now, go home. I'll catch up with both of you tomorrow. And tell me immediately if you find anything new.'

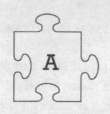

Fifty-One

'Please stay the night,' Edie said, as Liam dropped her at home. 'If I have to play the vulnerable old lady card, I will, but I'd rather you chose to stay. It makes sense. We should be together. Keep each other company.'

Liam's smile was blink quick. 'You've changed your tune.'

Across the road, Lucy's house was in darkness. The lack of a flashing Santa was unnerving. Edie might even miss him. She'd even miss being angry at the noise now that there was clearly to be no party at the Pringles' tonight.

'I never change my tune,' she said. 'I've simply put it in a different key. Now, do as your utterly exhausted Auntie Edie says and get inside.' The strange thing was, Edie really did feel a pull for him to stay.

Liam, though, shook his head. 'I can't, not while he's out there. I'll wear out your carpet through pacing or just start screaming.'

Edie felt drowned at being turned down. Rage burned to cover her shame. 'I reach out to you, and this is what I get.'

'I need to self-regulate, otherwise I won't be able to function.' Liam tried to touch her arm.

Edie pulled away. 'I was right in the first place. What

use will you be as a dad if you can't stay put when things turn to shit?'

'That's not fair.'

She couldn't stop etching hurt on Liam's face. 'But accurate.' Edie got out of the car and slammed the door, but her stomach lurched with loss as Liam drove away.

'It's been a hard day for both of you. He'll forgive you.' Riga was stirring a night-time tisane. Even paler than usual, she looked like she needed the potion more than Edie.

They were in the garden room. Outside, the garden itself was lit with hundreds of Christmas lights. Not long ago, Edie would have found them garish, but now she found them soothing. They reminded her of Sean.

Riga strained the tisane, stirred in honey, added more brandy, and presented it in a lidded cup for Edie. 'Take this home. It'll help you sleep, and you need your rest.'

They sat in their armchairs, crocheted blankets on their laps. 'Don't talk to me about "rest". Rest In Pieces has disturbed me enough. And I can't sleep, not while Sean's missing. Tell me about cyanide.'

'I really don't recommend taking that for insomnia. The sleep it would give you would be permanent.' Riga was smiling.

Edie was in no mood for their usual jokes. 'From the smell of almonds, and Dr Berkeley's physiological reaction, I'm assuming that he died via cyanide.'

'He must have been in such pain, even before he ate the marzipan.'

'How do you know all the details?'

'WhatsApp strikes again.'

Edie remembered Lucy Pringle sitting on the school steps, tapping at her phone. Receiving the glory of delivering gossip. 'Maybe he deserved the pain.'

'No one deserves that.'

'Let's argue this philosophical point another time. You must know about making it, through your herbalism stuff.'

'Why do you need to know?'

Edie's irritation was building again. Riga wasn't usually this slow to follow her thoughts. 'Look, I think the headmaster was the killer, and he decided to stop the jigsaw "game" before it was finished. There are still at least fifteen pieces missing. If the MO remained the same, after the death of someone else tonight, possibly from Beacon Street Medical Centre, I'd have been sent the remaining pieces, and then it would have been a race until midnight to find my baby. But if R.I.P. is dead, and I wish him anything but rest or peace, then Sean is out there alone, with no indication of where he's being held. *Any* information I have might help.'

'Okay, okay. I have several cherry trees and must ensure that no animals eat the pits or leaves as they could crunch through and release the prussic acid that makes cyanide so dangerous. I had to force-feed Nicholas activated charcoal on the way to the vet's once after he'd chomped on several pits.'

Nicholas the pug harrumphed on his chair.

'That doesn't help. I need you to inspire me, Riga.'

'I think you don't need me at all.'

Edie reared back in her chair. 'What do you mean?' She needed Riga so much she couldn't bear it.

'From R.I.P.'s notes, it seems you already have everything you need.' Riga stared at Edie with none of her usual sparkle.

'What are you talking about?'

'Right from the first Christmas card, they mention you being good at keeping "secrets", and cheating. I think R.I.P. was trying to get something out of you.'

Fear ricocheted through Edie, turning swiftly into anger. 'Are you saying Sean's disappearance is down to me? That it's my fault he's been taken?'

'No. But I think *you* think that.'

'Why are you turning on me?'

Riga's long exhale of frustration turned into a nasty cough. 'I'm trying to help. That what I'm always trying to do. But you don't listen.'

Edie thought of her conversation with Sky. She stood up, still clutching the tisane. 'Maybe that's because nobody is worth listening to. Including you.'

Riga looked away, sharp cheeks fairy-lit. 'Then I think you should go.'

Fifty-Two

December 24th – Christmas Eve

Somewhere nearby, church bells tolled twelve. Sean hoped it was Christmas Eve, but he had lost all sense of time. Christmas Eve was his favourite day of the year, though, so even if it wasn't, he'd pretend it was. Usually, he'd see in the early hours with a viewing of *The Muppet Christmas Carol*, singing along to every word. Then he'd drink mulled cider while wrapping up presents and making his way through a pile of mince pies. Tonight, however, he was just hoping not to die.

He tried to make sense of everything that had happened. Why would someone want to test and punish Edie? What had she done?

He knew that his aunt was no angel. She had hurt many throughout her life. Her all too often harsh truths had driven people away. Except him. Yes, she was cantankerous and swore too much and generally threw two fingers up at the world, but she was ferociously loving when she allowed herself to be, and he knew that it hadn't been easy for her, taking on a baby. But she'd done it, and his childhood – even without being able to celebrate Christmas properly – had been filled with love, laughter and puzzles. She had been with him for every birthday, parents' evening, judo tournament. She'd given him his first Doc Martens, his first Westwood. Held his hand when his heart had been broken, taken him to museums and shows. Advised him on the best gay bars and worst brands of poppers. She had always been there.

Apart from at Christmas. She'd always disappear from Christmas Eve through to Boxing Day, but when she re-emerged, she'd hand him a new jigsaw and a crossword she'd made just for him.

He knew why, of course. All those people leaving her, one way or another, at Christmas time. It was more than enough of a reason for a life to crack into pieces. And to hate Christmas.

When Sky had been with her, Edie had been better. One year, when they'd been particularly happy, she'd even let him have a lit-up tree and read *A Christmas Carol* to him. Admittedly, the tree was kept in the garden, and Edie had criticised Scrooge's character arc mercilessly, but it had felt more like the Christmases he longed for.

Even now, down here, he loved this time of year. If it was Christmas Eve, he had to hope that he'd get home. He remembered the opening scene of *A Christmas Carol* and recited the first line: 'Marley was dead, to begin with.' That wouldn't be him. He had to stay awake. He was so cold, and the pain in his head so bad, that if he slipped into unconsciousness again, he feared there'd be only one more sleep till death.

Edie's dreams were tinctured with death. Her own death. Strangers'. Sky's. Sean's. Riga's.

She woke herself by shouting, 'No!'

Turning on the bedside light, she checked her clock. Four in the morning on Christmas Eve. The very worst day of the year. At least she was in her own bed. Though Sean was not in his. He might never be again. All those years that she had tucked him up, kept him safe, only for this to happen. Now she'd lost him as well as everyone else.

Peggoty, Fezziwig and Mr Bumble blinked at her, then settled back down, curling into their corners of the bed. She tried to drown her pain by following them back into a velvet-lined sleep.

In the morning, Edie didn't get up to make herself a pot of tea. She didn't answer the door or the phone. Like every other Christmas Eve since Anthony had died, she ignored the world, but this time she didn't want to read or do puzzles or watch a DVD. All she could think about was Sean, lost, and his captor, dead.

Every second that she stayed here ticked away Sean's life, but her own internal workings had gone still. She couldn't solve anything, and she should never have tried to. She had kept the pieces back because she thought she was protecting her son. And she had lost him anyway.

Both she and Riga were right. It *was* her fault.

And now she'd managed to push away Riga and Liam as well, allies she realised she loved more than she'd known. What else didn't she know?

The light peeking round the curtains was already edged with orange. She thought of how many times Sean had begged for a 'proper Christmas', with an inside tree, fairy lights, stockings, turkey, tinsel, the lot, and she'd said 'no'. Any concessions she'd made had been minor, and only during Sky's time. She'd deprived her child because of her own Santa sack of baggage, and for what? She could have given him joy; instead she'd effectively gifted him death, wrapped up in a blood-red bow.

Maybe she too should pound cherry pits into paste and die.

R.I.P. Edie.

Downstairs, there was a knock on the front door. Her letterbox opened and clanked shut.

Edie almost ignored it, but couldn't quite bring herself to. Anyway, she had to top up the cats' bowls. She groaned out of bed and pulled on her dressing gown. The cats followed, knowing there were treats in her pockets.

An envelope rested on the YOU ARE NOT WELCOME mat. An R.I.P.-signature envelope.

Fifty-Three

R.I.P.'s latest charity card was the same as the others –
cheap and holly-covered.

```
Ms O'Sullivan (and you always insisted
on Ms, didn't you?),
  This is my last Christmas missive to
you before we meet. And we shall meet,
soon. If you want Sean to survive,
rearrange St Mary's memories and, in a
lone cameo, let your lips speak the
truth of who is at fault. You'll have
to remember it all: discover dug earth,
and revise the end word. No moths
depart in the sea.
  Then we can rest at last,
  Rest In Pieces
```

This time, Edie called Ama straight away.
'You didn't see who delivered it?' Ama asked.
'Do you always see who comes to your door?'
'Well, yes, but then I have a SmartFlat and a door camera
that goes to an app. I see everyone who arrives, and I can

choose who to buzz in. Sean saw it on my phone, and I think he might have suggested it to you?'

'More advice I should have listened to.'

'Not that it matters, probably. It could have been a pre-paid courier, which Dr Berkeley arranged before he killed himself. I'll check local courier services – they may be able to come up with a sender. Fill in some of the missing pieces of the case.'

'Has it been confirmed that Berkeley was the killer?'

'The safe in his study—'

Dusty.

'—contained a sack with a blood-stained hammer, a blood-caked tool used for carpet fitting, muddy boots which will probably match the earth from the woods, stained white gloves consistent with the fibres found on Veronica Princeton, four empty bottles of homemade cyanide . . . He's been very thorough; there's no real doubt.'

'Meticulous,' Edie said. *Meticulous = Omit us clue.* 'What about Sandra Challis?'

'The poor woman's in shock. He'd convinced her to lie about his staying with her on those nights, but it looks like she had no idea what he'd been up to, or what he had planned at the Christmas party.'

'But why would he kill them? He seemed to love Veronica Princeton.'

'We're thinking that jealousy was the motivation for Veronica and Carl – he couldn't stand to see them together. And, it turns out, Lorelei Berkeley was employed by Linus Cramer as his accountant.'

'No!'

'I've taken several statements from Cramer's employees attesting to dubious behaviour, both towards female staff and in his business practices. Now that he's dead, I think they're less likely to want his failings swept under the carpet, as it were.'

'What kind of behaviour?'

'The official story, told by Cramer to anyone who would listen, apparently, was that Lorelei stole money from the parent company, siphoning off tens of thousands each year into an offshore bank account. Somebody reported the missing money to HMRC, who brought in a forensic accountant, but the cash couldn't be traced. With no hard evidence against her, she couldn't be charged, but she could be sacked, and her reputation ruined.'

'And what's the unofficial story?'

'Lorelei uncovered Cramer's own dodgy tax trail and confronted him. And then the embezzlement charge was thrown at her. She never recovered, and killed herself not long after.'

There was something that didn't quite fit in all this, but Edie couldn't feel which piece it was.

'I also contacted Bridget Berkeley to tell her about her father. Poor thing, she couldn't stop crying. I managed to get out of her that she made the figures on the Christmas cake years ago.'

'Just as you thought, then. And Dr Newman? How does he fit into it?'

'He's still AWOL but . . .' Ama paused.

'Go on.'

'Current thinking is that Berkeley and Newman teamed up. And while Berkeley may have killed them all, Newman is the puzzler behind it. And he's still at large.'

An icy chill threaded its way down Edie's neck. It made sense for there to be two people behind the murders. She tried to ignore her own fear. 'Talking of which, there were more jigsaw pieces in the card. The centre of the puzzle is now complete.' Or at least it would be when she stuck the piece with Sean's watch on into place on the wall. She didn't want to move it from her pocket, though. It was as if completing the outline of the body made it more likely he would die. Edie hadn't known how superstitious she was.

'Do any of the pieces help us find Sean?' Ama asked.

'Not that I can tell. They're the same as the rest: shiny-as-new black and white tiles, thick chalk-like outline for the body, holly—'

'Surrounded by the sea. Yeah. Not much to go on.' Ama paused, and Edie could hear her tapping a pen against her notebook. 'So, it's down to you to solve the remaining clues.'

'No pressure.'

When Edie rang off, Mr Bumble lumbered over and leaned into her leg. He had a jigsaw piece stuck in his fur. She picked it out like a tick. It was the one with Sean's watch on it.

A sob rose to the surface. She'd let Sean down so badly, played everything wrong. Maybe it was time Edie prayed to that saint of fallen women everywhere, Mary Magdalene.

Something jolted inside her and she froze, overcome by the feeling that she knew something, just not quite what. It was when she thought of Mary, the apostle to the apostles. But why did that snag?

Edie read the last message over and over. It was alive with possible anagrams. It was clear in the construction – she often used 'rediscover', 'depart', 'revise' and 're-arrange' to suggest mixing up letters:

Rearranging 'St Mary's' could yield many different anagrams. *St Mary's = my stars. St Mary's = artsy ms. St Mary's = try mass. St Mary's = Ms Stray.*

So could 'dug earth'. *Dug earth = daughter. Dug earth = aged hurt. Dug earth = hate drug.*

Daughter. What had she said to herself so many times? You never stop seeing them as your child.

Then there was 'lone cameo' (*lone cameo = come alone; lone cameo = leone coma; lone cameo = ocean mole*), 'end word' (*end word = odd wren; end word = drowned; end word = red down*) and 'no moths' (*no moths = Thomson; no moths = so month*).

And the last phrase of the first message: 'you never were a good cheater'. *Cheater = hectare. Cheater = the care. Cheater = teacher.* It combined with the earlier message, the form tutor's classic phrase – '*it's your time you're wasting.*' On their own, they meant little. A load of nonsense; you can twist any pile of words to mean what you want. The problem, as Bishop Berkeley knew, was what to discard for things to fit together. And, as with all good puzzles, when a theme was applied, the message came through. Edie believed the theme was an event that she had weighted far down in her memory. One that haunted her, but she'd never wanted to dredge up.

Daughter. Drowned. Teacher. Try Mass. Come alone.

She looked at the front of the card with all its holly, and the back with its promise to donate ten per cent of money raised through sales to cancer charities. Each piece alone wasn't enough. But put them together and everything made a terrible sense.

Edie thought of Riga's unwanted advice from yesterday. She had to remember what she'd done wrong and confess.

But she'd weighted down the past for a reason. So much of her was screaming to run away, find anything else to distract her. *Distract her = cedar thirst.* But she couldn't be distracted, not anymore. She had to be in the presence of the past for Sean to have a future.

She let the memory swim up.

Flashbacks came in a torrent. It had been a month after Sky left. January afternoon gloom. Edie was standing on the beach, watching her class collect shells and driftwood from the shoreline to make art on the sand. Looking up, she saw Sky stride past on the promenade.

Edie had turned and followed Sky at a distance, keeping to the sand. She hadn't thought the kids would be in danger. Weymouth was in a bay, the sea gentle; barely a tide to trouble the town. When Sky turned off Esplanade and out of sight, Edie stayed still, staring. She didn't know how long for.

And then the shouts came. The screaming.

Edie ran back to a class now standing with winter waves

crashing over their sensible shoes. A girl in the school's characteristic red hat was in the sea, water up to her shoulders. She kept dipping into the waves and bobbing back up, gasping, 'I can't find her!' Another hat floated to the surface.

Edie waded in, hardly feeling the cold as the water soaked through her clothes.

'Who is it?' she asked, when she'd got to the girl.

'Holly Thomson,' she'd replied.

They'd looked for Holly, a student full of pizzazz and promise, for half an hour, joined by sea rescue services and lifeboats, but her body was never recovered. Edie knew that she too had never recovered.

The whole event was smoothed away, like the tide covering over 'HELP' written on the sand.

'It's in St Mary's best interests, and yours,' Mrs Singer, the headmistress, had said. 'You'll tell the police you were watching all the time and had told them to stay out of the sea.'

'I told all of them to not go beyond the water's edge, but I should have been there. One of them will have seen me leave.'

'The words of children can't be trusted,' Mrs Singer said. 'No one will believe what Holly's friends say.'

Edie couldn't at first remember the name of Holly's best friend, the girl who dove for her body. But now she was the one diving for memories, she could see her face; she had seen it in another context too, a few years later.

Edie came up from her reveries, breathless, lungs bursting with things she should have said. She had held all of this under the meniscus of her life for over twenty years. Told no one.

One of the messages said she must speak of her fault. Anything to do with the mouth or ear suggests a homonym or similar sounding or looking word. *Fault = vault*.

She looked again at the picture of the chalice, with the blood-red wine spilling out. Time to go further down into her memory vaults.

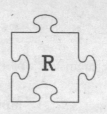

Fifty-Four

A queue was forming from the main doors of St Mary Magdalene's down the side of the church towards the graveyard. The congregation stood in woolly hats and scarves. Several children, up past their bedtime, rubbed their eyes.

'Will Santa have come when I get home?' a small boy asked as Edie passed.

'Santa will only visit when you're asleep, darling,' his mum said, pulling his coat hood over his hatted head, only for the boy to yank it off.

Edie had woken up on Christmas Day when she was four and found her stocking still empty, her mum dead and her infant brother in hospital. May no kid here, or anywhere, have to go through the same. And then she thought of Sean, never having woken up to a stocking in all the years he'd lived with her.

She made a silent promise, to all her saints, and to him, that she'd change that, from this moment on, if he lived.

The door leading to the crypt was at the back of the church. It was bolted shut, but opened easily, as if it had recently been oiled.

She had, of course, been down here before. And now

she was back, holding on to the rail with its flaky paint, slipping on moss that wanted to reclaim the stone. It reminded her of the crypt of St Michan's Church in Dublin, and the skeleton in the open coffin kept behind bars as if to stop it climbing out.

It was hard to stop ghosts. Even now, as she descended, it was as if she was stepping into the time when she had last led her class down the steep stairs and into the cold damp.

It had been one of her supply lessons, at St Mary's. She hadn't ever wanted to go back there again, but the agency still sent her sometimes, so she always took her classes on trips, though never to the beach. One time, she'd arranged with St Mary Magdalene's to come into the crypt, the vault, to get the children drawing strange things that sparked their imaginations. The floor then had been broken tiles. So dirty you'd never know the white ones were anything other than corpse grey.

One of the girls had been by herself, sitting on the dirty floor, sketching a figure of St Brigid. Edie went over to her. 'That's my favourite saint.'

The girl's head was down, long hair hiding her face.

'I know. You used to teach me.' She lifted her head but didn't look Edie in the eye. Her face was vaguely familiar.

'I'm sorry, I'm rubbish at remembering faces.'

She placed a hand on the saint. 'My name's nearly the same.'

'Can I have a look at your drawing, "Nearly the Same"?'

She had shyly shown Edie a sketch that showed little

promise. Some good shadowing, perhaps, a knack with charcoal, but nothing tangible. 'What do you think?'

'I think you should think of something other than art as a career!'

The girl shrank into herself.

'I don't know what else to do.'

'What do your parents say?'

'My mum's dead, and my dad doesn't care.'

Edie had hunkered down then, on hips that could still move easily. Face to face with the girl, she'd said, 'My mum died when I was a child, too. It can't help but shape you, leave a piece of you missing. It's why I do puzzles, to try and put myself back together. I never manage, but I try.'

'Puzzles?'

'Jigsaws, wordsearches, crosswords . . . things with answers, unlike life. Leave art and love to one side, like I did.' She looked around the crypt. 'Take my advice and find a secure job with answers. And keep trying to find that broken piece of yourself.' She'd felt proud of her advice at the time.

Now, Edie closed her eyes at what she had done. Then opened them. She couldn't hide from herself and others anymore.

At the bottom of the steps, Edie looked around in the darkness. 'Sean?' she called. Her voice echoed, but there was no reply.

Taking her phone out of her pocket, she switched on its torch function, noticing the lack of reception. She swept the beam around the crypt. There they were: pristine, new black and white tiles on the floor. The fundraising had been to replace the grey broken stone that had been there in her time.

Something moved towards the back of the crypt, in one corner. Edie hurried over and found Sean, lying on the tiles. When she lifted the tarpaulin that covered him, she saw he was arranged like the outline of the crime scene corpse. He was so still. His head lay on a prayer cushion, but the rest of him was on the freezing floor, next to a short pillar with a chalice on top. He held his inhaler in his fist, just as he had held her little finger when he was a baby.

She bent over him. He was breathing. Thank Brigid. Thank Monica. 'Hello, my darling Seanie. I'll get you out, don't worry.'

But he was so cold. He must have been here since he'd been taken. His leg looked like it was broken, his hip bleeding, his arm at a worrying angle. It would be impossible for her to get him out by herself. She'd have to go back outside and get someone to call for an ambulance.

Then, a shape moved slowly out from behind one of the larger pillars. In the shadows, with their St Mary's hoodie up, whoever it was looked like a wraith. As they moved into the torch's reach, Edie saw it was a youngish woman.

'You've got to help me,' Edie said, holding Sean's head in her hands. 'It's my son. He's going to die unless we get him out of here.'

'That's up to you, Ms O'Sullivan.' The hooded woman took a gun out of her coat.

Edie couldn't see her face clearly, but she knew who it was. 'Hello, Bridget,' she said. Equal amounts of hate and empathy collided inside her.

'I'm surprised you remember me – you never did when you taught me.' The woman – girl, really – spoke the words with spite-spiked sadness.

Even though Edie had been able to picture her when she was a child or a young woman, she didn't know this version of her.

'How did you know it was me?'

'You and your dad left enough clues to lead me here. At least I can save Sean, if not the others.'

'You were never meant to save them. Veronica, Carl and Cramer had to die, as you do. But I wanted to show you first that you're not the almighty Ms O'Sullivan who can solve every puzzle and person, cover up every mistake by rubbing it out and rewriting history. Sean was only meant to lead you here. My dad wasn't supposed to drive into him, just use the chloroform. Sean's done nothing wrong, but the rest of you have.'

'I know a little of the damage that's been done to you. I've guessed at some, and I'm in the dark about the rest. But I'd like to hear. I've learned lately that I don't listen nearly enough.'

'The point of all this,' Bridget said, her words seeming to come with difficulty, 'is for you to tell *me*.' She swayed slightly, the gun waving.

Edie shone the torch around the crypt. 'There are some chairs over there. I'll get them for you.' With Bridget's gun trained on her, Edie hurried over to a stack of church chairs and took two, one at a time, to near where Sean lay, barely breathing.

'Seeing as you're the one with the gun and the grudges, I'll start from the first corner of the jigsaw: Carl Latimer. Between a file dug up by Mrs Challis, additional information from Ama Phillips, and my own guesswork, I'd say you were one of the girls Latimer took advantage of, taking photos of you, and videos. He showed them to your friends, to everyone. And you were so very young at the time.'

Bridget started to shake. Despite it all, Edie wanted to hug her. But she was twenty-odd years too late for that.

'He was unfaithful, but I forgave him because he came back to me each time. And then his dad went away, and Carl started taking pictures of me. He persuaded me to agree, at first. Then he took them in my sleep, of him *doing* things to me.'

'I can only imagine how awful that must be.' Edie's voice had never sounded this gentle before.

Bridget closed her eyes. She rocked backwards and forwards. 'You couldn't see all my face, but everyone knew because he told them. The headmistress suspended him for a week, with nothing on his record, saying he had his whole future ahead of him. She called me a slut. I shut down, and I ended up leaving school before my A Levels. I moved north, changed my name. He stayed here, and got a job teaching, in the same school.'

'I imagine if Mrs Singer, the headmistress, were still alive, she wouldn't have been for long. She didn't listen to you.'

'On either occasion.' The implication was clear.

Again, they would come to that. It wasn't just playing for time that made Edie hold back.

'Your father was, I imagine, too busy to pay attention. A theme that will play out, I think.'

'So, you worked that out. What about Veronica? Why did she have to die?'

'Well, let's be honest. She didn't. She could easily have lived, if you'd let her.'

'No.'

'Fine. Then let's start there. She had a long-term affair with your father. I don't know when your mum found out, but it can't have helped when—'

'She'd suspected before, and he'd denied it, but she only knew for sure when I told her. I walked in on them. Dad and Veronica. Upstairs.' She looked upwards.

'They were in bed in your house?'

'Up *there*.' She pointed to the ceiling. 'I was at a Christingle service. I was a bit old by that point, but I was young for my age, and I loved the ritual. Dad was a lay preacher. Ironic really. They weren't supposed to lay members of the congregation. He slipped into a side chapel with her, and I followed. They were kissing, touching. I dropped the Christingle. Candle wax was dripping, the orange was burning, and they just stood there, staring, hands still on each other.'

'And when your mum died, he turned to Veronica?'

'He had no idea what I was up to; he was at her house all the time. I slept with Carl for months without Dad knowing. When I told him about the photos and videos, he just gave me a lecture on the philosophy of responsibility.'

Sean's teeth were rattling. He didn't have long. Edie looked to the door. 'Can we get Sean to hospital? You can have everything you want from me.'

'No. Tell me how it all fits.'

'One of the things I haven't worked out,' Edie said, 'was how the fertility clinic was involved. Or whether it was a red herring.'

'I came back two years ago, with my new name and new life. I wanted a family that actually loved and looked out for each other. Dad *said* he wanted to make everything up to me. So, when I decided to freeze my eggs, he persuaded me to use Family Ties.' She laughed at the irony of the name. 'I went along with it. Only Veronica didn't have the right facilities in place, and my embryos had to be "discarded". That's what she said. "Discarded". Like I was, so many times.'

'And your father helped cover it up.'

'Veronica was a councillor then, and knew who to talk to. And Dad obviously has connections too. Like Dr Newman and his other golf buggy buddies. Veronica wasn't penalised for losing those precious eggs and embryos, but the poor people who paid her were punished physically, emotionally and financially.'

'People like Lucy Pringle.'

'She's had twins, though. She doesn't get to complain.'

'Everyone in this case has a right to complain. Including you. But you do not have the right to kill.'

'I'm not interested in rights.'

'Clearly. As for Linus Cramer, your mum was treated badly by him, I believe.'

'The manager was a friend of hers and she'd gone to her in confidence. Her "friend" advised her not to make an official complaint; actually said, with no sign of irony, that she "should sweep it under the carpet".'

'And Cramer found out, and retaliated?'

'There'd been a few irregularities in the accounts, which Mum had also pointed out. When HMRC came knocking, they pointed the finger at her. She was sacked, humiliated, broke. A single mum. The night before she killed herself, she went to Dad at Veronica's house and begged him to come back. He shut the door in her face.'

'What about the fourth corner piece?' Edie asked. 'That wasn't supposed to be your dad, was it?'

Bridget's fragile voice cracked, rising in pitch. 'Dad promised me he would make things better. He said he wanted it to be as if he was smoothing away all of the bad things that had happened to me.'

'But he couldn't handle the murders.'

'When we planned it, he talked about the philosophy of ethics, death and justice. Once a chemist, he knew how to make the cyanide. But when the plan was in place, he was just a weak, feeble man. He thought he could take Charles Peacock's place, as if the jigsaw's picture wasn't fixed before we even started.'

'Charles Peacock – does he work at Beacon Street Medical Centre?'

'Dad was supposed to kill him last night and deliver you the last pieces of the jigsaw. Only, while Dad's flesh has always been too willing, his mind is too weak. If he'd been as strong in spirit as me, he'd have been able to resist temptation and avoid the easy path of fucking other women.'

'And if you'd been stronger in body, you could have done it all yourself.'

'Dr Peacock would have been dead at his desk in Beacon Street Medical Centre and the jigsaw would be complete. But now the picture will never be accurate.'

'Jigsaws,' Edie said, 'like the unfaithful's promises, are made to be broken.'

'He should be held to account.' Bridget looked towards her rucksack. 'Peacock dismissed the pain of hundreds of women, dismissing their diseases along with it, including polycystic ovaries, endometriosis and cancer.'

'Including *your* cancer.'

'So you figured that out,' Bridget said. 'I thought you weren't going to solve everything.'

'I only just realised. But it was there from the start – the charity card for cancer, with Holly on the front.'

Bridget nodded. Edie still couldn't see her face, but she could tell the young woman was pleased at the recognition. If only she could have had that in other ways.

'It's terminal, I assume. Your cancer. And that's what set off this death hunt.'

'Amen,' Bridget said, sarcastically. 'Brain tumour, inoperable. I can feel it inside my head, taking over.'

'And that just leaves my part in your jigsaw, doesn't it?'

'And who are you, Edith O'Sullivan? What is your jigsaw piece?'

'I'm the one who could have helped you. I should have stood in front of you when Holly died and taken responsibility for abandoning the class. I allowed my broken heart to break yours.'

'Holly shouldn't have died.' Her voice was childlike now. 'I was trying to hold on to her, but we were too far out. We panicked, kept dragging each other under. And then she didn't surface. I reached into the water. Her hair slipped like seaweed through my fingers.'

The image lingered in the crypt. Edie could almost smell the bladderwrack.

'You shouldn't have been made to take the blame when you were just playing. It's my fault, not yours.'

'And what else did you do to me?'

'I was in this crypt with you, and I swept away your dreams of being an artist. I told you not to reach for what you wanted. To go for certainty, not creativity. And I gave you the idea for the whole jigsaw.'

'*I* had that idea.' Bridget's voice rose. 'You can't take that from me along with everything else.' She stood, still unsteady, and took a bottle filled with something dark from her bag. She poured it into the chalice. The liquid smelled of sweet ether and marzipan.

Gun still pointed at Edie, Bridget said, 'Now that you've confessed, you must take Communion.'

Edie glanced at Sean. 'What will you do about my son?'

'Drink this, and I'll call for an ambulance, go to Mass, and then hand myself in. But you have to drink it all first.'

Edie nodded. There was fairness to this game. Keeping

her eyes on Sean's face, she held the chalice to her lips. 'I'm sorry. I apologise to you, Bridget, to Holly, to Sean, to Liam, to Riga, to everyone. And you did beautifully. I give you a gold star, an A, an A*, a First. You are my best pupil.'

Bridget took down her hood and smiled, sallow skin stretching over sharp cheekbones.

Edie knew her face, but couldn't quite place it.

'Drink up, Edie,' Bridget said, tipping the chalice up.

As Edie swallowed the bittersweet wine, she realised, too late, where she had seen Bridget recently – in Facebook photos of the Weymouth Runners. Small, so skinny, always standing apart from the others, like an island.

Isla. Sean's personal trainer.

Bridget Berkeley, aka Isla, tied Edie's hands, and fastened Sean's watch around her wrist. 'I hope it's quick for you.'

Laughter came from the nave above them. The church organ played a melancholic chord.

Bridget looked up, her smile the saddest Edie had ever seen. She seemed lost in a dream that would never now come true. 'Time for Midnight Mass.'

Then Edie gasped, lurching forwards off her chair. The chalice clattered to the tiles as she clutched at her closing throat. She kicked out at the floor, eyes wide, but it was no use.

Sean stirred, groaning.

'I love you, Seanie,' Edie tried to say, but there was no breath left. Her heavy lids fell, as did the dark.

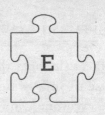

Fifty-Five

Bridget walked with difficulty up the stairs, trembling. She didn't know why she felt so bad at seeing Ms O'Sullivan die. It was what she'd been planning for so very long. And Ms O'Sullivan deserved it, for not protecting her and Holly. Maybe Bridget's spirit was as weak as her father's, after all.

She managed to get the door to the outside open, but couldn't push the bolt back in. Her body had been failing her for a while now. If her clients hadn't been so self-obsessed, they'd have realised that she posted times on the app, yet never actually ran; they'd have worried about her weight loss, not congratulated her for it. But she was stronger than all of them. She'd been strong enough to put the final piece of the jigsaw in place. And now she had the inner strength to keep her word, even to Edie O'Sullivan. Unlike her father, *she* saw her promises through. She'd had her revenge on all of them, for herself, for Holly.

With the ambulance and police called, she joined the queue to enter the church. Bridget felt she could breathe properly for the first time in decades. The brain tumour that Dr Charles Peacock had dismissed as 'hormonal headaches' would soon take what was left of her life, and she too would die.

But before that, she would cleanse herself, and confess.

The Purbeck choir stood to sing. The words of 'Away in a Manger' made her think of children who were lullabied and loved, not lied to or left. She confessed, then, in her head and heart, to all she had done. But she was not sorry.

When her turn came to take Communion, Bridget knelt on the cushion and took a sip of the wine. The priest wiped the cup and made the sign of the cross on her forehead. Peace descended.

Outside, sirens wailed, singing along with the choir.

She opened her mouth and the hooded lay priest, head bowed, placed the Communion wafer on her tongue. She closed her eyes and waited for it to dissolve.

But it wasn't melting. It was too solid. Too cardboard.

Reaching into her mouth, Bridget took out a jigsaw piece. She stared at it. Its edges had been worn smooth, and at its centre there was a picture of Sean's watch.

'I don't understand.' Her head was pounding.

Above her, the hooded clergy raised a hand in forgiveness and benediction, and something glinted in the candlelight. Bridget squinted at it. Sean's watch was on the lay priest's wrist.

She froze. 'What's happening?'

Slowly, the priest drew back their hood. Edie O'Sullivan stood before her.

'It's a Christmas miracle,' Edie said.

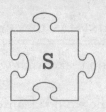

Fifty-Six

Bridget gasped and steadied herself against the prayer rail. 'I don't understand.'

Edie hurried to help, knowing that this too would be a trauma for the sick young woman.

The deacon coughed in a way that suggested he would rather they took this somewhere else. Ama Phillips was now at Edie's side, holding both her and Bridget up. The congregation whispered as she led them into the St Brigid side chapel.

Edie, woozy from the poisoned wine, tried to catch her breath while Ama gave Bridget the 'you do not have to say anything' spiel. 'Glad you got here,' she said at last.

'I'm glad you called us before you went in,' Ama replied.

'Is Sean—'

'The paramedics are with him, as is Michaels, and Liam.'

Edie wanted to cry and break down, but she couldn't, not yet.

Bridget looked like she wasn't listening, just staring at Edie, the reborn ghost. 'You should be dead. You're the final piece. You should be lying on the black and white tiles!' She stamped on the centuries-old stone.

'I had several pints of activated charcoal at my friend Riga's house before I left. I hoped it would counteract the cyanide I suspected you'd use.' She'd also apologised profusely to Riga, and asked her out on a date, should she live.

Riga had said yes.

'I'm sorry that I broke up your jigsaw picture, just as I broke up your life. But I need to paint my own. I'm eighty and I want to live much more.'

'At least I taught you something,' Bridget said. 'A life is made up of pieces that are taken away and added to each day.'

'I was *your* teacher. I should have helped you find ways to put yourself back together. Please forgive me.'

Bridget doubled over, racked with sobs. Edie held her. Two broken women. One crone mothering a maiden. Behind them, St Brigid held out her arms.

As Ama was about to take Bridget gently away, she said, 'You have to make a statement, Edie. We need to get all the information before you forget it.'

'Are you suggesting that someone my age will lose the memory of nearly being murdered?'

'No, it's just . . . I want to know how you figured it out.'

Edie felt her vision blur again. 'I'll tell you at the hospital. I've ingested poison and need my stomach pumped. But first I need to see my great-nephew. And you'll get nothing more from me until I have.'

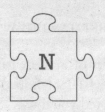

Fifty-Seven

December 25th – Christmas Day

Sean's hospital room, just off the ward for privacy, was as full as a Christmas morning stocking. DCI Leyland was sitting in the corner, sulking. He looked like he was chewing a particularly fetid sprout. Michaels was next to him, matching his scowl. Ama, however, seemed to be enjoying every second. She was peeling chocolate coins and slotting them into her mouth. Her eyes were bright.

Sean lay on the bed, looking around, baffled. Head bandaged, leg and arm in casts, hips bruised, bloodied and bandaged, but not broken. He was alive, and Edie had to pinch her hand to stop herself crying. Liam was sitting on one edge of the bed, and she wasn't about to leave Sean's other side for anything. She gripped his hand.

'Are you going to tell us what really happened?' Michaels scowled at Edie. She appeared truly annoyed to have to ask, as if livid at Edie for her own curiosity.

'Once I'd put all the clues in the messages and the jigsaw together,' Edie explained, 'I knew that Sean would be in the crypt. I was there with Bridget once, a long time ago, and I had the chance to help her when she needed it, but I didn't. And when it occurred to me that the red spatters might be spilled wine, and thought about my spiked words to Bridget, I suspected that, if another person *were* involved, they'd likely commit murder with poisoned wine, probably laced with cyanide, given what happened to Dr Berkeley. So, I drank charcoal before entering the church for Midnight Mass, which of course was taking place at the time specified in the first message.'

'I'll never think a lump of charcoal is a punishment again,' Liam said.

'I also put wadding and tissues down my top and up my sleeve, and spat the wine out when she wasn't looking, like I do with gum.'

'Who said chewing gum was a bad habit?' Ama said, reaching over to high-five Edie.

Sean shook his head, grinning. 'Aunt Edie's ability to spit out gum discreetly has always amazed me.'

'Old punks know how to spit. And, fortunately, Bridget was preoccupied with what was going on in the nave upstairs. I pretended to collapse and, when she'd gone, I took the lino cutter out of my deep pocket.' Edie pointed a finger at Ama. 'Make sure you always have trousers and skirts with pockets.'

'And absorbent sleeves,' Liam added.

'What were you thinking?' Leyland said. He'd been staring at her as if she were a wild animal in a zoo. 'What if you'd taken in too much poison? What if it hadn't been cyanide? You could have both died.'

'Well, we didn't.' Sean sat up higher in the bed, wincing

and holding his side. 'What's happened to Isla, I mean Bridget?'

Leyland sat up straighter, becoming more official. 'Bridget Berkeley has been charged with multiple counts of murder, and conspiracy to commit murder. But according to the doctor who saw her in the early hours, it's unlikely she'll make it to court. The tumour is advancing quickly. She'll likely die awaiting trial.'

'Hopefully being made as comfortable as possible?' Sean asked. Edie squeezed his arm. Even now, even for this woman, he was full of empathy.

'There are mitigating factors that may help,' Ama added. 'I spoke to her colleagues at her former gym in Harrogate, and they're all baffled by her behaviour. They described her as kind, thoughtful and devoted to her clients. What she did seems to have been completely out of character, and the doctor said the tumour may have affected her thinking and personality.'

'And what about Dr Newman?' Edie asked.

Leyland coughed, embarrassed. 'My friends found him in a bad way, in a casino in Bournemouth. He has a gambling addiction and a lot of debt. We're paying for him to go to rehab.'

'We?' Edie asked.

Sean coughed to tell her to shut up. She knew he'd fill her in another time.

'Now you know the whole story,' Sean said, 'I don't want to be rude—'

'You nearly died,' Edie said. 'Be as rude as you like.'

Sean gestured to his colleagues. 'Then you lot can

bugger off, so I can rest here today, hopefully be signed out tomorrow, then go home and start my Christmas on Boxing Day.'

'I will allow you to speak to me like that once and once only, Sean.' Leyland stood and walked to the door.

'You give the best presents, DCI Leyland,' Edie said sarcastically.

Leyland hovered in the doorway. 'Although I must say you have done well.' He looked across at Edie. 'You *and* your aunt. I'm sure the commissioner would like to hear all about it. Maybe you could both join us on the golf course at some point soon.'

Edie laughed. 'Golf? You can fu—'

This time it was Liam who coughed into his hand to stop her.

She sighed, loudly. 'You can fundamentally count on me wearing plaid capri pants on the course.' The things Edie did for her great-nephew.

'I'm not sure golf is for me, sir,' Sean said. 'Unless it involves a windmill. But I'd happily take you on in a game of darts.'

Leyland laughed, then left, whistling 'Driving Home For Christmas'.

'Happy Christmas, boss,' Sean called after him. Michaels followed, leaving the room with a parting shot. 'You'll be lucky to get a doctor to see you on Christmas Day, DI Brand-O'Sullivan.'

Ama waved them goodbye with an angelic smile on her face. Edie marvelled at those young people who life had yet to get to. Long may it continue for them.

'I *am* lucky, though.' Sean leaned into Liam's shoulder. 'Tell her.'

'Tell me what?' Edie grabbed his hand.

'Sunny has said she'll recommend us as Juniper's official adoptive parents,' Liam said. 'And, if her mum wants it to go ahead, we'll be adopting her brother or sister too.'

'But you were in danger,' Edie said.

Sean grinned with pride. 'Sunny was impressed by Liam's honesty, and the teamwork the family showed, including you, Edie. *And* she said that gay couples statistically make highly successful adoptive parents.'

Edie felt the customary twist in her heart as she thought of the vulnerability of children. Of how, as of now, there might be two more O'Sullivans to protect.

She looked, then, at Sean and Liam, holding hands. They were going to be okay. And so was she. 'Congratulations!'

'And to you,' Sean smiled at her. 'Great-Aunt Grandma Edie.'

'This time, I'm going to be a great one.'

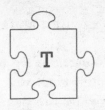

Fifty-Eight

December 26th – Boxing Day

Liam's face when he opened his front door to find Edie on the doorstep was a picture of shock. He was wearing reindeer antlers and a butcher's apron.

In one hand Edie was holding two makeshift stockings – 120 denier plaid tights severed at the crotch. She waggled them at him like a raunchy Santa. 'It's me. Your Aunt Edie.'

'What's happening?'

'I've come to Christmas dinner, on Boxing Day! Sean said you were doing the full works.' She brought her other hand out from behind her back. 'And I bring Bolly.'

'You have?' Liam kept blinking, as if that would help him absorb the news. It probably didn't help that she, the famous Christmisanthopist, was wearing a festive red jumper, borrowed from Riga, with black sequins that spelled out 'Christmassy as Fuck'.

'I believe you both invited me. Will you let me in? I want to see my other nephew.'

Liam backed away as if she were a bomb about to go off, and she was, but this time with joy.

Sean was in the lounge, his leg up and poorly arm in a cast. The bruises on his face were even darker than the day before, and he winced in pain as he twisted to see her.

'Don't move! I'm coming to you.' She placed the stockings by the fireplace and took off her coat, thrilled by Sean's eyes boggling at her jumper.

'I have no idea what's going on,' Sean said at last, shaking his head but smiling.

'I've brought you a stocking each, mainly stuff from the house as no shops are open, and some of Riga's healing tinctures. And a crossword I've made just for you, in case you get bored.'

'Thank you.'

'I've kept Christmas from both of us for far too long. Time we got into the spirit together.'

The house was warm and smelled festive – tatties roasting, turkey resting, spiced cabbage broiling, wine breathing, bread sauce bubbling, gravy gulping, sprouts jostling, chestnuts splitting, Bucks Fizzing and coffee brewing. These and the scent of the fir, ivy and pomander swags that writhed over every surface combined to create an olfactory cacophony. And it was perfect.

Liam came back through from the kitchen.

'I'm sorry,' she said. 'For being an arsehole. I'll do better.'

He held out his arms and she tentatively entered them. His hug was warm and smelled of eucalyptus. 'That's okay. And we knew you'd turn up one day if we just kept asking.'

'We hoped, anyway.' Sean was grinning his big silly grin.

She may have felt like she was the one looking after him, but, really, he'd been watching over her for years. He had believed in her, and he was right. She would follow his lead. Trust that people intended the best, up until they showed their worst, at least.

'Well, here I am.' She looked around the room with its cheery, warm fire. 'I love it in here.'

Liam and Sean shared a shocked look. Liam recovered quickly. 'Let me show you around,' he said.

They had redecorated since she was last here, including putting the Lacroix wallpaper she'd given them last year on the long wall in the living room. Edie saw splashes of herself everywhere, right down to framed pictures of her and her crosswords. Even the tchotchke near their wedding portrait turned out to be, on closer inspection, a snarky Post-it she had once hidden at the bottom of the biscuit tin Sean consistently raided as a teenager, now enshrined in a glass paperweight. The love they had for her was clear; why had she hidden hers for so long? She hoped the clues had always been in plain sight.

'And this is going to be Juniper's room,' Liam said. 'The baby, if he or she arrives, will go in with us till they're old enough for their own room.'

'And Juniper will be here in a month?'

'Or sooner. I can't believe it!'

'Shame she's missed Christmas,' Edie said, when they were all back in the living room, drinking champagne. She thought of the kids already being here, unwrapping presents on the living room floor.

Sean covered his mouth in mock shock. 'Who are you, and what have you done with my Great-Aunt Edie aka "Mum"?'

Edie cupped her great-nephew aka son's face in her hands. 'I'm right here, Sean. I always have been. I got wrapped up in other things for, well, ever. But I'm very much present, and in the present. Talking of which . . .'

Breaking away, she popped into the hall and picked up her bag. Returning, she presented its contents with a flourish. 'Open your main gift now. Well, go on then.'

'Ah, yes, Aunt Edie, it's definitely you.'

He took the large box covered in tin foil, the nearest thing she'd had to wrapping paper in the house, and began to unwrap pots of paint and paintbrushes. 'Thanks, Edie. Though I don't think I'll have much time for a new hobby.'

'They're not for you.' Edie opened a pot of bright red paint and dabbed at it with a brush. 'I was going to give you yet another jigsaw, but that seemed inappropriate this year. So, I thought I'd paint a mural for Juniper.'

'What's it going to be?'

'A rainbow to welcome her, then I'll paint whatever she wants.'

Liam's eyes shone. Sean's were as tear-filled, but he was smiling. 'You've got paint on your face already.'

Edie looked at her reflection in the silver tray holding the glasses and now-empty Bolly bottle. Her nose was tipped with a smudge of red. She carefully took the reindeer antlers off Liam's head and placed them on her own. 'Just call me Rudolph.'

'We need a toast.' Liam looked to Sean, who turned to Edie.

She cleared her throat. 'I haven't been the best great-aunt, friend, lover or person. I've been broken and not wanted to look at the pieces of my life. But there is always time, and we have it. The past is here with us, and we should drink to its ghosts, but I'm never going back again to being the person who lives in the past. So, let's also drink to those ghosts of the present, and most importantly the future, and your beautiful family.' She thought of Riga's advice and just put her lips together and went for it. 'And I love you all.'

Both men smiled as she stood and raised her glass. 'To the brilliant shape of things to come!'

Liam and Sean raised their glasses.

Edie's love for them fizzed over like the best champagne. 'Merry Christmas,' she said, and, for the first time, she meant it.

Acknowledgements

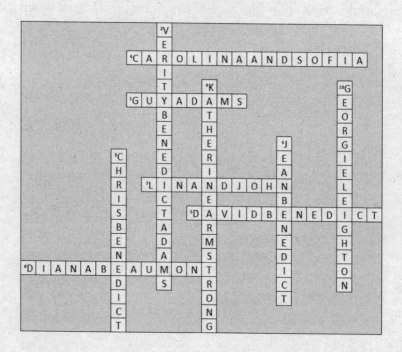

Across

1. Gaudy Sam
5. Vindicated Bed
6. Cool Naiads Farina
7. La Hon Djinn
8. Unabated Aim On

Down

2. Embraced A Tidy Invest
3. Etch Inscribed
4. Need Jet Cabin
9. A North Rink Gamester
10. Heroine To Giggle

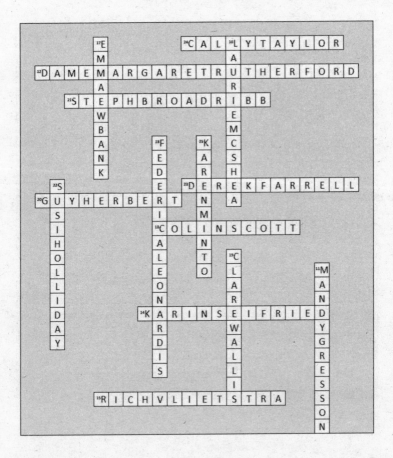

Across

12. A Radar Reformed Truth Gem
13. Tonic Colts
14. Inked Rarifies
15. Cart Silver Hit
20. Ruby Her Get
21. Barb Striped Hob
23. Drake Err Fell
24. Call Royalty

Down

11. Earns Gym Nods
16. Maria Clues, Eh
17. Mama Web Ken
18. A Clarified Endorse
19. Lace La Swirl
22. Daisy Lush Oil
25. Remain Knot

ALEXANDRA BENEDICT

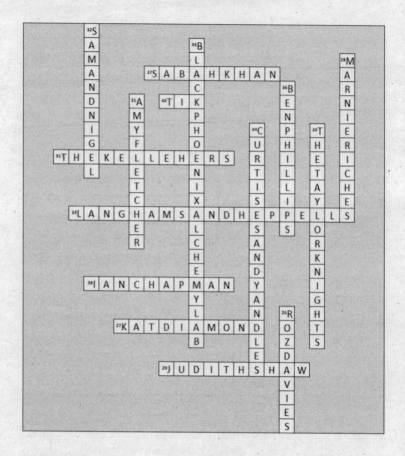

Across

27. Kinda To Dam
29. Wish Jut Had
31. Lee Thresh Elk
33. Ms Panhandle Plash Leg
37. Hank Abash
38. Chip A Manna
40. Kit

Down

26. Savior Zed
28. Hernia Crimes
30. Lathery Goth Knits
32. Galena Minds
34. Truly A Candidnesses
35. Alchemy Fret
36. Lip Nib Helps
39. A Bony, Hemp, Helix Callback

Anagram answers

A Christmas Carol – 'armchair, cats, Sol', p.211

A Tale of Two Cities – 'wife? A Costa toilet!', p.12

Dombey and Son – 'nobody amends', p.84

Great Expectations – 'excerpt. A gestation'; 'a target. Exceptions', p.142

Hard Times – 'this dream', p.228

Nicholas Nickleby – 'chilblain, once. Sky', p.174

Oliver Twist – 'vows. It relit', p.76

The Battle of Life – 'the toilet baffle'; 'that fleet foible', p.245

The Chimes – 'chemist, he', p.316

The Cricket on the Hearth – 'hock. thirteenth teacher'; 'the tchotchke near their', p.331

The Haunted Man – 'death hunt. Amen', p.317

The Signalman – 'hangman stile'; 'light means an', p.253

Fleetwood Mac songs

Riga's Christmas Livener

(Makes a killer measure for one person, but share if you must)

Glugglug of good red wine
Jolt of brandy
Jigger of whisky
Judder of rum
1 teaspoon orange bitters
1 tablespoon of brown sugar
1 tablespoon of finely grated ginger
Cinnamon sticks
Sprig of rosemary for remembrance
Pinch of nutmeg

First, boil a kettle. Place the brown sugar in a mug and pour over around 25ml just-boiled water. Make yourself a cup of tea at the same time, if you fancy. Stir the sugar solution with one of the cinnamon sticks and leave to sit together for ten minutes while making a fervent wish or intention. You could always make a big batch of magical cinnamon sugar syrup and use at your leisure.

Pour the sugar syrup into a bevelled glass to catch the light. Add the ginger, bitters and nutmeg, then the whisky, rum and brandy. Muddle. Gently heat the wine for a few minutes if you wish, for a warming livener, or just add the wine. Stir widdershins with the rosemary sprig, wishing yourself and the world well.

Serve with a cinnamon stick, but mind you don't poke yourself with it.

Drink until livened, or dead drunk.

P.S. Drink responsibly.

Edie's Dorset Apple Cake

225g self-raising flour
115g unsalted butter, in chilled cubes
115g light brown sugar
1 large egg, beaten
1½ tsp ground cinnamon
Firm grating of fresh nutmeg
8 tbsp milk
240g cored, peeled and grated cooking apples, from
    Dorset if at all possible
80g sultanas
Mug of spiced rum
4 tbsp Demerara sugar

Soak the sultanas in the rum overnight. In the morning,
sieve out the sultanas and pop the spiced rum on your
porridge.

Pre-heat your oven to Gas Mark 4/180°C/160°C fan.
Although if your oven is as temperamental as mine,
you'll need to adjust according to its temper and idea
of temperature.

Grease and line a deep round baking tin, preferably 20cm, with parchment paper. I like to write rude words on the paper but I have, as yet, not noticed a difference with the rise.

Sieve flour and spices into a big bowl. Add the cubes of butter and rub in with your fingertips until you have a fine rubble. Stir in the sugar, beat in the egg and add the milk.

Mix in the apples and rum-soaked sultanas. Plop the batter into the prepared tin and shake to level the surface. Sprinkle the Demerara sugar evenly over the top to give it a crunchy crust.

Bung the tin in the oven and cook until a skewer spiked in comes out clean; this usually takes 35–45 minutes, but your experience may vary, because ovens are as capricious as people.

Leave to cool in the tin for 20 minutes, if you can, then place on a wire rack.

Serve slightly warm, with clotted, single, double, ice or brandy cream. After all, it is Christmas.